voice that brims with wit

Everything Romantic

'[MacAlister's] world-building is excellent' *USA Today*

'Wild [and] zany' *The Best Reviews*

'The paranormal romance equivalent of soul food'
Errant Dreams Reviews

'A humorous take on the dark and demonic' *USA Today*

'Smart, sexy and funny – Katie delivers!'
Christine Feehan, *New York Times* bestselling author

'With its superb characterization and writing that manages
to be both sexy and humorous, this contempary paranormal
love story is an absolute delight' *Booklist*

'A book rich with humour, loaded with sexual tension, and
packed with interesting, if sometimes slightly off-beat,
characters' *Romance Reviews*

'Readers who delight in satiric romances will want to
learn the ___ of A Girl's Guide ___
Midwest ___

About the author

Award-winning *New York Times* bestselling author Katie MacAlister has a passion for mystery, a fascination with alpha males, and a deep love of history that qualifies her perfectly for the fiction she writes. She lives with her husband and dogs in the USA.

www.katiemacalister.com

Katie MacAlister

DRAGON FALL

A Dragon Fall Novel

HODDER

First published in Great Britain in 2015 by Hodder & Stoughton
An Hachette UK company

1

A CIP catalogue record for this title is available from the British Library

Paperback ISBN 978 1 473 61112 2
Ebook ISBN 978 1 473 61111 5

Typeset in Times

Printed and bound by Clays Ltd, St Ives plc

Hodder & Stoughton policy is to use papers that are natural, renewable
and recyclable products and made from wood grown in sustainable forests.
The logging and manufacturing processes are expected to conform to the
environmental regulations of the country of origin.

Hodder & Stoughton Ltd
Carmelite House
50 Victoria Embankment
London EC4Y 0DZ

www.hodder.co.uk

Dragon Fall

Dragon Fall

One

Two years ago

Arvidsjaur Center for the Bewildered
Entrance interview conducted by Dr. Kara Barlind
English translation

Dr. Barlind's note: The following is the interview held at the admission of Patient A upon the demand of her family members. Clear signs of schizophrenia were demonstrated, and a reluctance by Patient A to admit that her story more resembled a fantastical movie than real life. She expressed a great desire to tell her story, however, which was encouraged and which we hope will facilitate recovery.

INTERVIEW BEGINS:

Dr. Barlind: Good afternoon, Miss A. How are you feeling?

Patient A: I've been better, and my name is Aoife, not Miss A. It's Irish, and pronounced EE-fuh.

Dr. Barlind: My apologies. Aoife. Some patients choose to be anonymous in our reports, but I will make a note of your preference. Would you like to tell us what happened that made your brother and sister decide you needed our care?

Patient A (*shuddering*): I'd rather not think about it, but I suppose if anyone is going to do anything about it, then I'll have to tell you what happened last night. It was last night, wasn't it?

Patient exhibited signs of distress and was reassured that the triggering event had occurred the past evening.

Patient A: Okay, good. I thought I'd lost some time there, too, which, let me tell you, isn't as freaky as it sounds. Where should I start?

Dr. Barlind: Wherever you are comfortable beginning.

Patient A: I guess it all started with the date. I had no idea that anything...weird...was going to happen. I mean, Terrin looked perfectly normal. He certainly didn't seem like the type of man who could die and resurrect himself at will.

Patient A shuddered again and rubbed her eyes as if wishing to remove mental images, but ceased before self-harming.

Dr. Barlind: Why don't you start with your date with this man, then.

Patient A: Yeah. The date. It started all right. Nothing fantastic, but pleasant enough...

"Isn't the band great?"

A dense wall of throbbing bass surrounded us, thickening the night air and making me feel unusually...needy. In a sexual way.

"What?" My date shouted the word at me. He had to in order to be heard over the noise of the Swedish band that was playing.

I eyed him. I'd only known Terrin for a few days, having bumped into him while attending the traveling circus known as GothFaire. We'd both been in line to have our palms read and had struck up a conversation, ending up with me meeting him for the concert that was now under way.

"I said the band was great. You like it, don't you?" I yelled, almost into his ear. We were bobbing along with the dense crowd of people, not exactly dancing but moving in time with the music, as if the steady, pounding drumbeat triggered a primal need to move. I was a bit worried about whether Terrin was enjoying himself, not because he looked old—he appeared to be around my age, in his midthirties—but because he gave off a vibe that I couldn't help but classify as "accountant." He was the personification of the word *nice*—everything about him was mildly pleasant: his brown eyes were innocuous, his voice had absolutely no accent, his brown hair was cut short but not super short, and his face was indistinguishable from a thousand other men. He looked like a perfectly respectable, ordinary, white-bread kind of guy.

Whereas I was anything *but* white-bread. At least, ethnically speaking.

"It's quite effective, isn't it?" he answered at the same volume as my question.

"Effective?" I bellowed back.

"The glamour, I mean. Even back here, at the fringe of the crowd, it's very potent."

I stared at him. What the hell was he talking about? Maybe I'd made a mistake agreeing to a date, but I had figured that a public location like the GothFaire was safe enough. I must have misheard. "I've never heard the band before, and my family has lived in this area since I was a little kid, but they're good. Different. The music makes me feel..." I stopped, not only because my throat was starting to hurt from shouting everything, but also because I hesitated to admit the odd feeling that had come over me.

Terrin might be giving off the vibe of being just an ordinary guy, but I wasn't about to risk saying something that could have very bad consequences.

"Horny?" he asked, still bopping along to the music.

My eyes widened. Could he tell that I was suddenly possessed with a desire to kiss him? To touch him? To feel his skin on mine...Desperately, I shoved down those thoughts. Terrin may very well be a nice guy, but that didn't mean I should be thinking about him touching me, and vice versa. "Er..."

"That's all right," he yelled, putting an arm around me and pulling me against his body. He smiled, his eyes not expressing anything but friendly interest. *Trust me*, they seemed to say. *I'm a clean accountant.* "There's no reason to be embarrassed. It's not as if you could resist the urge."

I leaned into him for a moment, breathing in the smell of soap, shampoo, and nice man. My inner hussy swooned at the feel of him and the clean smell that surrounded him, but my brain pointed out that there was nothing so special about him that warranted his last comment.

"Um...yeah." With more strength than I thought possible, I pushed away from him. He didn't look offended, thankfully. He just gave me a bland smile and took my hand.

We listened to the band until the song ended, at which point he suggested that we see the rest of the Faire.

"I've seen most of it already," I told him when we left the big tent. It was located at one end of the U-shaped arrangement of vendor and attraction booths that constituted GothFaire proper. I pointed to the sign that hung off the entrance of the tent. "I saw the main magic act earlier today, and *herregud* was it amazing. Have you seen the magician? It's a father-and-son act, and they do this trick with eggs that gave me goose bumps."

"*Herregud*?" Terrin's brows pulled together in a little puzzled frown.

"Sorry, it's a Swedish colloquialism. It's kind of on par with *holy cats*, or *oh my God*, or something like that."

"I thought you were American?" Terrin asked, his hand still holding mine as we strolled down the main aisle of the Faire. There were a few people out still, visiting the various booths to have their fortunes told, palms read, or any of the other fun faux-creepy things that the Faire people offered up.

"I am. Mom is from Ireland, and my dad is from Senegal. He met my mom while he was in New York City studying to be an architect. She was playing the harp in Central Park; he stopped to watch her and said he fell in love with her right on the spot." I stopped talking, wondering why on earth I was telling him so much about my family.

"How did you end up here?" he asked, waving a hand around that I took to mean Sweden, rather than the Goth-Faire itself.

"Dad got a job with Ikea. And, no, I don't know how to put furniture together. I'm all thumbs when it comes to things like that."

He held up my hand and pretended to admire it. "Your fingers look perfectly fine to me. So, what would you like to do? We've already had our palms read. Have you been to the personal time-travel advisor? I'm told she's very good."

I looked at the booth he pointed to. "Not really my thing. I'm perfectly content with the here and now."

"Ah. A traditionalist? Let's see ... piercings?"

We both looked at the body-piercing booth, then looked at each other.

"No piercings," Terrin said with a pinched look about his mouth.

I laughed. "Yeah, I'm not into pain or stabbing bits of things through body parts. It was all I could do to get my ears pierced when I was sixteen."

Terrin stopped in front of a red-and-black-painted booth. "Hmm. There's to be a demonology demonstration in half an hour. That might be interesting."

"Eh, demons," I said, making a little face at the booth and moving forward. "I can take 'em or leave 'em."

"Really?" He looked mildly surprised. "You have depths, my dear, positively unplumbed depths."

"Yeah, we Irish-Senegalese Americans living in Sweden are often deep. What's that?" I pointed to a sign with a camera. We stopped in front of the booth in question so I could read the text. "What's a soul photograph?"

"I assume it's a euphemism for an aura photo, but I could be mistaken."

"Oh, I think I read about those somewhere. A picture together might be fun, don't you think?" I swung our hands and gave him a winning smile, then suddenly worried that he might think I believed in auras. "Not that they're real."

"The photographs?"

"No, auras."

He handed over some money to the bored teenager who was manning the front of the booth and held up two fingers to indicate we wanted a photo together. "I'm a bit surprised that you want a photo, then."

"Oh boy, did I just put my foot in my mouth?" I gazed at him in consternation. He didn't look offended or angry, but then, I wasn't sure someone with his calm, unemotional personality type got upset about things. "You believe auras are real, don't you?"

"It's difficult to dismiss something that you've seen, yes." He held aside a long black curtain so I could enter the tent. Ahead of us stood an old-fashioned camera on a tripod, the kind with huge bellows and large square glass plates, just like something out of a silent movie. A woman was seated on a low bench having her photo taken. The photographer, a bald little man with a fringe of carroty red hair and an elaborately curled mustache, was behind the camera, telling her to think happy thoughts.

We moved to a couple of chairs that had been placed to form a makeshift waiting area.

"You've really seen an aura?" I asked Terrin in a low voice.

He nodded. "In photographs, yes. I don't have the ability to see them with the naked eye, unfortunately."

"Oh." I relaxed, feeling much better. I tried to pick out judicious words. "I read an article on a skeptical website that talked about how people make those, you know. Evidently there are some things you can do before the film is developed to make pretty halo effects appear around people's heads and whatnot, and of course, digital images are super easy to mess with."

His eyebrows lifted slightly, just enough that told me he was disconcerted by the fact that I was dissing his aura photos. I hurried to try to smooth things over—there was no need to ruin the evening by being a big ole party-pooping skeptic. "Lots of people are taken in by them. Even experts! And I suppose they don't really do any harm, do they? It's just a picture, after all."

"It is that." He was silent for a moment, still watching me with those eyes that expressed mild interest. "I find it curious that you desired to visit the GothFaire since you don't particularly believe in things like auras."

"Are you kidding?" I gave a jaded laugh that I tried to nip in the bud before it got away from me. "We're not exactly in the hotbed of fascinating life here in northern Sweden. The nearest big city is hours away by train, and there isn't a whole lot that's interesting to do or see except rivers and snow and fishing and that sort of thing, and most of the year it's too freaking cold to do anything but huddle around the fireplace with a stack of books and a bottle of brandy. When Rowan—he's my brother—told me that a fair was coming this far north, I leaped at the chance to see it. I've been here every one of their three days."

"Ah. I see the attraction of the fair, then."

The photographer waved us forward, took the slip that Terrin had been given, and told us to arrange ourselves on the bench in whatever manner we liked.

We sat somewhat stiffly side by side while the photographer fussed with extracting a plate and inserting another.

"It's not that I don't appreciate other people's beliefs and such," I told Terrin. "It takes all kinds to make the world go, and I'm certainly not going to bash someone if they really believe that such things as demons existed, or time travel, or auras. I mean, it's really kind of a suspension of disbelief, isn't it? Like when you're watching a movie, and people suddenly burst into song with a full orchestra that isn't there. You just go with the flow and believe it in order to have fun."

The photographer told us to angle ourselves slightly toward each other, then to turn and look at the camera.

"That seems to be a sensible attitude to have," Terrin agreed.

"Hold that for seven seconds," the photographer said, and disappeared under the black cape that hung off the camera.

"But you think I'm wrong?" I asked without moving my lips from the smile I'd presented to the camera.

"Not so much wrong as perhaps imperceptive."

There was a click from the camera, and the photographer emerged. He got out another large, glass square plate and swapped it into the camera. I turned my head to look at Terrin. "Imperceptive? So you believe that all the stuff here, at the GothFaire, is real?"

"Yes." He didn't look at all disconcerted by admitting that. His face held the same placid, pleasant expression as it had all evening.

"Hold the pose, please."

We held our pose. I waited until the photographer emerged a second time from the depths of the camera cape and rose when he told us that the photos would be ready in fifteen minutes. We exited the booth just as an older couple entered.

"So, you believe in that?" I asked, pointing at the booth next to us.

"Scrying? Of course. Have you ever had someone scry for you? It's fascinating, truly fascinating."

"I didn't even know what it was until the first day here, and then I had to ask the lady who does it."

"It's a shame the booth is closed, or I'd treat you to a session." We strolled along the one long arm of the Faire. I noticed that Terrin didn't take my hand again and damned myself for questioning him about his beliefs.

And yet... dammit, I was trying to decide if I wanted to pursue a relationship with him, and in order to do that, I had to know if we were going to be compatible. Which is why I nodded to the booth across the broad center aisle and asked, "That doesn't strike you as just a wee bit too Harry Potter?"

"The spells and charms booth, you mean?" He gave it due consideration. "I see where you might think so, but I blame popular culture for that more than the woman who runs that stall selling tangible forms of magic."

"Uh...yeah." I had many other things to say but kept them behind my teeth.

"The proof is all around you, my dear, if only you choose to see it. For instance..." He gestured toward something behind me. I turned to see a tall man with shoulder-length black hair striding across the open space of the center aisle, obviously heading for the parking area. Next to him was another man, also dark-haired, who kept glancing around as if he was looking for someone. "Dragons."

I stopped admiring the way the first man filled out his black jeans and turned back to Terrin with an obvious gawk plastered all over my face. "What about them?"

"Those two men," Terrin said, gesturing again toward the two men in black. "They are dragons. Black dragons, I'd say, although they could be ouroboros. I'm afraid I'm not terribly up-to-date on the happenings within the weyr since it was destroyed."

"And a weyr is...?"

"The collective group of dragon septs."

"Of course it is. So, you're saying—" I stopped, shook my head, then pointed at the two men in question as they disappeared behind the booths. "You're saying those two guys—those two perfectly normal-looking guys—are dragons? The big-scaly-wings-and-tail-and-eats-medieval-virgins dragons?"

"I'm sure the virgin sacrifices stopped a long time ago," he said gently. "But to answer your question, yes, they are dragons."

"They looked like men," I couldn't help but point out.

"If you had the choice of appearing in dragon form or that of a human, which would you choose?"

He had me there. "Point taken."

"So you see? There is more to be seen than what's on the surface. The same can be said for auras."

"Oh, come on," I said, unable to keep the words from escaping my mouth. It was pretty clear to me that he wasn't going to be boyfriend material. He had the right to believe what he wanted, of course, but I could see that there would be countless arguments and debates about the differences in our respective points of view. Opposites may attract, but that didn't mean they could live together in harmony.

His eyes twinkled at me, positively twinkled at me when he dug into his jeans' pocket before holding out his hand, palm up. Lying on it was a gold and beigey-white object. "Still don't believe me, hmm? Perhaps I can change that. Would you like to see some magic, Aoife? *Real* magic?"

I looked from the ring that lay on his hand and back to his eyes. The latter were still full of amusement. "You have a *magic ring*."

Disbelief fairly dripped off the words.

"I do. In fact, I have no doubt that it is this very ring that has drawn the pair of dragons to the area. You may touch it if you like. It won't harm you—since it was remade, it has developed what, for lack of better words, might be described as a mind of its own. It cannot be used if it does not wish the user to do so and thus far has shown affinity with very few people. Its original creator was one, and the woman who re-formed it is another, but she has no wish to use it and turned it over to me for safekeeping. I've been trying to find out if it is simply inactive or choosy about who it reacts to."

I took the ring, of course. I like jewelry, and it looked old and worn, and I wanted to get a good close look at it, but I really didn't expect anything magical to happen the second I touched it.

And nothing did.

"I guess I won't be joining those two special people," I said, running my fingers around the outside of the ring. It appeared to be made of ivory, or something like that, with the outer edges bound in gold. There was nothing inscribed on it, and no design scratched into the ivory, but it still felt nice in my hand. "Wouldn't the person who created it want it back?"

"The originator?" A fleeting expression of amusement passed over Terrin's face. "I'm quite sure he would give much to have it in his possession again, but that would not be at all wise."

"Oh?" I slid the ring onto my finger and admired it. "He's not a giant orange eyeball, is he?"

"Nothing so dramatic to look at," Terrin said with a little laugh, glancing over my shoulder when, behind me, someone gave a little screech. It was impossible to tell if it was just some kids being kids or someone who just discovered what a Prince Albert was. Given that the piercing tent was down that way, I thought nothing of it. "But nonetheless, extremely dangerous."

"So why do those two men who you think are dragons want it if it's so bad?"

"The ring is not bad in itself; it's the user who dictates whether it is used for good or evil. And all the dragons, not just those of the black sept, have sought the ring since the weyr was destroyed. But that is a long story, too long to tell you now."

"Uh-huh." I held out my hand and looked at it. "Since I didn't disappear when I put the ring on, I don't quite see what's magical about it."

He chuckled. "It's not a Tolkien sort of ring. Its magic is...unique. That is, it's unique to whoever wields it and whatever the ring wishes to be used for."

I looked at the ring, half expecting a wee pair of eyes to look back at me. "Wow, that's...weird."

"As I said, it is unique."

"It's pretty, though. I just hope," I said, starting to pull the ring off, "this isn't one of those bad kinds of ivory, like from an elephant or something. I'm a firm believer in karma, and I don't want to think what sort of horrible thing will happen to me because I admired a dead elephant ring."

"Ivory? Oh no, it's horn." That twinkle was back for a moment. "Unicorn horn, as a matter of fact, and I can assure you that the unicorn in question donated her horn for the purpose of reinforcing it."

"Riiight," I drawled, and removed the ring. I was just about to hand it back to him when a blood-chilling scream ripped high into the night air, so loud we could hear it clearly over the throb of music.

Two

Terrin was off before I could even process the fact that someone was in serious trouble; mercifully, it wasn't long before my wits returned, and I legged it after him. I thought at first the screaming was coming from the demon tent but quickly realized that the noise came from beyond it, toward the big open field that served as a parking area. Two other people were running in the same direction—a big, blond man who seemed to be made of muscles and a small elderly woman with black-and-white hair. I passed by the latter, but the blond dude was well ahead of me. As I raced around the tent and hit the open area, I stumbled and would have fallen if the elderly woman hadn't caught my arm before I fell.

Ahead of us, lit by a small portable light, were four rows of cars. Terrin stood in front of the first row, facing a tall, thin man who seemed to be wielding some sort of sword. A woman lay prone on the ground between Terrin

and the man, and before my brain could process what I
was seeing, the thin man with the sword flung his arms
upright for a moment, so that the sword glinted dully in
the night sky. With a terrible flash, he brought it down,
right on Terrin's shoulder, slashing downward through
him, almost completely severing his arm. I was left sick
and numb with horror, a great yawning pit of terror seem-
ing to open at my feet. I tottered on the edge of it, trying
desperately not to faint.

The mangled Terrin fell almost on top of the woman.

The blond man ahead of me leaped on the Terrin-
killing man, and for a second, I saw something silver flash
between them. Then the sword-man was gone—there one
second and gone the next—leaving only a thick curl of
black oily smoke that hung heavily in the air before slowly
dissipating. I stopped dead where I stood, trying desperately to make some sense of what had happened, my brain
shrieking that I had to do something to help Terrin.

The old lady passed me and reached the spot where Terrin lay dead, lightly vaulting over an inky pool of blood that
stretched out from his inert form just as the blond man spun
around and picked up the immobile woman.

I dropped to my knees, my legs suddenly unable to
hold my weight, and watched with disbelieving eyes as
the man staggered back toward me carrying the woman,
while the old lady trotted beside him, talking rapidly in
a heavily accented voice. "Take her to my trailer, Kurt.
She isn't harmed, just stunned, although it was foolish of
her to try to deal with the demon on her own. It's not as if
she's a Guardian…"

Neither of them spared me so much as a glance as they
passed by. I stared after them for a second before turning

back to look at where the dead and mangled body of my almost-boyfriend lay.

"Hey," I tried to yell, but the word came out a scratchy whisper. I cleared my throat and tried again. "Hey, you can't just leave him. He needs help."

By now the couple was almost back to the center of the Faire and evidently didn't hear me, or didn't care, because they kept walking.

Bile rose in my throat when I looked at what remained of Terrin. I knew I should do something—maybe he wasn't dead. Maybe he was just stunned? Maybe his arm could be put back on.

I retched at the last thought, doubling over and heaving up everything I had eaten before the band started playing. When my stomach settled again, I crawled over to where Terrin sprawled, tentatively reaching out to touch his neck.

He was still warm, but I didn't feel a pulse.

I got to my feet somehow and instinctively stumbled my way back toward the lights and noise of the Faire, back to where there were people other than me who could take charge of the situation and make the nightmare end.

By the time I reached the closest booth—closed now—I was gasping for air. Up and down the aisle all the booths had closed down. Music still pulsated from the big tent, but there wasn't a single person to be seen. A few crows hopped around, pecking at spilled popcorn and other debris, but other than them, there was no living creature to be seen.

With a shaking hand, I pulled out my cell phone and dialed the emergency number. "There's a man…a friend…Some guy hacked him down with a sword, then disappeared into a puff of smoke," I told the woman who answered. My throat was so tight that my voice came out like gravel. Sharp, pointy gravel.

"Smoke?" the woman repeated.

"Yeah, black smoke. He was there, and then he wasn't."

"People do not turn into smoke, madam."

"This guy did. Can you please get the police out here?"

"Your location?" the woman asked.

I told her where I was and that the murder took place in the parking lot.

"Are you sure your friend is dead?"

"Yes," I squawked.

"Did anyone else see this alleged attack?"

"Alleged? It wasn't alleged! It happened right in front of me. Look, I realize it sounds odd, but the sword guy attacked my friend and then just went *poof*! Disappeared! And, yes, there were two other people there who saw it, so would you please send the police out? Who knows where that madman is, and my friend is lying dead on the ground, and he has no pulse and... and..." I broke down, unable to take it anymore.

She assured me that medical help would be sent immediately, as well as police, and asked if I wanted to remain on the line. I told her no and clicked off, although I remained clutching the phone as if it were a lifeline to sanity. I wiped my face (and nose, I'm ashamed to say) on my jacket sleeve, wishing like hell that I could restart the day.

Flashing lights in the distance got me moving again. Way across the pasture that was being used for the fair, I could see an ambulance and a couple of police cars, zooming across the long, flat valley floor. I made my way back toward the place where Terrin fell, intent on waving the ambulance over so they could cart him away.

He wasn't there.

I spun around wildly, my heart in my throat, my eyes huge in an attempt to find where Terrin's corpse had fallen. "He was here," I said aloud, jogging down the line of cars before stopping and running in the other direction. "I know he was here. Right here. Oh my God, the murderer came back for him!"

That's how the police found me—running up and down the line of cars, babbling to myself. I clutched at the nearest cop and dragged him over to the spot where the ground was still stained with Terrin's blood. "There! He was right there! And now he's gone!"

The policeman and his buddy examined the ground. The ambulance pulled up, lights flashing silently as the medics hurried over.

"Did you see anyone move the body?" one of the cops asked.

"No! It has to be the murderer. He probably de-poofed and hacked poor Terrin to bits and went off with Terrin chunks stuffed into a bag!"

Both cops and the two medics stared at me. "De-poofed?" one of the cops finally asked.

"He turned into black smoke after he struck down Terrin," I said, wringing my hands. Why weren't they searching the parking lot for signs of the murderer? "Surely there must be a blood trail you could follow!"

The second policeman took out a notebook. "Would you describe the deceased?"

"Before he was hacked to pieces, I assume?" I took a deep breath and tried to marshal my madly running brain.

"He was about an inch taller than me, midthirties, slight build, brown hair and eyes, square chin, gold-rimmed glasses. His hair was starting to recede, but not really far back, just a bit. Um…" I tried to remember what he was wearing, but the vision that rose before my eyes was one of blood and an almost amputated arm. "He had on a pale blue checked shirt, blue sports coat, jeans, and black shoes."

The cop was writing down the description. "Did he have any tattoos or scars? Was he wearing any jewelry that stood out?"

"No, none of those." I suddenly remembered the ring that I'd been holding when Terrin was murdered. My hand went to my pants pocket, where I'd evidently absently stuffed it. At least that was safe—although now it was too late to give it back to him. "He looked like exactly what he was—a nice guy."

"Something like that gentleman?" the first cop asked, nodding over my shoulder.

I turned to look and felt the world come to a grinding halt. At least my world did, for standing next to the nearest booth, deep in conversation with the blond man who'd hauled off the unconscious woman, was…Terrin.

I took a step toward him, wondering if the world had suddenly gone insane. He didn't look the least bit like he was favoring his arm—the one that had almost been severed—let alone like he'd been attacked at all.

"That's…that's him," I heard myself saying.

"Him? That man there is the victim?" the cop asked.

I took another step toward Terrin. "Yes, that's him. Only…he's not dead now. He was dead. He had no pulse, and his arm was almost off, but now he's…not."

Terrin looked over at that moment and saw me. He smiled and lifted his hand in greeting until he saw the cops and ambulance behind me. His smile faded as my legs suddenly recovered from the shock and marched me toward him.

"You're alive," I told him, well aware that the cops and ambulance dudes were right behind me.

"Yes, I am." He looked slightly confused. "Should I not be?"

"You were killed. Just a few minutes ago. By that tall, thin man with the sword." I poked him on the shoulder that had been severed. It felt solid as all get-out.

Terrin blinked at me for a moment, then shot a smile over my shoulder. "Good evening, Officers. Is there some problem?"

"This lady claims that you were assaulted earlier. *Gravely* assaulted."

"He was!" I protested. "He was dead."

"Clearly not," the first cop said, giving me an odd look.

"I know what I saw." I turned to the blond man to whom Terrin had been speaking. "You were there, too. You saw what happened. Tell them that the sword guy killed Terrin and then disappeared in a puff of smoke."

Blondie pursed his lips for a moment, then shook his head and said something in German. One of the cops asked him a question in the same language, and Blondie answered in Swedish. "I saw no one dead. One of my colleagues was feeling unwell, and I escorted her back to her trailer. That is all."

"You're lying!" I admit that I was close to shouting at this point, but I was righteously enraged. I pointed at both Blondie and Terrin. "They're both lying. I saw what I saw."

Cop number two consulted his notebook, while cop number one stopped the ambulance guys from leaving. "You said that you saw this gentleman here get struck down, his arm almost severed completely from his body, and his body lying in a pool of blood. You also state that his attacker *disappeared into a cloud of black smoke.*"

The emphasis was impossible to miss. Nonetheless, I ignored it. I marched over to the spot where Terrin had fallen and gestured to the stain on the grass. "Look. Right there. See that? It's blood. His blood, from where he was killed."

"I'm not dead, Aoife," Terrin said gently. He peered over my shoulder at the ground. "That looks as if someone spilled some fruit punch."

"Look, I don't know what's going on," I told the cop, who was now muttering in an undertone to his partner. "I don't know if this Terrin is a duplicate or something, but I didn't hallucinate the killing. I saw him get killed. That blond guy there saw it, too, despite what he says. Obviously they're trying to cover something up, but it's not going to work, do you hear me? I know what I saw!"

"Calm down," policeman number one said, taking me by the arm. "There is no sense in getting yourself upset. As you can see, your friend is alive and well."

"That's not my friend!" I shouted, frustrated to my back teeth with the fact that no one seemed to be listening to me. "That's an imposter. Or his twin. Or something, but it's not the man I saw get killed *right before my very eyes*!"

"I think you should come with us now," the ambulance man said, taking my other arm. "You are upset and a little time away from the situation should calm your mind."

"My mind is perfectly calm," I told him, digging in my

heels to stop them from dragging me to the ambulance. "And don't think I'm not aware of what you're doing. You think I'm deranged, don't you? Well I'm not! They are!"

The second ambulance guy got to me at that point, which was a shame because he intercepted my run for freedom.

I won't go over the next few hours because they were tedious and frustrating beyond belief. The more I protested that I was telling the truth, and that the impossible really had happened, the more people gave me the look that indicated they didn't believe a word I said. The people at the hospital where I'd been taken were all very nice, but none of them listened at all, and they certainly didn't believe me. They shot me up with something that made my brain feel like it was full of molasses and put me to bed in a room with bars on the windows. The following morning my sister Bee and brother Rowan showed up. I explained to them what happened and requested release.

"I'm sorry, Aoife, but the doctor says you've had a mental breakdown," Bee told me. "He said it wouldn't be good for you to be out on your own just now."

Rowan smacked her on the arm. "You weren't supposed to tell her that."

"Breakdown?" I sat on the edge of the bed, wearing only my underwear and the loose hospital gown, wanting nothing more than to go home and curl up in my own bed. "I haven't had a breakdown. I saw a murder conspiracy! An impossible one, yes, but I know what I saw."

"What you said happened was impossible," Bee said with a shake of her head. "You couldn't have seen it. You must have imagined it. Did you have anything to eat before the event? Perhaps your date drugged you."

"Drugged me?" I gave her a look that dealt with such a ridiculous idea. "Of course I wasn't drugged. No, I did not eat or drink anything in Terrin's company, so you can scratch that off your list of possibilities and just accept what I'm telling you."

"That you saw a man disappear into smoke?" Rowan looked doubtful. "Aoife, that just doesn't happen."

"Just get me out of here, and I'll make you understand," I begged. "I'll take you to the GothFaire, and you can see the place for yourself, not that there's probably much to see, but if you were to stand where I was standing, then you'd see that I couldn't mistake what was happening right in front of me."

They slid each other a glance, and to my horror, Bee shook her head. "We had a long talk with the doctor, and he really thinks that if you spend some time with people who know how to deal with situations like what you're going through, you'll be right as rain in no time."

Fear crawled up my skin at her words. "You're not... you don't mean—"

"We're signing the papers to have you admitted to a facility. It's called the Aardvark Center for the Deranged."

"Arvidsjaur Center for the Bewildered," Rowan corrected.

"Same difference. The doctor says it's really nice, and very modern, and we'll visit you just as soon as they say it's okay."

"I am not crazy!" I wailed. "You can't do this to me! All I did was see a man die and another man disappear in smoke—"

"Aoife, love, this is for your own good," Bee said in a calming tone of voice.

Rowan, thank the gods, looked a little less sure. "I don't

know, Bee—putting her away like this does seem to be a little...harsh."

"Very harsh!" I said, panic filling me. I had to get out of here, get away from them so I could get my wits together and present my case calmly and intelligently.

"Maybe if she stayed with you in Venice for a few weeks—" Rowan suggested.

Bee sent him another unreadable look and gave a little shake of her head. "It's for the best, it really is. She'll be well cared for."

I lost it at that point. I didn't know why my sister was so adamant to have me locked up or why she didn't believe me when I told her what I'd experienced, but I wasn't going to argue with her anymore. I made a dash for the door.

It was, of course, the wrong thing to do, and by the time the nurse shot me full of more brain-molasses stuff, Rowan and Bee were gone. The next day I was driven down south to the booby hatch.

I don't care what anyone says happened. I know what I saw.

Three

"I don't see how this can possibly be a good idea, Bee."

My sister looked up from where she was throwing some clothing into a suitcase. "Leaving you by yourself? Dr. Barlind says you're perfectly fine to be on your own—"

"Of course I'm fine to be on my own. Two years of intensive therapy have done wonders," I said with a bright, "I'm not insane anymore" smile.

"Me going to Africa, then?"

"No, of course I think *that's* a good idea. You're going to be helping all those people get fresh water."

She dumped her drawer full of undies into the suitcase, glancing around the room. "I don't know why you want to stay here by yourself, I really don't. Rowan won't be back for a couple of months, so you'll be alone here in the house." She shot a look out the window. Beyond a scraggy hedge, the dull gray and brown sand could be seen stretching out to pale bluish gray water. Overhead, a couple of gulls rode the currents, searching for signs of food, and even through the insulated glass I could hear their high, piercing cries. "I wouldn't wish that on my worst enemy."

"That's because you're a city girl now, Miss Lives in Venice." I rubbed my arms and leaned against the wall, looking out at the endlessly moving water. "I like the isolation of the Swedish coast. Especially after spending two years in a house with forty other people. You can hear yourself think here."

"You're lucky if you can hear anything over the constant sound of the gulls. Never mind, you don't have to tell me that you love it here. I know that you do. You take after Dad that way." She paused and glanced at the family picture that sat on her dresser before turning back to the suitcase. "You promise to call me if you have another... incident?"

"I'm not going to have an incident," I said, standing up straight and giving her another brilliant smile. I tried to remind myself to tone down that smile just a bit, since Bee was much more perceptive than Dr. Barlind had been. Bee always was able to tell when I was bluffing her, and the last thing I wanted right now was for her to cancel her trip in order to babysit me.

"Of course you aren't. Still, I don't understand why Dr. Barlind insists that you confront your inner demons by returning to that weird fair that started everything. Oh." She cast a perceptive glance at me, which made me swear under my breath. "*That* is what you were talking about not being a good idea, wasn't it? Well, I agree. It's just bound to lead to all sorts of grief for you."

I rubbed my arms again and turned my back to the beach. Unlike my metropolitan-loving brother and sister, I could happily spend hours wandering up and down our little stretch of the coast. "I don't know about grief... It's not like just seeing GothFaire again is going to make me snap, and I see Dr. Barlind's point about confronting my personal bogeys. She's very big on cathartic experiences and thinks that until you directly confront what is giving you issues, you can never really be cured. To be honest, though, I don't have any desire to see GothFaire again. What if the people remember me as the woman who wigged out? I would die of embarrassment."

Bee lifted her shoulders in a half-shrug. "What if they do? They don't mean anything to us." She paused in the act of gathering up toiletries. "Would you like me to cancel my trip and stay here with you for the next month? Maybe it's too much asking you to stay on your own right after your release—"

"No," I interrupted firmly. "I'm fine, I really am. Dr. Barlind wouldn't have let me go unless I was, right?"

"Mmm," she said doubtfully. She placed the items in her bag and zipped it up, turning to face me. "Aoife, you're a smart girl. If you don't think you need to go to that fair, then don't go. Why stir up all those unpleasant memories? With all due respect to your precious Dr. Barlind, you're out of danger now, and that's all that matters."

"I never *was* in danger," I started to argue, then stopped myself. I took a deep breath, remembering Dr. Barlind's favorite saying: *think twice before you speak once*. If I made too much of a fuss, Bee would cancel her trip, and

I very much wanted time to myself where I could sort out
the shattered remains of my life. I didn't want to go back
to the GothFaire, didn't want to see the face of the blond
man who had lied, and certainly didn't want to see the
same field where I'd seen...but, no, it was better not to
think of that.

"Aoife?" Bee prompted.

"You're right," I said, deciding that it was worth a little
white lie if I could get her off on her trip. The thought of
two lovely months of solitude was damn near priceless in
my eyes. "I'm sure it would be better for my mental peace
to avoid GothFaire."

She smiled, clearly relieved, and patted my cheek in
that annoying way older sisters have. "Good girl. Ack!
Look at the time! I'll be late for my flight if I don't leave
now." She set down her luggage to give me a hug and a
kiss on both cheeks. "Call me if you need me. Or Rowan.
You know we both love you."

"Love you, too," I said, walking with her to her car.
"Take care of yourself. Don't get yourself kidnapped,
because you favor Mom's side of the family more than
Dad's."

"Ha. As if. Smooches!"

She drove off with a wave, and I reentered the
house, leaning against the door and sighing at the blissful silence. Really, there wasn't a more ideal place than
the house that my father built when he moved us to
Sweden.

"I miss you," I told the last family portrait we had
taken, about seven years ago. My mother's face beamed
out of it, her red hair and freckles making her look like a
stereotypical Irish girl, whereas my father's gentle brown

eyes and dark chocolate skin radiated quiet warmth and love. Tears pricked painfully behind my eyeballs, but I blinked them away. "Dr. Barlind says that while it's fine to regret loss, there is no sense in holding on to grief and that one way to let go is to state your feelings. So that's what I'm going to do. I feel sad. I miss you both. And I'm angry that you went to Senegal even though you knew it was risky. I'm furious at the men who killed you and even more furious at the politics that caused the situation. But most of all, I love you, and I wish you were here so I had someone to talk to."

The picture didn't answer me—of course it didn't! That would be crazy, and I was as sane as they came. I laughed out loud at that thought and pushed down the nagging little voice in my head that pointed out that no matter what I told Dr. Barlind, no matter how many times I repeated that I had been mistaken and confused and not quite with it mentally speaking two years ago, no matter how often I told everyone that I had learned much during my stay at the Arvidsjaur Center and had come out a better person for it, the truth remained buried deep in my psyche.

"I'm not listening to you," I told that voice. One of the side effects of the therapy was that I now spoke aloud to myself. Dr. Barlind said it was a perfectly normal habit and that to stifle it would be to cease communication with the emotional self, and *that* was the cause of half the world's problems. "I'm quite normal and not at all weird, and I will not think about things that are impossible, so there's no sense in trying to stir up trouble."

The voice didn't like that, but if I had learned anything

during the last two years, it was not to let the voice in my head push me around. Accordingly, I padded barefoot into my room and considered the small suitcase that sat on the chair. In it were the things that I'd brought with me from the Arvidsjaur Center but that I hadn't yet unpacked. There the suitcase sat, almost taunting me, implying that although I could ignore the little voice in my head, I couldn't pretend reality didn't exist.

"Right. You can shut up, too," I told it, and with my chin held high, I opened the case and took out the bag full of paperbacks that Bee had brought me over the duration of my stay. Clothing was the next to be removed in the form of the pajamas and utilitarian bathrobe that had been given to me, followed by the pants and shirt that I'd been wearing two years ago when I was carted off to the loony bin.

A small vanilla envelope lay underneath the last items, my name and admission date neatly printed in block letters. Inside were the contents of my pockets when I'd been hauled to the hospital—driver's license, a little money, keys, and the jewelry I'd been wearing. I tossed the necklace and earrings into my jewelry box but stood frowning down at the remaining object.

It was a ring.

"Terrin's ring," I said, prodding it with my finger. I'd forgotten all about it, but there it was, sitting there looking like a perfectly normal ring.

It's magic, he had said. I closed my eyes, for a moment swamped by the memories of that terrible night, but I hadn't been ignoring the voice in my head for two years without learning some tricks.

"Fine, you want to be magic?" I shoved the ring on

the fourth finger of my right hand. "You just go ahead and try."

I held out my hand, but of course nothing happened.

"You're no more magic than I am," I said with a snort of derision, and proceeded to put the rest of my things away in their proper place.

Swayed by Bee's comments, I almost didn't go to the GothFaire, but the memory of Dr. Barlind lecturing me on the subject of confronting issues rather than avoiding them resulted in me driving to the next town where the Faire was being held. "Fine, I'll do it, but I refuse to have a cathartic experience," I grumbled to myself as I parked in a familiar field. The GothFaire had returned to the same spot it had been in two years before, and just as it had been on that fateful night, people were streaming into the big tent, no doubt waiting for the band to start that night's concert.

I sat in my car for a few minutes, my hands gripping the steering wheel in a way that had my knuckles turning white. My breath came in short little gasps.

"I can do this," I told the silence around me. "It's just a traveling circus. It's not like Terrin is even here."

Who's to say he isn't? the annoying voice in my head asked.

I got out of the car slowly, trying hard to hang on to the sense of calm that Dr. Barlind said would get me through the worst experiences.

Anxiety is your mind being a bully, she had said during a very bad week when she had ordered electroshock therapy. *Don't let it make you a victim. If you can master your fear, you can master anything.*

"Easier said than done," I muttered, shoving away the

memories of that horrible week and locking the car before I followed a group of three girls heading straight for the big tent.

As I passed by the first row of cars, I couldn't help glancing down the line, just in case a body was lying there. "Ha, smarty-pants brain. There's nothing there, so you can just stop trying to freak me out and get on board with the 'a whole mind is a healthy mind' program that Dr. Barlind says is the key to happiness."

The Faire was much as I remembered it—weird booths, loud music, and people indulging in the sort of excited laughter and high-volume chatter that went along with a day's adventures. I strolled up and down the center aisle, not entering any of the booths but watching people with an eye that was soon much less vigilant.

"No Terrin," I breathed with a sigh of relief. I hadn't really expected him to show up, but as my brain had pointed out, who was to say he wouldn't have? "See, inner self? Nothing here but a circus full of pierced people and demonologists." I passed by a booth with a sign that read SPIRIT PET PSYCHIC. "And ghosts who talk to animals. Nothing at all out of the ordinary."

I swear I could feel my brain pursing its lips in disbelief.

Ten minutes later I started up the car and bumped along the field toward the exit.

"Leaving so soon?" asked the young man who collected the money for parking. He had been sitting on a folding chair, a camping lantern next to him and a book in his hand. "You didn't stay long. Do you want your money refunded? I'm afraid we don't normally do that, but since you weren't here long enough to partake in any of the delights to be found at the GothFaire—"

"That's not necessary. I was just here...er...to check on something."

"Oh? Did you find it?"

"No. As a matter of fact, it was anticlimactic in the extreme," I answered with a friendly smile. "But no worries—now I can tell my therapist to relax. There's no chance of me having another mental breakdown."

"Er..." The man backed away from my car. "That's good."

"It is indeed!" I gave him a cheery wave, and the car lurched off the grass and onto the tarmac. I hummed to myself as I zipped along, enjoying the feeling of freedom after two years of incarceration.

"I have a bright new life ahead of me," I told no one in particular. "Dr. Barlind said she was certain I have great potential in something. I just have to figure out what. Maybe I should try painting again. Or writing. Oh, poetry! Poets are always tortured and angsty, and after what I went through, I bet the dark, tormented poems would just ooze out of— Son of a fruit bat!"

The car fishtailed wildly when I slammed on the brakes, the horrible thumping sound of a large object being struck by the bumper echoing in my brain, but not even coming close to touching the sheer, utter horror I felt at the thought of hitting something. Ever since I had been a child and my father had hit a deer in a remote section in northern Sweden, I feared running down a living thing. And here I was, happily yacking away to myself and not paying attention to the road...

With a sick heart and even sicker stomach, I got out of the car, peering through the darkness at the road behind me.

"Please let it be something old and ready to die... please let it be something old and ready to die," I repeated as I stumbled forward a few steps.

Just a sliver of the moon was out, but we were far enough north that we got the midnight sun effect—since the sun didn't fully set at night, the sky wasn't as pitch-black as it was elsewhere. Instead, we suffered through what I thought of as deep twilight—too dark to read but with enough residual light to see the silhouettes of large objects.

My heart sank at the sight of the big black mound in the middle of the road.

"Please be an elderly deer that was ready to die, please oh please oh please." My voice was thick with the tears that were splashing down my face. I felt perilously close to vomiting, but I could no more leave whatever it was I hit lying on the road than I could have sprouted a second head.

The black mound resolved itself into the shape of a large black dog. "Oh my God," I moaned, guilt stabbing at me with hot, sharp edges. "I've killed someone's beloved pet!"

I knelt next to the dog, the tears now falling on my hands as I ran them over the animal, my heart aching with regret. If only I had been paying attention. If only I hadn't been so caught up in myself. Right at that moment, I would have given anything to take back the last five minutes and live them over again.

Heat blossomed under my hands where I touched the dog. There was no visible blood, no horribly mangled limbs, but the animal wasn't moving. "Noo!" I wailed, wanting to hug the poor thing and make it all better. "No, this can't— Sweet suffering succotash!"

To my astonishment, the dog jerked beneath my fingers, then leaped to its feet and shook. We're talking a full-body shake, the kind where not only the head and ears get into the action, but also the sides, tail, and evidently, copious amounts of slobber. He was big, with thick black fur and droopy lips from which stretched tendrils of slobber that lazily reached for the earth.

"You're not dead. You're okay?" Hope rose inside of me at the sight of the dog. "Did I just stun you? Man, you're big. You're the size of a small pony, aren't you? Let me just look you over and see if there are any serious injuries..." I patted him up and down his body, but he didn't seem to react as if he was in pain. In truth, he looked more dazed than anything. He kept shaking his head, which sent long streamers of drool flying out in an arterial pattern. My left arm took the brunt of much of that slobber.

"But I don't mind," I told the dog, getting to my feet. "So long as you're all right."

He sat down and promptly howled, causing me to wince in sympathy.

"All right, you're not quite unharmed, but at least you're not dead, and that's the important thing. Here... um..." I looked around but didn't see signs of any nearby houses. "Damn. Houses here can be a mile or more apart. Looks like you're my responsibility now. Great. Ack, don't howl again! I'll take care of you, I promise. What we need is a vet. Can you walk? This way, boy. Or girl. Whatever you are, here, doggy. Car ride!"

I opened the door to the backseat. The dog looked

at the car, then looked at me. I patted my leg. "C'mon, doggy. Let's go for a ride in the car!"

He cocked his head for a moment, then got to his feet and limped over to the car, hopping nimbly onto the backseat. "Well, thank heavens I don't have to haul you into the car. I'm not sure I could do it if I had to. You look like you weigh about as much as me. Right, let's go find you an emergency vet hospital."

Two and a half hours later, I emerged from a twenty-four-hour animal hospital, the Swedish equivalent of $180 poorer. "I don't quite see why I should be the one to take him home."

"You ran over him," the vet, an older woman with a no-nonsense haircut that perfectly matched her abrupt manner, told me. "He's your responsibility."

"Yeah, but you have a kennel where you could keep him until his people come to get him."

"He has no collar, no identification of any form, including a microchip, and you said you ran him down on a rural stretch well outside of any town."

I flinched at the "ran him down" mention.

"Therefore," she continued, opening up the rear door of the car. The dog hopped in and plopped himself down, taking up the entire backseat. "He's your problem. We don't have the space or the resources to take care of him."

"Yes, but—"

She pinned me back with a look that had me fidgeting. "If you insist on leaving him here, he'll be collected by the animal welfare people in the morning. A dog of his size is virtually unadoptable. He might be a purebred Newfoundland, or he might not. Either way, he would be put down in less than thirty-six hours. Do you want that on your conscience?"

"No," I said miserably, and got into the car. The rest of the trip home was accomplished in silence . . . if you didn't count the snores of a 150-pound dog.

Four

"You can stay here for the night," I told the dog when we got home. "But my sister is allergic to your kind, so it's just a short visit for you, and then we'll find somewhere else for you to go."

The dog wandered off as soon as I let him out of the car. "Hey!" I shouted after him when he ran across the dirt drive and the scrubby grass that was the only thing that would grow so close to the water, and bounded over a large piece of driftwood and onto the rocky beach. "Dammit, dog, don't make me chase after you. Wait, are you going home? Do you know your way home from here? Home, doggy, home!"

I followed after him, half hoping he'd head back to the road and to wherever it was he belonged, but instead, he turned down the beach and loped along the edge of the water until he disappeared into the semidarkness.

"Great. Now he's gone. Oh well, at least the vet gave him a clean bill of health."

I walked back to the house, trying to convince myself to forget the dog, but I couldn't even get across the threshold.

The vet was right—the dog *was* my responsibility. He might not be hurt, but I had hit the poor thing, and since I had opposable thumbs and he didn't, I had to see to it that he was either returned to his people or handed over to folks who would find him a new home.

"Yo, dog," I called, doing an about-face and heading down the beach after him. The weak light from the horizon seemed to glow across the now-inky water, making it possible to see the large rocks and tree trunks that dotted the shore. A familiar scent of seaweed, damp sand, and salty air filled my lungs. "Here, boy! Treaties! Or there will be once I get you into the house."

Ahead of me, over the soft sound of the water lapping at shore, I heard a muffled *woof.*

"Doggy?" I yelled. My nearest neighbor was a good three miles down the beach, so I didn't worry about waking anyone up. "Hey, dog, if you found something dead and stinky and are planning on rolling in it, I'd like to encourage you to change your mind. For one, it's not nearly as attractive a smell as you think it is, and for another, I don't think you'd fit in my bathtub— Oh no, not again!"

By now I'd come upon the dog, who was standing with his nose pressed against a black shape that was slumped on the ground.

"If that's a dead seal or something equally nasty..." I started to warn him, but stopped when I got a better look at the shape.

It was a man.

A dead man lay at my feet.

Right there on the beach. The tide was going out, leaving the ground sodden with seaweed, the tang of the night air stinging my eyes. I stared at the black shape, wondering who was screaming.

It was me.

"No!" I said in protest, wanting to turn on my heels and run away from the horrible sight. "No, no, no. I can't have this. I can't have men lying dead at my feet. The last time that happened, I ended up hooked to a machine that zapped me full of a kajillion volts. I refuse to be crazy anymore. Therefore, you, sir, cannot be dead. I forbid it."

I reached down to turn the man onto his back, jerking my hand away when a static shock to end all static shocks snapped out between my fingers and his arm.

"What the hell?" I rubbed my fingers, wondering if the man had some sort of electronics on him that had gotten wet. But before I could ponder that, he moaned and moved his legs, his head lifting off the rocks for a few seconds before he slumped down again.

"What is this, my day for seeing dead things that aren't really dead?" My mind shied painfully away from that thought. "Hey, mister, are you okay?"

It was a stupid question to be sure—he was facedown, obviously having been deposited on the shore by the tide, and clearly unconscious. But at least he was alive.

Tentatively, I reached out a finger and touched the wet cloth of his sleeve. "Mister?"

There was no static shock this time, so I tugged him until he rolled over onto his back. His hair, shiny with water and black as midnight, was plastered to his skull, while bits of seaweed and sand clung to the side of his cheek and jaw. His chin was square and his face angular, with high cheekbones that gave him a Slavic look and made my fingers itch to brush off the sand. There was a bit of reddish black stubble on his jaw that I really wanted to touch. I was willing to bet that it was soft and enticing...

I shook that thought away. What the hell was I doing thinking about a man's beard when he was lying at my feet, possibly near death?

"Stick to what's important," I told myself, noting that his chest rose and fell in a regular rhythm. Although a quick examination didn't show any obvious signs of injury, it was clear he needed medical attention. Accordingly, I pulled out my cell phone and called the emergency services number.

"What is your emergency?" a coolly impersonal voice asked.

"There's an unconscious man on the beach next to my house. He's alive and breathing okay and I don't see any blood or twisted limbs, but he might have hit his head or something."

"And your location?"

I gave her the address of the family home.

She tsked. "You are very rural."

"Yeah, I know. My parents liked that. How soon can you get someone here? The breeze is picking up, and I should probably at least cover the guy up until the paramedics arrive."

"There has been a large fire in Maslo," she answered, naming the largest nearby town. "I cannot send anyone to you for some time."

"You've got to be kidding," I said, shocked by such

a callous response. "This guy is unconscious. He could have a brain injury!"

"You said he was breathing on his own, and there was no blood or signs of external injury."

"No, but—"

"The nearest hospital to you is . . ." I could hear her fingers tapping on a keyboard. "Seventy-two kilometers in Kirkeist."

I knew exactly where that hospital was. I'd spent a horrible night locked up in the psych ward two years ago. "Are you suggesting that I move an injured man? What if he has back injuries?"

"You must move him with care if you believe that to be the case."

I shook my head in disbelief. "I can't believe that you'd tell me to haul this poor guy to a hospital so far away. That's almost inhuman. Aren't the emergency guys obligated to come and help?"

"Not in your region, no. There is no funding for emergency services. They are provided by regions that have them, but on an as-needed basis, and I just told you that the aid units are dealing with the fire in Maslo."

I gritted my teeth and fought back the need to punch out the woman on the phone. I'd never before had such a violent reaction to anyone, but frustration and a long, emotion-packed day had pushed me close to the edge. "There's got to be a clinic closer than Kirkeist."

Tappity-tappity went her computer keys. "There are two, but neither has emergency hours. There is a doctor four kilometers from you who is listed as an emergency resource, but his hours are not stated. If you like, I can provide you with that information."

"You do that little thing," I snarled, patting myself to find a small notebook and pencil. I wrote down the doctor's name and address and thought seriously about giving the woman a piece of my mind, but Dr. Barlind's strictures on "a calm mind is a happy mind is a sane mind" had me simply snapping a terse "Thank you" and hanging up.

"So, doggy, I guess this is my day to rescue everyone. Hmm." I eyed the man. He looked pretty solid. I doubted I could lift him and carry him to my car. I shifted my gaze to the dog. "I don't suppose you've ever pulled a sled?"

The dog sat down and squinted at me.

I sighed. "I didn't think so. Not to mention the fact that I don't have a sled anyway. Stay here, doggy, and watch over the man while I go grab a blanket or something."

To my surprise, the dog was still there when I returned. "All right, you get bonus points for loyalty. Now, if you could grow a couple of thumbs, I'd be delirious with joy. Ugh. Sorry, mister, this is going to be slightly unpleasant for you."

Fifteen minutes later, swearing mightily and huffing and puffing in a way that bespoke of someone who hadn't had much exercise while confined to the booby hatch, I managed to get the man onto the blanket and hauled off the beach onto the sandy dirt drive that led to the house.

"I sincerely...bloody, buggery hell...hope you don't have a back...son of a seagull...back injury because if you do, then I'm making it a hundred times worse. Holy mayonnaise and all the little condiments." I collapsed against the side of my car and panted, rubbing my hands in order to take away the sting of blanket burn.

The man lay on the ground, still not awake, but every now and again one of his arms or legs would twitch, and he'd mutter something unintelligible. I wondered if he was dreaming or hallucinating.

"Doesn't matter which," I said with an effort, shoving myself away from the car in order to grab him under the armpits. "I just hope my Good Samaritan efforts aren't going to end in a lawsuit by your family. Upsy-daisy."

With a very unladylike grunt, I managed to heave the man into the car, arranging him on the backseat in as comfortable a manner as possible. The dog watched me with bright, interested eyes, and when I hesitated, unsure of what to do with him, he walked over to the passenger door and waited for me to open it.

"Sure, why not," I said. "By all means, come with me to see the doctor who may or may not grace us with his expertise. The more the merrier, right?"

When my parents moved to Sweden, they had chosen an underpopulated section of the northeastern coast to build a house. They wanted isolation, and they got it in buckets. The closest house to ours was a good three miles down the road, and the nearest town—if you could call a collection of weather-beaten buildings and a small bait shop that doubled as a post office and miniscule grocery store a town—clung to the coastline with the tenacity of a limpet. The folks there were mostly fishermen, people like my parents who didn't mind living on the back side of nowhere. I drove through the town and down the road that led toward several other small communities that dotted the area. The largest of them, about nine miles away, had a few more amenities, including one Dr. Anders Ek, physician.

"And here we are," I said as my phone's GPS directed me to a small green house with a white picket fence. I glanced at the time. "Ouch. He's probably asleep. Oh well, let's hope he has a lot more compassion than the emergency lady. Stay, doggy. Guard the guy. Not that he's going to go anywhere..."

It took a few minutes of pounding on the front door before a light went on behind the fan window above the door. A few seconds later an elderly man in pajamas and a fuzzy sea-green bathrobe peered at me. He had salt-and-pepper hair that stood on end, reminding me of an old picture of Albert Einstein.

"Yes? What is it? Who are you?"

"My name is Aoife. Are you Dr. Ek?"

"Yes, yes. What time is it?" The doctor squinted up at the sky. "Bah. It is impossible to tell this time of year. Are you ill?"

"No, but I found a guy on the beach, and the emergency people had some big fire that they had to deal with, so they told me to bring him to you."

He didn't look any too pleased when I gestured toward my car. "I was sleeping."

"Yeah, well, I couldn't very well leave him on the beach, could I? And you know how far away the hospital is."

He clicked his tongue and reluctantly told me to bring the man in, turning to walk back into his house.

"By myself?" I called after him. "I barely got him into the car as is, and being dragged along the beach probably didn't do his head any good, assuming his brains aren't already scrambled."

The doctor said something I didn't hear, waving one

hand dismissively at me. I had quite a few things to say about that, but mindful of the happy psyche stuff that Dr. Barlind insisted was the key to a successful life, I kept them under my breath. I had the man half out of the car when a metallic rattling caused me to whirl around. The doctor was wheeling out an ancient gurney, the kind used in old black-and-white movies. Still, it had wheels, and it meant I wouldn't have to drag the poor man in by his heels.

It took some time for us to get him around the side of the house, where the doctor evidently had a room devoted to emergencies, with what looked like a massage table, a cabinet full of gauze and bandages and a few stainless steel medical tools, and even a bottle of oxygen. We wheeled the man in and I stood back, wondering if I should leave or sit outside and wait for the prognosis.

"Is that your dog?"

I glanced over my shoulder to where the dog sat on his haunches, watching us with those eyes that seemed uncannily knowing.

"Not really, no. I kind of ran over him earlier in the evening, but he wasn't hurt, and the vet couldn't keep him, so he's staying with me until I find his people. I don't suppose you recognize him?"

"No."

"I figured that was too much to hope for."

"Here," the doctor said, shoving a chipped enamel basin into my hands. "You hold that."

"Um...I was going to head on home. It's late, and—"

"This is your man," he said, peering over the tops of his thick-lensed glasses. "You can't leave him here. I will patch him up, and then you must take him away."

"You're a doctor," I said, feeling a strange déjà vu.

"I have no room for him. I am retired, you know, and only help out occasionally when I'm needed. No, don't tip it. Hold it steady." He poured some alcohol into the basin and tossed into it a pair of scissors, forceps, and something that looked like a scalpel before bending over the man, pulling up one eyelid and flashing a tiny light right onto the man's eyeball. "Hmm."

"Hmm?" I wanted to look at the same time I wanted to be away from there. My curiosity won out. I peeked over his shoulder. "Is he badly hurt?"

"I haven't examined him yet, but he's not showing signs of a concussion."

"That's good." I stepped back when the doctor spun around, selected a pair of scissors from the alcohol bath, and used them to cut the sodden shirt off the man's body.

"Ah."

"Ah?" I felt like a human parrot, repeating his words. "Is that a good ah or a bad ah?"

"It is an ah that means I see no obvious injuries."

Once again I looked over the doctor's stooped shoulders, bracing myself for the sight of blood or at least a gaping wound that had been washed clean by the sea. There was neither. What there was made me blink in surprise. The man's chest seemed to go on forever, with lovely swells of muscles at the pectorals, rippling down to a six-pack that would have done any Hollywood actor proud. "Wow," I said, drinking in the magnificent sight. He had what I thought of as a reasonable amount of chest hair, not so much that he looked like a monkey, but he was no plucked goose, either. A line of hair disappeared into the waistband of his pants.

I had a sudden, almost overwhelming hope that the doctor would cut off those pants.

Inappropriate smutty thoughts aside, I looked back at the man's face. There was something about those high cheekbones and black hair that rang a distant bell in my memory. Was he some sort of a celebrity that I'd seen pictures of? Mentally, I shook my head. The memory was on the edge of my consciousness, hovering tantalizingly just out of reach.

Dr. Ek hummed to himself when he pulled out a stethoscope and listened to a couple of different spots on the man's chest, then with a grunt, rolled him onto his side and listened to his back before letting him return to his resting position. "No water in the lungs. That, my dear, means your man was most likely conscious when he went into the water. It is a good sign."

"He's not really my man," I protested.

One fuzzy white eyebrow rose over the lens of his glasses. "You were certainly ogling him as if he was."

My face heated with embarrassment. "Oh, uh… I was…" I cleared my throat. "I was just glad to see he wasn't hurt."

"Mmm-hmm." He didn't sound like he believed me, and I couldn't blame him. Not with the blush that was burning up my cheeks at being caught all but drooling over an unconscious man. "We might as well take his trousers off, if you think you can control yourself."

"Hey! I may have admired the way his chest has all those muscles and the cute little nipples and the six-pack, but that doesn't mean I'm going to pounce on the man the second you get his pants— Sweet sizzling soupspoons!"

While I'd been speaking, the doctor got the belt

unbuckled, the zipper lowered, and jerked the sides of the jeans down to the man's knees. Unfortunately—or fortunately, depending on how you looked at it—the man's underwear went with the pants.

"Well, there's the myth about men and cold water blown all to hell and back again," I said, staring at the man's groin before I realized that the doctor was asking for my help. "Oh, sorry."

Hurriedly I set down the basin and helped the doctor divest the man from his shoes, socks, and pants. The doctor, with a glance at me, tossed a towel over the man's privates.

"I'm quite in control of my libido, I assure you," I told him with much dignity.

"It's no concern of mine what you do with your man," he said, giving a little shrug before continuing his examination.

I tried to adopt a nonchalant "I don't care if there's a naked, seriously hot man in front of me" expression and held the basin in case he needed one of the tools.

He didn't.

"I don't see any marks on him," the doctor said. "Nothing that would indicate he'd been tossed around by the tide, as you said he was."

"I said I thought he'd been rolled ashore with the tide, but maybe he swam there and then collapsed. Do you think his brain's okay?"

"I can't tell without a scan, but I don't see any signs that there is damage." He straightened up and peeled off a pair of latex gloves. "Let's see if we can bring him around with a little chemical aid."

He snapped a small plastic vial under the man's nose.

The smell of ammonia made my nose wrinkle, but it took about ten seconds before the man suddenly coughed, blinked, and tried to shove the doctor's hand away.

"Ah." The doctor smiled at me. "That is a good ah. He awakens."

"So I see." I stepped to the side to look at the man. He was squinting up at us, one hand shielding his eyes against the bright examination light.

The doctor tipped it down so it wasn't shining right in the guy's face, and asked, "How do you feel?"

The man looked first at the doctor, then at me, his eyes narrowed in confusion and, I thought, suspicion. He said something that I didn't understand.

"Um... did you catch that?" I asked the doctor.

"No. It sounds Russian, or like one of those languages."

"Russkie?" I asked the man.

He started to shake his head, yelped, and put a hand to the back of it, wincing.

"That would be the goose egg you have back there," the doctor said, pushing his hand aside to gently probe around the area. "It didn't feel too worrisome to me, but evidently you're feeling it now, eh? Your head hurts, yes?"

The man said something else, carefully holding on to his head as he swung his legs over the side of the table.

The towel slithered down off his lap, leaving him exposed. He looked down at himself in surprise, then up to me.

I kept my eyes firmly on his face as I knelt to pick up the towel, handing it back to him. And if you think that was easy, you're dead wrong.

"You don't speak Swedish?" I asked him as he tucked the towel around his hips.

He just looked at me.

"English?" I switched to that language. "I hope you're not Russian, because I never did pick up any of that language."

"I'm not Russian," he said, his voice a husky baritone that seemed to brush over me like a wave of velvet. He had a slight, very slight accent that I couldn't place but seemed vaguely Slavic. He frowned first at me, then at the doctor. "Who are you? Why have you beaten me on the head and captured me? If you intend to kill me, I must inform you that my brother, although not currently on speaking terms with me, will avenge my death."

"Wow. Straight from who are you to avenging your death? That's some pretty big leaps of logic right there."

"You are conversing with him?" the doctor asked, evidently not understanding English.

"Yes. He says he's not Russian and warns us that if we kill him, his brother is going to come after us."

"Will he?" The old man looked interested. "Who is his brother?"

"No clue. I'll ask." I turned back to the mystery man. "The doctor—and he is a doctor, not some deranged head-bonking murderer—wants to know who your brother is."

"I will answer none of your questions," he said with what I thought was a whole lot of dignity considering the fact that he was naked except for a small towel. He got to his feet, clutching said towel, and weaved for a moment but managed to remain upright.

I had to admit that for a man who'd been unconscious and bashed around a bit, he looked pretty damned good.

His chest had a few scars around the ribs and a nasty line across one pectoral that interrupted that nice chest hair, but the rest of him wasn't at all hard to look at.

"What did he say?" the doctor asked.

"He refused to answer."

The man glanced around the room, a dark frown on his brow. "Is this where you intend to torture me? You should know that my brother will, eventually, avenge that as well."

"This is an examination room, not a torture chamber," I said with a mixture of impatience and amusement. What a drama queen he was.

"Then you will take me to my cell," he said with haughty indifference. "And bring me some clothes, unless you intend to expose me to the elements in an attempt to kill me that way. Not that such treatment will have the effect you desire. It's been tried before, and I survived for many years before I was freed."

"Someone tried to kill you before?" I asked, aghast at the idea. My gaze dropped to the scars on his ribs. "Maybe instead of asking us who we are, we should be asking you just who the hell you are. So I will. Who the hell are you?"

He made a sound like he was annoyed. "I am Kostya. What is your name, mortal?"

I gave him a look to let him know I didn't appreciate the condescending attitude. "Aoife. This is Dr. Ek."

"What is he saying now?" the doctor asked, plucking at my sleeve.

"His name is Kostya, and someone tried to kill him before."

"You will cease speaking in whatever Nordic language

you are speaking. I cannot understand it, and it irritates me."

That sort of attitude didn't go far at all with me. I ignored Kostya. "He seems to think we're holding him captive, and evidently likes to threaten people with his brother, whoever he is. He's also demanding that we bring him clothing."

"Is he? Your man is quite obstinate."

"Annoying, isn't he? And for the record, he's not mine."

Kostya glared at us both. "You are clearly making plans for my demise. Very well. I cannot stop you, but I can repeat that my brother—"

"Yeah, I know, your brother's going to beat us up if we kill you. What sort of people do you hang with that you get those sorts of scars, and are left exposed to the elements for years, and have to threaten people with your big brother?"

"Drake is my younger brother," he said, clearly offended.

I laughed right out loud, which obviously offended him all the more.

"I'm sorry," I said, putting a hand out and touching him on the arm before I realized what I was doing. He stared at my hand as if it were a three-headed crab. "I don't like laughing at anyone, but you looked so enraged, it was impossible to stifle. Look, we seem to be at cross-purposes, so let's start over again. I'm Aoife, and I found you lying unconscious on a beach outside my house. This is Dr. Ek. He's retired but kindly offered to take a look at you when I hauled you out of the ocean. Neither one of us is interested in killing you or torturing you or leaving you out in the cold naked, although it's July, so it's really not that cold right now. Evidently you took a smack to the head—I don't suppose you remember what happened to you?"

"What have you done with my clothes?" he asked, moving slightly away from me so that my hand dropped off his arm.

"I didn't do anything with them. Dr. Ek cut off your shirt, so it's probably not wearable, although your other clothes are behind you, on the chair. They're sopping wet, though. Why aren't you answering my question? I asked it nicely enough."

"You have nothing to offer me for the answers," he said dismissively, turning to grab his clothes, then obviously realized that he was exposing his butt to me. I got an eyeful before he whipped the towel around with one hand while grabbing his pants with the other. He held them up with a look of distaste. "They are wet."

"How very nice of you to confirm what I just told you."

"Your man's clothes are wet," Dr. Ek said, evidently wanting to join in on the let's-say-the-obvious fun. "I suppose I could part with a pair of trousers. You wait here with him and see that he doesn't break into my drug cabinet."

Dr. Ek bustled past me to the door, where the dog, which had been lying down, sat up and watched him leave.

"Where is he going?" Kostya demanded. He now had the chair between us, using it as a shield for his modesty. "Is he fetching those who would destroy me?"

"You really do have a one-track mind, don't you?" I spread my hands to show him that they, at least, were empty of threat. "He's gone to get you some dry clothes, as a matter of fact. And if you think I'm going to pay you to answer a couple of civil questions, you're more nuts that I ever was."

He was about to answer, but some movement behind me must have caught his eye, because he stepped to the side and stared for a moment before turning a surprisingly furious expression upon me. "What are you doing with Jim?"

"Jim who?" I asked, confused.

He pointed to the door. "Do not deny that you have captured Jim. Or has it been sold into your employ?"

"I think Dr. Ek's first name is—"

"Not the mortal. Jim," Kostya said, pointing again. I turned to look. The dog sat there watching us.

"Oh," I said, understanding dawning at last. "That's your dog? I had no idea. I mean, he wasn't near the beach at all when I ran him—er—found him. But he did snuffle you a lot when you were lying on the beach. Talk about serendipity, huh?"

"Jim is not mine," he snorted. "It belongs to my brother's mate, Aisling."

"Really? That's still odd that I should find both of you." I turned to the dog and patted my leg. "Hey, Jim. Come here, boy."

The dog cocked his head but didn't move.

"He doesn't seem to know his name very well. Does your sister-in-law say it differently?"

"Jim," Kostya said, a disgusted curl to his lip, "tell this mortal who you are."

Warning bells went off in my head. I mean, big-time warning bells, the kind that deafen you for a moment before leaving you with the overwhelming desire to get the hell away from the man who thought dogs could talk.

"Um," I said, backing away from Kostya very slowly,

so as not to capture his attention, "sorry, but that's my cue to leave."

I turned and bolted to the door, but just as I was about to fling it open, Kostya was suddenly there, all warm, naked skin, pressing me against it, his breath hot on my face as he demanded, "You will go nowhere, woman. Now you are *my* prisoner."

Five

"I don't know whether to be more disturbed by the fact that you think a dog can talk or that you can stand there, stark naked, without so much as a stapler as a weapon, and hold me prisoner." I adopted a quite reasonable, conversational tone, the sort intended to calm deranged people and keep them from committing acts of violence. I tried very hard not to notice just how nice the naked Kostya felt against me, the unyielding planes of his body being softened by my curves. It was a wonderful demonstration of how men and women fit together, but now was not the time to dwell on that subject.

His eyes were black, I noticed as he scowled down at me. Not dark brown but black, as black as his pupils, but a shiny black, one that glittered with little specks of silver. Unfortunately, at that moment, the glitter took the form of ire. "What the hell are you talking about?" he demanded to know. "What stapler?"

"There's no stapler," I said, finding myself suddenly blighted with several conflicting desires, ranging from the urge to grab his head and kiss him to laughing at the crazy situation, stomping on his toes, kneeing him in the naked noogies, and running away.

He looked even more irritated. I tried to ignore the heat of his body pressed against mine. "Then why did you bring it up?"

"I was using it as an example of just how vulnerable you are," I said, deciding to go with amusement. Dr. Barlind was big on the subject of using humor as a coping mechanism for trying situations. "You know, if you need someone to talk to about things, I know of a top-notch therapist. She really helped me when I was super-confused."

My brain made a comment about denial and what happened to people who refused to admit the truth just because that ended up in shock therapy, but as usual, I paid it no attention.

"I have no need of therapy," he scoffed, then must have realized just how hard he was pushing me into the wall, because he glanced downward. My breasts were smooshed up against his chest, making them bulge upward in a way that I would have found annoying in any other situation, but at that moment, they were deliriously happy with where they were, and that disturbed me more than anything.

"Stop ogling my boobs," my mouth said before I could approve such a thing.

His gaze snapped up to mine. "You ogled me earlier."

"You were naked. And you're not at all bad-looking, despite those scars. I would have had to be inhuman to not ogle you at least a tiny bit, and I want full marks for handing you that towel without once looking down. It wasn't easy, but I managed it, and I think credit should be given where credit is due."

"Then you cannot damn me for looking at your breasts when they are flaunted in front of me," he countered.

"That's because you have me pinned to the door." I waited for the count of five for him to step back. He didn't. "You're still doing that, by the way. Pinning me to the door, that is."

"You are my prisoner," he repeated.

That was the point where I noticed the fact that he smelled like the spicy mead that is sometimes served during regional festivals—the warm, summery hint of honey overlaid with a sharper note that seemed to sizzle along my skin. Despite the knowledge that I should be getting away from him as expeditiously as possible, I had the worst urge to tilt my head back and brush my mouth against his.

That was a crazy thought, and I didn't have any more of those. So without disputing the fact that he had me prisoner, let alone the idea that he needed any such thing, I did the one thing that I knew would cause him to back off...I reached around him with both hands and squeezed cheek.

He leaped backward just at the moment when Dr. Ek opened the door, sending me stumbling forward straight into Kostya's arms again.

"Couldn't wait until you were home, eh?" Dr. Ek said, peering at us over his glasses. He held a stack of worn clothing that he offered to Kostya. "That bodes well for the bump on the head your man took. If he gets nauseous, though, you shall have to take him to the hospital. They can scan his brain there."

Kostya donned the clothing and lectured me for at least five minutes about why it was unfair of me to accuse him of ogling my breasts when it was clear I lusted after his body, while at the same time Dr. Ek gave me instructions on warning signs to watch for should Kostya suddenly fall victim to some undetected head injury. I let them both talk until they ran out of steam, then turned to Kostya to say, "I wasn't making a pass at you, so you can just drop that line. I grabbed your butt so you'd back up and let me go. And, Dr. Ek"—I switched to Swedish—"I appreciate the fact that you are being conscientious and all, but I'm not going to be around to see if he has any of those reactions. I've told you that we're not a couple, and he's clearly got a screw loose upstairs somewhere, which means I want nothing to do with him."

"We must be kind to those who are not as fortunate as we are," Dr. Ek said, bustling us toward the door. To my surprise, Kostya allowed himself to be shooed, having first snagged his wet clothing and shoes. "You should not spurn a fine man simply because he is not entirely right in the head. Now, then, if you have a credit card, I would prefer that for payment over a check."

Jim the dog—I'll assume Kostya was correct about his name—followed us, bumping his nose into the back of my leg when I stopped suddenly at the front door. "What? Oh, yeah, you want payment. Um"—I switched languages and addressed Kostya—"the doctor wants to be paid. I don't suppose you have any cash? Doesn't matter if it's wet or not."

Kostya's black eyes spoke volumes, none of which were the least bit helpful.

"Fine," I snapped, pulling open my purse, which was

strapped across my body. "You can owe me. Visa okay, Dr. Ek?"

It was, and after a couple of minutes, we found ourselves on the flagstone pathway that led across a tiny green lawn. The sun was still in twilight mode, leaving the trees beyond the road silhouetted against a hazy amber sky. Dark shapes flitted across the sky every now and again— bats out for the evening's hunt. I drew in a deep breath, catching a faint note of lilac on the air, but mostly it was Kostya's intriguing scent that filled my awareness.

I turned to Kostya and took his hand, giving it a firm shake before dropping it and saying in a bright, chipper voice, "Well, it was interesting meeting you and having my breasts squished against your chest. I hope your head feels better. I'm sure you can take the dog to your sister-in-law. You can donate the money for your doctor bill to whatever charity strikes your fancy. Good-bye."

I turned and walked to the car, well aware that both the dog and the man were right behind me. I sighed when I reached the car. "You don't have a car, do you? Fine, I'll take you into town; then you can find your own way to wherever you're going."

"I will be tracked if I rent a vehicle. I will use yours instead," Kostya said, then reached around and grabbed the keys from my hand, ignoring my protest to open the door and get into the driver's seat.

"What the— Oh, you are not going to steal my car on top of everything!" I snarled, jerking open the back door and shoving Jim into the car before leaping in after him. And just in time—Kostya had started up the car before I could get the door closed.

"Where do you live?" Kostya asked.

"What? Are you insane? You actually think I'm going to tell you where my house is? You're carjacking me!" I managed to get myself disentangled from the dog and sat up, considering how best to disable Kostya without causing him to crash.

"I'm not insane. I do not know where I am, but evidently you have a home here. We will go there, and then you will tell me everything I wish to know, following which I will return to my home and continue my quest to rid the world of all red dragons."

Red dragons? Oh no, he was just like Terrin, believing in people who were secretly dragons. And if that didn't scare the pants off of me, nothing would.

"You are so setting off my crazy alert warning bells," I told the back of his head. I searched for something with which I could conk him on the noggin, but only halfheartedly—for one because it was dangerous to disable a driver in that manner, but mostly because the poor guy already had been walloped hard enough to leave a lump.

Poor guy? the sane part of my brain asked. *Poor guy? He's kidnapping you!*

"Look," I said in my most calming, reasonable voice, the one I found went really far in convincing Dr. Barlind that I had no more need of such heinous things as shock therapy and mind-altering drugs. "I know how it is when things around you get a little…intense. But kidnapping isn't the answer. Why don't you pull over, and we can talk about this. I'll help you as much as I can, I promise."

To my surprise, he pulled over to the grassy verge on the edge of the road. We were out of the tiny town, driving through the seemingly endless grassy pasture-land where sheep and cows rubbed elbows with elk and reindeer. "I need a secure location from which I can evaluate the situation. I must determine if I'm being stalked or if they believe me dead. If they saw you rescue me..."

"They who?" I asked when he didn't continue. For some reason, I felt a wave of empathy toward him, despite the fact that he wasn't as sane as I first thought he was. "Are you implying that someone would have an issue with me pulling you out of the water?"

"They would likely kill you if they knew, yes," he said matter-of-factly. "After they tortured you to find out what you know, of course."

"Of course." To my surprise, my empathy grew. I'd been in that poor man's shoes, when no one believed me, and I knew well how much a sympathetic person could mean to one's peace of mind.

"I won't let them do either," Kostya suddenly said, piercing me with a glittering look from those onyx eyes. "You have shown me kindness, and for that, I will not allow harm to come to you."

"That's very noble," I answered, touched by his statement despite the unusual circumstance. I felt oddly protected, which wasn't a wholly unwelcome feeling, although I could have wished my erstwhile protector had a few more wits about him.

"Will you take me to your home?" he asked.

I hesitated.

"I have sworn that no harm will come to you," he said, correctly interpreting my unspoken concern. "That includes from me. I pose you no danger."

"Well..." I bit my lip, weighing common sense with the understanding of what it was like to be cast adrift where no one would listen, really listen, to what it was you were saying. Kostya clearly had more than one screw loose in that attractive head of his, but that's what others had said about me. I knew well what it was to have judgments made about me without having my voice heard, and I had sworn that I would never be in that position again.

Didn't I owe it to deal with him as I wish I had been treated?

"All right," I heard myself say. "It's late, and I don't suppose there's a hotel or B&B we could park you at, so you're welcome to spend what's left of the night at my house. So long as you understand that should you attempt to assault me in any way, I will not hesitate to defend myself. And I know how to shoot my father's guns."

He made a face in the mirror. "I do not force myself on women, if that is what you fear."

"It's what *every* woman fears," I told him, and got out of the backseat when he exited the front, holding the door open for me. I got behind the wheel, giving him a cautious look when he slid in beside me. I pulled back onto the road, saying, "There's one thing I think you should know. I recently spent time in a facility for people who have a certain amount of mental confusion about life, and for that reason, I don't put up with people who think it's funny to poke fun at mental health, or the lack thereof. So you can just drop the references to dragons, dogs that can talk, and that sort of *Alice in Wonderland* crap because it's not amusing."

The look he sent my way was thoughtful. "Mental confusion? You were in an asylum? You have a sickness of the mind?"

"Yes, yes, and no, of course I don't have a mental illness." The tiny voice in my head cheered and waved a wee little banner at my show of support. It dropped the banner with the words that followed, however. "There was an event that I was at a couple of years ago, and I thought I saw something. Something...impossible. No one else saw it, so I was sent to an expensive clinic where they helped me realize that I was wrong."

The sense of inner disappointment at my words was great. I felt a tiny little part of my mind curl up into a ball of despair.

"What event?"

"Hmm?" I dragged my thoughts from the absurdity of feeling guilty over hurting part of my own psyche to what Kostya was asking. "Oh, it was a traveling circus that had all sorts of creepy stuff."

"Was it named GothFaire?" He frowned. "I recall coming across such a circus a few years ago. What impossible thing occurred?"

Something pinged at the edge of my awareness but wouldn't come into focus. I drove for a few minutes in silence, trying to decide if I should tell him or not. In the end, my miserable inner self got its way. "I saw a man get killed. Right before my eyes. And the man who killed him turned into a black puff of smoke when another guy did something to him—I didn't see what, although I think he stabbed him with a knife—but then the guy who I saw get killed came back and wasn't hurt at all."

My fingers started to hurt with the grip I had on the steering wheel. I made an effort to loosen the hold and didn't look over to Kostya to see what he thought.

"Ah," he said at last, and then I couldn't stand it and slid a glance his way. He was leaning back in his seat, looking out of the passenger window.

"Ah? That's all you have to say, just 'Ah,' like someone tells you every day that she sees a man murdered and
miraculously resurrected? You don't think that's in the
least bit odd?"

"Not really." He turned his head to look at me, his
black eyes unreadable in the dim light. But there was no
sense of mockery in his voice, or even sympathy, which
I personally found a thousand times worse. "You saw
someone who was not mortal nearly slain by a demon. It's
not a common occurrence, but it's certainly not unknown.
Not every demon is as civilized as Jim."

The hairs on my arms prickled. "You aren't trying to
say . . . no, you can't. Because if you were that crazy, you'd
be strapped down to a table right now while Dr. Barlind
stood over you telling you that the shock therapy should
help you break down those mental blocks that are keeping
you from being well again. You can't possibly mean that
the dog in the backseat of my car is a demon. I must have
misheard you."

"You did nothing of the kind." He turned his head to
look back out of the window. "Jim is a lesser demon—I do
not rightly recall its class, although given experience with
it, I assume it's a low one; nonetheless, it possesses all the
qualities inherent in a demon. I do not understand why it
refuses to speak, though."

"Dogs can't talk," I said in my super-calm voice. This
despite the warning bells shrieking in my head.

"Demon ones can. Jim, tell the mortal you can speak."

"I can?" The car jerked violently to the side at the
sound of a male voice from the backseat. "Oh, wow, I
can talk. How cool is this? Lookit me, I'm talking! Talk,
talk, talk. I can talk. Whoa, babe, you may wanna watch

the road and not look at me, because that tree is getting awfully—aieee!"

I slammed on the brakes, the rear of the car sliding with a horrible noise along the dirt and grass before we came to an abrupt halt less than a foot away from a stone fence.

My entire body shaking, I carefully unstrapped the seat belt and turned around as far as I could to look at the backseat.

Or rather, the dog that sat on it. He was panting, his eyes round, but there was nothing at all odd about him.

Other than the fact that I'd just heard him speak.

"You can't talk," I told him.

"I think I can," he answered.

I blinked.

"Okay," I said, raising a shaky hand to rub my forehead. "I'm having some sort of episode. Some...I don't know, psychotic flashback or something."

"Maybe the dude better drive, then," the dog said sympathetically. I closed my eyes, wanting to scream and cry and run away as fast as I could. "'Cause you look like you're going to ralph all over the place."

"This is not happening," I said, still rubbing my forehead. "I'm going to have to call Dr. Barlind, and she's going to lock me up again, and I don't want to be locked up! I'm sane, dammit! I'm perfectly sane!"

"I don't know about that, but I agree with Jim that if you are going to vomit, I should drive," Kostya told me.

I opened my eyes to glare at him. "This is all your fault!"

"I reject your accusations," he answered with lofty disdain, then ruined the effect by asking, "How is it my fault?"

"You put the idea of a talking dog into my head! If you hadn't, I'd be perfectly fine." I smacked him on the arm.

"Dammit, if I'm going to be locked up again, then so are you. I'm going to tell everyone what you said about that . . . dog . . . being a demon."

"Hey, you don't have to say the word *dog* like I'm made of poop or something," came the protest from the backseat. I ignored it. It was just a delusion, nothing more. "And what do you mean, demon? I'm a demon? I thought I was a dog? That's what the vet said. She told Aoife here that I was a handsome specimen." In the mirror, I could see the dog looking down at himself. "Really handsome, I should say. Hey, I got a white spot on my chest. That's cool."

To my surprise, Kostya looked startled at the dog's words. "What do you mean, are you a demon? Of course you are. What game are you playing?"

"I dunno. Spot the white on a black dog?" Jim the impossibly talking dog shrugged. I swear to all the gods, he shrugged! "What game do you want to play?"

"Why are you not with Aisling?"

"Twenty questions, is it?" Jim's eyes narrowed on Kostya. "Okay, I give. What's an Aisling?"

Kostya stared at him for the count of seven before turning a speculative gaze on me. "Order it to answer the question truthfully," he said after another couple of moments' thought.

"Huh?"

"Give it a direct command to answer the question truthfully."

"What question?"

"Why it is not with Aisling."

"I'm sorry, I can't . . . this is all . . . I swear to you, I'm sane. I'm perfectly sane now, but I can't indulge my hallucinations this way. Dr. Barlind says—"

"To hell with Dr. Barlind, whoever he is."

"She."

Kostya made an annoyed gesture. "You are not insane. The dog is a demon. It is speaking, and it belongs with Aisling. Order it to answer the question truthfully."

"This is stupid—fine! I'll ask him, but you get to go first for the shock therapy." I turned around again to face the dog. "Dog—"

"Jim. Say its name."

"You really are enough to drive someone nuts, you know that? Dog whose name is evidently Jim, at least according to the man next to me, please answer—"

"Command it."

"Gah! Jim, I command you to truthfully answer the question of why you are not with someone named Aisling."

The dog pursed his lips, scrunched up his nose, and said, "I don't know anyone named Aisling."

"Happy now?" I turned back to Kostya.

He sat back in his seat, a slight frown pulling his brows down. "No. Although this explains the rumors that Jim was no longer seen with the green dragons. It must have been given to another... but no, Aisling would not part with it. It was too dear to her."

"Okay, this is going to sound like a ridiculously pedantic thing to say given that we're both quite, quite mad, but why do you keep referring to the poor doggy as *it*? He's a boy dog, if you were wondering."

"Demons are always referred to with gender-neutral pronouns," he answered absently.

"Hey! My gender is very much not neutered!" Jim said, bending over to snuffle himself. "Look, right there, two magnificent noogies, just as big as you like. Well, maybe not *you*, because you'd have to stuff them into your pants, but I think they're perfect for parading around in front of the lady dogs."

I looked at Kostya, feeling as if I were standing on the edge of a precipice. One step in the wrong way and I'd fall into a pit from which there was no return. Kostya sat in deep thought, staring out the front window, one hand rubbing his stubble-laden chin.

"Kostya, I command you to truthfully answer whether or not that dog in the backseat just said something about his balls."

The disbelief in his eyes was almost comical. "It doesn't work on me, mortal!"

"Sorry. I just figured that since you wanted me to do it for Jim—"

"Jim is a demon. You are evidently now its demon lord, although what Aisling will have to say about that, I do not care to think. Thus, you may give it commands and it must obey."

I stared at him for a moment. "I'm what, now?"

"A demon lord." He turned back to the window. "I wish that I was able to contact Drake. There might be a reason that Jim was separated from Aisling."

I shook my head to myself, then decided that if I wanted to retain even the slightest shred of sanity, there was only one thing to do. I did it.

"Where are you going?" Kostya asked when I got out of the car and started walking down the road.

"Away from you."

"Why? I have done nothing objectionable." I didn't even hear his footsteps when he caught up to me. I just kept walking. "I have made no untoward comment about the fact that you have mental instability, or that you pushed your breasts against me in a blatant invitation, or even that your driving skills are not as impressive as I had hoped."

I stopped to glare at him. "*My* driving skills? I drive just fine, you arrogant son of a sea witch!"

"My mother is not a sea witch, although I admit that there are times when I would relish calling her that—"

I smacked him on the arm. "I drive wonderfully. I couldn't help being startled by Bo-Bo the Talking Dog!"

"It's Jim, evidently," the dog in question said, strolling up behind us. "Are we going walkies? Because I think I need to drop a load, and you probably don't want to be downwind when I do."

I pointed to the field across the road. "Go over there and do that."

He grinned at me, a real grin, one with teeth, and curved lips, and an amused look in his eyes. "You've got it, oh master."

"Stop that!" I snapped, then turned back to Kostya. "Go away. And take the demon dog with you. You can have my car. I'll find a way back home somehow."

Kostya took my arms in his hands, giving me a little shake. "You appear to be denying the existence of Jim, among other things. Is that it? You do not wish to admit that I am a dragon and Jim is a demon?"

"Oh, now you're a dragon, are you?" I asked, stifling the urge to laugh hysterically.

"I have always been a dragon." His tone implied that he was vaguely insulted, but before I could make a comment about his sanity—let alone mine for even having that conversation—the world as I knew it came to an end.

Or rather, the world that I had lived in for the last two

years ended. Before my unbelieving eyes, Kostya's form seemed to shimmer for a moment before morphing into that of a black dragon, complete with glossy black scales, ivory claws, and a trickle of smoke coming out of one nostril. I froze, staring, my brain trying to come to terms with the impossible being in front of me, but before I could do more than squawk, the dragon shimmered again and Kostya stood in its place.

That was the moment that my sad little inner voice stood up and shouted with joy, filled with vindication after two years of denial.

"Holy sex me now!" I said, the rest of my brain still having problems coping with the fact that a dragon—*a dragon*!—had stood before me, his claws on my arms.

Told you so, said the formerly sad inner voice. *Guess Terrin was right all along, huh? Now we can get on with life. I wonder what a demon lord does?*

And that's when the penny dropped. "You're the black dragon I saw at GothFaire that night the world went insane. You're the guy Terrin pointed out to me."

"I do not know anyone named Terrin. As for your request—"

"What request?" I asked, confused, while my mind was busy pushing bits of puzzle pieces into place. No wonder Kostya looked familiar to me. But that meant that everything Terrin told me was true. Which in turn meant I wasn't the least bit gaga. Relief swamped me when I added, "I didn't ask you for anything."

"You did. You asked me to sex you now. I realize that you desire my body," Kostya said to me in the same stern tone of voice that my father had used whenever I was caught doing something I oughtn't, "but *now* is hardly the time or place for such actions. I will admit, however, that the thought is not displeasing to me. You are quite comely. Later, we will have the sexing. But for now, we must remain focused."

I giggled. I couldn't help it, the giggle just slipped out.

His frown returned. "You find me amusing?"

"I find your phrasing amusing. *Comely*, to be exact. I don't think I've ever heard it used outside of a Georgette Heyer novel. And for the record—" I had to stop for a moment to get a grip on myself. Apparently, my brain decided that giggling was good, and there was no reason to cease that action. "For the record, I do not desire your body. Not that you're hideous or anything, far from it. Even with those scars, your chest is really nice, and I like your legs because they aren't scrawny, and you have nice shoulders and naughty bits, but I've never been one to put physical attributes ahead of more important things."

"Such as?" He had his hands on his hips when he asked the question, which just made me want to giggle again.

"Intelligence, a sense of humor, and oh yes, not being a mythical creature." I swallowed another giggle. "Not that it wasn't a cool form, but still. I like my men without the sort of baggage that must go with being a shape-shifter."

"Is that so?" One eyebrow lifted.

"Yes."

"Then you will not like this." He pulled me against him, his mouth moving into place on mine, his breath hotter than I could have imagined. And then he kissed the very wits right out of my brain.

For about five seconds, after which my brain began to formulate thoughts again, all of which were highly positive about his kissing technique. My body gave that a thumbs-up and went into immediate seduction mode, which is why I found myself sliding my hands into his hair, careful to avoid his injury, and tugging gently to make him turn up the heat a notch.

It felt like fire was sweeping through me as he obliged, deepening the kiss, his tongue busy in my mouth even as his hands stroked down my back to dig into my behind. I wiggled my hips against him, causing him to moan into my mouth, a sound I wanted to echo. His lips were hot, but his tongue was pure fire, leaving little burning tingles that seemed to light other fires within me, deep fires, secret fires.

I was just seriously contemplating stripping the clothes off him and molesting him right there on the side of the road when he pulled back. Even in the dim twilight, I could see a glow in his eyes, as if they were lit with an inner power that glinted with silver moonlight.

"No," I said, unable to think of anything else to say. "No, I didn't enjoy that in the least. Do it again so I can not enjoy it some more."

His lips curled slightly at the corners, and tiny lines appeared at the edges of his eyes. "If I were to do so, you would end up naked on the backseat of your car. And as much as I might desire that, we would not be safe. Someone could come upon us, and I do not wish to place you in a position of risk."

"All things considered, that's really thoughtful of you, but I doubt if we're in any actual danger. Sweden is a pretty safe country." I let go of his hair and stepped back, simultaneously embarrassed that I reacted so strongly to his kiss and filled with a strange, empty sort of wanting that I hadn't felt before. "I concede the point that maybe I don't find you wholly repugnant. And you're right—we shouldn't do that again. I'm not at all the sort of woman who kisses strange dragons when she comes across them. Wow, I can't believe I just said that sentence. Are you impressed with how well I'm coping? Because I am. I'm not screaming, or ranting, or even calling the cops and having you hauled away. No, sir, I'm just standing here perfectly normal and natural even though my entire world has just been shaken to the core. There are demons who look like dogs, and dragons who look like handsome-as-sin men, and men who get killed and come back without a scratch on them. Really, I think a major award is in order to acknowledge just how well I'm coping, especially after all I've been through."

"If you're getting an award, then I want one, too," said Jim as he approached, evidently now refreshed. "It ain't every day you find out you're a demon and can talk. How come you're beet red, Eefies?"

"My name is Aoife. It's really not that hard to say: EE-fuh."

"Nicknames are a sign of affection, babe. So what's the plan? We going to walk to your house or drive like civilized peeps?"

I looked at the dog, then up to Kostya. It took me a minute to stop looking at his mouth and reliving that kiss, but at last I managed to ask, "You said I'm a demon lord. I assume that means that I am his boss?"

"Yes. There are eight demon lord princes who rule Abaddon, but they have legions of demons, not just one. I know of no other demon lords who are not princes of Abaddon."

"Abaddon being...?"

"Mortals based their concept of hell on it, but it's not the same thing. Similar in some respects," he allowed. "But not identical. I am hungry, and my head hurts. I wish to eat and then rest for a while, but if you do not want to drive, then I will."

"So I have legions of demonic dogs at my beck and call?" The skin on my back prickled at the thought.

"Not so far as I know. A demon lord is technically anyone to whom a demon is bound. For some reason that I do not understand, Jim appears to be bound to you. Do you wish to drive or not?"

I gave in to his prompting and returned to the car, part of me still marveling at how well I had shifted mental gears and gone from denial of all things impossible to a new world where dogs talked, and men were dragons, and I was smack-dab in the middle of it all. "I'll drive. But don't you be turning into a dragon while you're in the car. I don't want those claws poking holes in my nice upholstery."

He gave an exasperated look heavenward as he got into the car. I let him think whatever thoughts were possessing him, my own attention focused on driving while trying to sort through the thousands of questions zipping through my mind.

It wasn't until fifteen minutes had passed that I thought to ask the obvious. "What were you doing unconscious on the beach outside of my house? Was some...I don't know...dragon killer after you? Is there such a thing? St. George and all that?"

"St. George was an asshat."

I blinked at him in outright surprise.

"Is that not the right word?" His brow wrinkled. "I read it online. Should it be asscap?"

"No, *asshat* is the correct word. I'm just...I don't know, kind of surprised that a dragon knows about asshats. And the Internet, for that matter."

"Of course I know about the Internet." The look he hefted my way was filled with scorn. "I may have been held captive for more than forty years, but I am not an imbecile. Once my brother freed me, I learned what advances had been made in society. I have a laptop, and a tablet computer, and an intelligent phone."

"Smartphone."

"I can send texts. I am extremely wired," he added with a sense of pride that I didn't want to squash by giggling again.

"Clearly, I was wrong, and you are Mr. Technology. So tell me, why do you go around looking like a hunky man if you're a dragon?"

"Human form is easier to fit into cars. Not to mention sitting upon chairs," he said complacently, his gaze once again turned to the window at his side. "Dragon form is generally reserved for mating and fighting. We found over the years that it was simply easier to blend in—physically speaking—if we resembled those around us. Do you wish to mate with me?"

The car jerked again, but this time either my reaction had improved or such surprises were getting to be old hat, because I continued on regardless of the squawk from the backseat. "Is that an offer or a question?" I finally managed to ask Kostya.

He flexed first one shoulder, then the other, followed by a stretching of his neck to the left and right before he leaned back in the seat, his eyes closed as he answered. "Which would you like it to be?"

"You know, I think I can honestly say that I've never, ever been propositioned so quickly after meeting a man. I don't want either, and no, as I said a few minutes ago, I have zero interest in mating with you, assuming dragons do that the same way we do."

"We are flexible. We can do it either as mortals or as dragons. The latter is much more pleasing but requires a bigger space, as well as grounds for the chase." His voice sounded drowsy now, as if the fatigue of the evening's events had finally caught up to him. I knew just how he felt, with the added bonus of all the stress that I'd gone through. "That is so... I mean, they have a word for sex that way, assuming you are talking about doing it while looking like a tiny T. rex, and while I'm saying that, ew."

"Dragons do not look like tiny T. rexes. We have excellent forms that none can duplicate." He lifted a hand in a vague gesture. "You would not say ew if you knew the pleasures to be found in dragon form. Is it far to your home?"

"About forty minutes. You can take a nap if you like. I'll wake you when we get to town."

"Mmm-hmm."

He sounded very tired now, and it didn't take much longer for him to drift off to sleep. Jim was soon snoring from the backseat as well, leaving me the rest of the way home to think about the way my life had suddenly changed.

What on earth was I going to do with a large black demon dog? How was I going to break it to my sister and brother that I was now a demon lord? Would they even believe me when I did tell them, or would they try to stuff me back in the loony bin?

More worryingly, would I be able to survive the rest of the night with Kostya so temptingly close in my house without succumbing to the lure of his lips?

I sighed to myself and drove northward, my thoughts tangled, but at least there was one thing I knew for certain: "I'm so going to call up Dr. Barlind and tell her that I'm not crazy after all. And then I'm going to send my demon squad to break that electroshock machine."

Six

The scream ripped through my dream, bringing me instantly to full consciousness, if a little confused and dazed by the sudden waking. I sat up in bed, no stranger to the sound of distant screaming. The occupants of the Arvidsjaur Center sometimes vocalized their issues in ways that were at first frightening and later just became part of the background noise.

But I wasn't at Arvidsjaur. The sunlight that streamed around the partially closed curtains wasn't that of the Center, but my own home. The echo of the noise still bounced around my head, but I didn't know if its origins were from a dream or something external.

A black shadow moved, then stretched and resolved itself into the shape of a large black dog. I stared at it for a few seconds, my brain still muzzy enough that it took until the count of eight before I remembered.

"Jim!"

"Hiya." Jim stretched again and shook his whole body. "What's up with Kostya?"

It was on my lips to ask who when the vision of the handsome man rose before my eyes. I was on my feet and wrapping myself in my bathrobe when another scream sounded, this one hoarse and ragged.

"Sweet simmering sauceboats!" I sprinted down the hallway to my brother Rowan's room. With Jim hot on my heels, I flung open the door and plunged into the semi-darkness of the room, half expecting it to be filled with . . . well, I wasn't quite sure what. Something bad, that's all I knew.

Kostya lay tangled in the sheets on Rowan's bed, his chest and belly exposed, along with one naked leg. He was on his back, one arm flung out, his chest glistening with perspiration. I flipped on the bedside lamp, looking around to make sure something or someone wasn't hiding, but it was just Kostya in the room.

He moaned and said something unintelligible, his brows pulled down into a fierce scowl. Beneath his eyelids, his eyes were moving, his fingers flexing in an odd rhythm.

"Dreaming, huh?" Jim said, coming over to the bed to stare at Kostya. "I wonder if dragons run in their sleep like dogs do?"

I gave him a look. "He's not an animal, silly. And yes, I think he's having a nightmare. A very intense one if the fact that we are standing here talking without waking him is anything to go by. Kostya?" I eased myself onto the edge of the bed, told myself it was not polite to ogle a guest, no matter how tempting, and put my hand on his arm to gently shake him awake. "Kostya, you're drea—"

Suddenly, I was on my back, and a naked Kostya loomed

over me, one hand around my throat. The fingers were black, with wickedly curved white claws that pricked into my flesh.

"No!" Kostya barked, and even in the light of just one lamp I could see his eyes. Despite the fact that he was nearly strangling me, I reached up and touched the lines radiating from one of his eyes, trailing my fingers down to his stubbly jawline. For over a year, I'd seen just such an expression every time I glanced in a mirror.

It was pain, betrayal, and hopelessness, not stark and fresh, but long remembered and still very potent.

Once again, a sense of empathy filled me. Someone had damaged Kostya's psyche; someone had betrayed him to the point where it was haunting his dreams. I knew well the anguish of that sort of torment, and it made me want to wrap my arms around him, comfort him as I would a distressed child.

But he was no child, and I had my own emotional scars to contend with.

"Who hurt you?" I asked, my voice husky with both sleep and the pressure on my throat.

His hand shimmered and returned to that of a human. He loosened his hold, looking slightly appalled. "It is you. I did not...I must have been dreaming...I apologize. I would never have attacked you if you had warned me of your presence. It is dangerous to come upon a dragon in just such a circumstance."

"That dragon arm thing was pretty cool, Slick," Jim said, his eyes taking in the fact that Kostya was quite obviously naked. "And, hey, nice ass for a human form. Bet you could bounce a bowling ball on it. Eefables, you should really see this."

"My name is Aoife," I snapped, but nonetheless peered around Kostya in order to get a glimpse of his butt.

It was, as Jim said, really nice. Kostya made an annoyed noise at the back of his throat, shifting to the side so he was no longer looming over me. He also twisted the sheets around his waist. "What are you doing here in my bed? You said earlier that you did not desire me. You made that face that women make when I tell them that I have no interest in mating activities with them. And yet, you are here, touching me."

"I was trying to wake you up. You screamed twice in your sleep, so I figured you must be having a dilly of a nightmare." I slid around him and got to my feet. "And dammit, after all that 'do you want to mate with me' business, why didn't you tell me you were gay? Not that I was hitting on you, but still."

"I'm not gay," he said with as much dignity as a man can have while wrapped in a sheet and newly awoken from a raging nightmare. "I have learned that women are not to be trusted, and I do not wish for any more involvement with them. As for your outrageous claim, I reject it. I do not scream."

"And yet you did. Right, Jim?"

The demon, in the process of snuffling Kostya's clothes, nodded. "Made my hackles stand on end. Man, you don't even have so much as a stick of gum in your pants pocket. Hey, now that everyone's awake, think we could have some breakfast? I'm so hungry I could eat something large and Swedish, the name of which I can't think because apparently my memory loss includes food. But I do know I'm starving."

"Hardly that," I said, eyeing his large form. "You look a little chubby to me."

Jim sniffed. "You clearly do not know your superior sort of demon from the run-of-the-mill variety. My form is obviously a deluxe model and will require ample and frequent applications of food. So why don't we all go out to the kitchen and see what you have to keep me from perishing?"

A glance at the clock showed it to be morning, making any further attempt at sleep senseless. I opened the door for the dog, wanting to ask Kostya a question and preferring to do so without an audience. "Feel free to go out and get some bacon and eggs started."

Jim sat and gave me a long-suffering look. "Ain't got no opposable thumbs, babe. Don't actually have any non-opposable thumbs, either. See?" He held out a big black paw. "Not even a dewclaw."

"Then go take yourself outside."

His head tipped to the side. "How'm I supposed to open the door?"

"I'm sure you'll figure out a way."

"You want me to put my mouth on a door handle? Do you know the sorts of germs that are on it?"

"Oh, for the love of the good green earth, go!"

He sniffed again but followed my finger that pointed out the door, saying over his shoulder as he left, "Boy, you must really want to jump Kostya's bones if you can't even be with him five minutes before demanding alone time together."

I muttered something quite rude under my breath and turned back to face Kostya, who had been suspiciously silent during the whole exchange. He had, in fact, busied himself with dressing while I was distracted.

"I, too, desire breakfast," he said, buttoning up his shirt. I had a small moment of regret at that lovely chest being covered up, but hid my feelings well. "Following that, I will have you contact Aisling. I cannot speak to her or Drake due to the curse, but you can."

"It's like you're speaking English, and yet you're not," I said pleasantly, moving to block the doorway when he was about to leave the room. "Whoa, there. I think you owe me a few answers, and now that we've all had a little sleep, I'd like them. Let's start with the big one of how you got to my beach in a state that appeared to be near death, although obviously wasn't as close as I first thought."

"I am hungry. I will eat breakfast now, and then you must contact Aisling to ask her why Jim is in Sweden without its memory and bound to you."

I put my hands on my hips, blocking the exit. "First, *you* answer questions. Then if you ask nicely, I may make some food. But only if you— Hey!"

He put both hands around my waist and heaved upward. I rose a couple of inches, but when I kicked my legs out in protest, he dropped me like a hot potato. I thought at first that I must have connected with him, but since he didn't double over clutching whatever I had kicked, I decided I was mistaken.

Plus there was the expression of befuddlement on his face. "What did you just do?" he demanded to know, standing so close to me I could feel his breath on my face. Normally, I'm very strict about personal space and don't like people puffing on me, but Kostya somehow managed to breach the perimeter of my safety zone without setting off any of my mental alarms.

In fact, I had just the opposite reaction. I wanted very much to smoosh myself up against him. I told my body to knock it off and focused on what was important. "Did

I kick you? I didn't think I made contact, but if I did, you deserve it for trying to pick me up and move me so you could walk through the door before I'm done talking to you."

"You did something," he said, frowning down at me. Hesitantly, as if he was afraid of what would happen, he put both hands on my arms. "One moment you were fine, and the next it was as if you weighed a ton."

I pinched his side. "That is so rude! I know I'm not one of those anorexic skinny models, and I might need to lose a few pounds—okay, maybe twenty pounds—but that doesn't mean that you can make cracks like that. Men are supposed to admire real-sized women! Get with the program."

"Your body shape and size pleases me," he said, but his frown was still in place as his gaze zipped up and down my front. "I would not want you to starve yourself thinner. It would not suit you. That was not, however, what I meant when I said that you did something." His eyes narrowed. "Did you cast a spell? You do not appear to have that ability, but it could be that the blow to my head has somewhat confused me, and I am unable to see you as you really are."

"What sort of a crack is that? I am exactly what I am—there is no seeing-me-as-I-really-am business. And, no, I did not cast a spell. I'm not a witch!"

"You did something, though," he insisted. "It was as if you did not wish to be picked up, and you blocked me doing so. Look, I will try again."

His hands slid down to my waist, and I braced myself, my hands on his arms. I did not want him to move me away from the door—I had questions, and he had answers, and I'd be damned if I let him get away without satisfying at least part of my curiosity.

He grunted in his attempt to lift me.

"You're just doing that on purpose," I accused. "Despite that very nice comment about how I shouldn't go after the twenty pounds of flab that comes from being stuck in a nuthouse with little to do but read, you're doing passive-aggressive shit, and I don't like it."

He released my waist, his expression turning thoughtful. I tried hard to resist the urge to brush back a lock of hair that had fallen forward on his forehead, but it was too much for me. I reached up and pushed it back. He jerked backward as if I had struck him.

I thought at first it was because I had touched him, but he grabbed my hand and twisted it, saying, "The ring!"

"Huh? Oh, that."

"Where did you get it?" He all but shook my hand at me, which struck me as an amusing thing to do.

"It was given to me by a guy I dated. Well, not really *given* to me. I mean, he handed it to me to look at, but then he was killed, and later came back from the dead, but by then I was taken away to the home for the deranged, so I never got to give it back to him. It was the same guy who pointed you out to me. Except there was a second dragon, too."

"That was Anton. The red dragons killed him shortly thereafter. Who is this man who gave you the ring? You said his name was Terrill?"

I twisted the ring around my finger. To be honest, I'd forgotten that I'd even put it on the day before, but the idea that it could keep Kostya from picking me up—twenty extra pounds aside—was ludicrous. "Terrin."

"I do not know him. Who was he? Why did he give you the ring? Why did he not demand it returned?"

"He was just a guy I met at the GothFaire. At least I thought he was just a guy. Now I realize that there was more to him, too, than I thought. But why all the questions? It's just a ring. Yeah, Terrin said it was magic, but it doesn't do anything."

Kostya's range of expressions ran from dark and brooding to slightly amused. "It is not just a ring. It is the very reason that I am in this area and also why I was almost killed and likely why Jim is here."

"You're kidding, right?" A memory struck me, one of Terrin telling me that the dragons sought the ring for some reason, but I couldn't quite remember what it was.

Kostya's lips thinned. "Do I strike you as if I am joking?"

"Well . . ."

He adopted an outraged expression. I had to give it to him, he did outraged well, although it seemed to strike my funny bone more than make me feel apologetic for offending him.

"I do not laugh. I do not smile. I see no enjoyment in kidding, intentional or otherwise. I am Konstantin Nikolai Fekete, wyvern of the black dragons! I have been tortured for many decades and left to die a slow and lingering death. I survived the wholesale destruction of my sept and had a deranged naiad force me to declare her a mate before the entire weyr only to later run off with a minor deity, the embarrassment of which would have killed a lesser dragon!"

I did laugh at that. "Oh, so that's why you're so gun-shy of women? Got dumped by someone who embarrassed you, huh? Weyr . . . I've heard that word before, although I don't remember what it means, or naiad, for that matter.

It sounds like something out of Greek mythology. Isn't a wyvern a two-legged dragon?"

"Yes. It is also the name of the leader of a dragon sept. Answer my question about the ring."

"Tell you what, Mr. Bossy Pants, we'll play you answer one, then I'll answer one, okay? You go first. How did you end up on the beach outside my house?"

"Why do you have the ring?"

"Why would someone leave you to die a slow and lingering death? Wait, was it the chick who dumped you?"

He ignored my question. "How long have you had it? Did you use its powers to revive me?"

"What did you mean that you were almost killed because of the ring? It's been locked away with my possessions for two years, and I only just put it on last night, before I went to the GothFaire. Man alive, that was just last night, wasn't it? It seems like weeks ago." I shook my head and held up my hand when Kostya opened his mouth, obviously about to ask yet another question. "This is getting us nowhere. Let's do this step-by-step. Why were you almost dead on my beach?"

"You are stubborn enough to be a dragon," Kostya surprised me by saying. The warm, admiring look in his eyes was just as surprising. "That pleases me. I dislike women who pester me—the naiad was forever challenging everything I said—and unlike her, you present your opinion without whining. Nor are you cowed by your circumstances. This is good."

"I'm so happy you approve," I said with a little laugh, half annoyed and half flattered by his no-nonsense appraisal of my personality. I had to admit, though, it was refreshing to find a man who didn't form an opinion on me based on the color of my skin. Kostya was…different. He was brusque and arrogant, but underneath that, I sensed a need in him that resonated with something deep in me.

It was as if he had a hard exterior shell that protected his sensitive inner self. I envied him that shell.

He gave a sharp nod. "If I were to ever take a woman again, which I will not because after Cyrene, I made a sacred oath that no other woman would ever tempt me, but if I were to be tempted, I would allow you to act out all of your lustful desires upon me."

I addressed the most important thing in his outrageous statement. "I do not have lustful desires about you!"

"You kissed me. You enjoyed it. And you like touching my chest and are pleased with my ass."

"*You* kissed *me*, and chest-touching and ass-looking are totally allowable, especially when the parts in question are naked," I said with much dignity.

He leaned forward so that his chest rubbed against my breasts. A little moan escaped me as my body seemed suddenly to come alight. He tipped his head down, the strand of hair falling down over his forehead again, this time brushing against my face. It sent shivers down my spine, shivers that soon faded into fire when he murmured, "You are too enticing for your own good, mortal. There is something about you that speaks to me…"

That was when his lips touched mine, and his tongue swept along them, causing me to gasp with the heat of his body that was suddenly pressing me against the wall. He caught the gasp in his mouth, his hands setting my hips on fire when he grasped them, an inferno of desire sweeping through me and catching me wholly off guard.

I swear that the kiss was so hot—*Kostya* was so hot—that

perspiration prickled on my forehead as his tongue slowly and thoroughly explored my mouth. I've never been one to particularly enjoy such things, but apparently I just hadn't yet properly experienced exactly what a tongue could do. Kostya's tongue seemed different, more sensual and... for lack of a descriptive word, hot. Red-hot. Think the spiciest of cinnamon candies that burns almost to the point of pain, but not quite over the line.

It wasn't until he snapped his head back, asking, "What is that?" that I heard the sound.

A shrill *BEEP BEEP BEEP* was echoing through the house.

"That's... holy hellballs, it's the smoke detector. Something is on fire. It's my room! Ack! And me! I'm on fire!"

I stared in utter horror at my feet, which were fully engulfed in flames. Kostya wasn't at all touched by the fire, and although there were little patches of it around the bedroom, I stood frozen with fear until Kostya, with an odd look at me, flicked his fingers. The fire circling my feet died down.

He leaned forward and sniffed the air next to my head.

"What the hell?" I asked, jerking away, trying to get my mind to stop shrieking while at the same time well aware of the fact that I didn't feel anything in my feet. Clearly, they had been burned to nothing. "What are you doing smelling my hair at a time like this?"

"I'm not smelling your hair, although you have a nice scent overall. Not chemical, like many mortals who use perfume. I like that. I was smelling you to see if you had any dragon blood that I did not ascertain earlier. You appear wholly mortal, however."

"Sweet salted saltines!" I screamed, ignoring his babble

for what was important. I grabbed his shirt and tried to shake him to drive home the horror of the moment. "My feet are gone! I don't feel anything in them—they're burned to a crisp. Aieee!" I stopped shaking him and instead tried to climb him like he was a ladder, but of course, you can't climb a ladder if your feet have been burned away.

He clicked his tongue and pried me off his chest. I tried to punch him, which just resulted in me stumbling backward until I collapsed on the bed. "Now you are being hysterical. Cease such emotional outbursts. This smoke detector noise irritates me. Where is it originating?"

I was so incensed by the fact that he didn't even take the trouble to notice that I no longer had feet—I was afraid to look down and see how bad they were, since the sight of blackened, burned stumps would no doubt snap what was left of the sane part of my mind—that I focused on him rather than the fact that I wasn't actually in any sort of pain. I jumped to my feet-stumps and stomped over to him, poking him in the chest while saying, "How dare you!"

He had the gall to look surprised. "How dare I do what?"

"Make that annoyed noise! No, don't give me that look like I'm crazy—you proved to me that I'm not and I never was, and despite your attempts, I refuse to let you drive me insane. That tsking thing you just did. That is the sort of noise you make when you discover you're in a bathroom stall with no toilet paper, or that you've run out of stamps, or that someone drank the last of the milk and didn't tell you. That is not the appropriate response when someone has had their feet burned off!"

He looked pointedly down at my feet. "Do you have some sort of anti-derangement medication? If so, you might wish to take it."

I walloped him on the arm. "How dare you!"

"You already said that," he pointed out.

"And I'll say it a third time if I like! How dare you cast slurs about my mental stability when you know full well that you being a dragon and Jim being a talking demon dog means...Hey." During the middle of my (wholly righteous) rant, I had glanced down to take in what remained of my feet, but there weren't any remains to notice. They were perfectly normal. Two feet, all ten toes present and accounted for, adorned with pink toenail polish and stuffed into my favorite pair of sandals. There was nary a singed mark to be seen, let alone a stump, burned or otherwise. "Why are my feet okay? They were on fire."

"That was my dragon fire. Somehow you managed to harness it." He gave me another one of those speculative looks before tsking again. "No, it is worthless to question how you accessed my fire. You are not a mate, and even if you were, I do not want you."

"Oh!" I gasped.

He made a sharp gesture of dismissal. "Will you make that machine cease the noise? It is giving me a headache."

"For a man who doesn't want me, you sure end up kissing me a lot," I snapped, casting yet another glance at my feet before looking around the room. There was no fire to be seen, and only the faintest black smudge on the floor where the little pools of flames had been. "But I'm going to let your overbearing arrogance—"

"I am not arrogant."

"—and self-centered egotism—"

"I am a wyvern! The welfare of my sept falls on my shoulders."

"—go, because this fire thing just freaks the bejebus out of me. Wait a minute—dragon fire? That's a thing? A real thing?"

"Dragons control their fire, yes," he said, looking impatient.

"I object to that," I said, pointing at his face. "You can't give me that impatient, 'How did you not know that dragons have fire, let alone control it' look when that's so out of the bounds of normalcy that it never even struck me as possible. Well, to be true, the same can be said about dragons, but still! You didn't tell me that the whole fire-breathing dragon thing was real."

"You are an odd woman," he said thoughtfully.

"Odd good, or odd bad?" I couldn't help but ask.

"I have not yet come to a decision. Dragon fire is different from mortal fires. It does not generate as much smoke, and dragons and their mates are not harmed by it. To us, it merely feels . . . warm."

"That's it exactly," I said, thinking about how my feet felt when they were on fire. "Warm and tingly. Where did the rest of the fire go?"

He was still giving me a speculative look, but that ended when he shook his head and said softly to himself, "No. It is fine for Drake, but I swore never again would I bind myself to a woman. What? As soon as I realized your room was alight, I put out the flames, of course."

"There's no 'of course' about it. You didn't move," I said, wanting to crawl back into bed and pretend the last twenty-four hours hadn't occurred.

Except, my mind pointed out, that would mean Kostya never kissed me. Twice. And despite his protests that he didn't want me, and my own common sense that told me to hook up with a man who had a dragon side was nothing short of folly, I very much enjoyed those kisses.

Once again, I sensed a need in him that called to me to give him succor. His was a soul in unrest, and as someone who'd lived through her own hellish nightmare, I felt a kinship that threatened to blossom into something warm and fuzzy.

And if that wasn't the most ridiculous thought I'd ever had, I don't know what was.

"I did not need to move. Why are you stalling?"

"It's called trying to wrap my poor, beleaguered brain around something like dragons and fire, not stalling. Oh, all right. I admit that sound is annoying." I opened the bedroom door and went into the hallway, where the nearest smoke detector was screeching away.

The hallway was filled with smoke.

"I thought you said—" That was all I got out before Kostya, swearing profanely, grabbed me by the waist and tossed me over his shoulder. He raced down the hall, the breath knocked out of me sufficiently to leave me speechless for about five seconds. When he ran across the living room, I stopped trying to squirm out of his grasp.

The house was on fire, seriously on fire, and I knew without him saying a word that this was no dragon fire that he'd lost control of—smoke, thick and choking, boiled around the room while the kitchen walls were fully engulfed. So was the door to the beach. Kostya spun around and bolted back down the hallway to my bedroom, not stopping even when I squawked to be let down. He simply shifted his weight, smashed one foot through my bedroom window, kicked out the glass shards, and flung me through the gaping hole.

I fully expected to hit the dry, scraggly grass outside my bedroom, but instead I hit something hard that fell backward under my weight. I screamed, thrashing my arms and legs in an attempt to gain purchase on whatever it was, my hair and burning eyes blinding me for a few seconds. Voices shouted nearby, and hard, grasping hands suddenly clawed at me, jerking me to the side.

I kicked out and had the satisfaction of hearing the grunt of pain in response. Just as Kostya leaped out of the window after me, I managed to roll to the side and get to my knees.

The man—and it was a man I'd been flung onto—grappled with Kostya in the very best action-movie manner. Kostya snarled and suddenly shifted into the shape a large, angry black dragon. I gawked when the other man did likewise—only his black was tinged with a dusky red color, with little yellow flecks that dotted his torso.

"Holy cheese on whiz!" I stumbled backward, my eyes huge as I watched the two dragons fight. Tails whipped through the air as bodies twined around each other, claws slashing and drawing crimson arcs of blood that splattered on the yellowish-brown grass.

"What the— Fires of Abaddon! Is that Kostya?"

Jim had come at a run, evidently having been taking a stroll down the beach, judging by the amount of seaweed clinging to his legs.

"The black one is. I don't know who the other guy is. Nooo!" This last wail was directed to my home when with a roaring *whoosh*, the roof suddenly collapsed, blasting us with a bank of scalding air. I grabbed Jim and pulled him backward toward the beach, my gaze flitting between the house—now fully engulfed in flames—and the two dragons rolling on the ground locked in deathly combat.

"I dunno either, but he has friends," Jim said, looking around me. "Wow, they're dragons, too. Kinda cool-looking, huh?"

I spun around to see three more men come running around the burning house. They didn't even pause, shifting in midstride to a similar dragon form as the one whose head Kostya was bashing on the ground. Kostya got to his feet, leaving the other dragon twitching and groaning.

"Behind you!" I yelled, pointing at the oncoming dragon horde.

He spun around, stared for a minute, then hurdled the downed dragon and raced straight for them. "Use it!" he yelled over his shoulder at me. "I will hold them as long as I can, but you must use it. They will come for you once they kill me. Use it now!"

"Use wha— Oh." I looked down at my hand where the gold of the ring glinted gently in the sun.

"What's he talking about?" Jim asked, watching with interest as Kostya, with a battle cry, flung himself on the three other dragons, sending them all tumbling in a mad whirl of legs and tails and claws.

"The ring. Terrin said it was magic, but I don't know how it works."

Another wall of my house crumbled in a roar of flames. Jim and I stumbled backward another few yards. I dragged my gaze from the sight of my childhood home being destroyed to where Kostya fought. One of the dragons was crawling away, his arm at an odd angle. The other two were wailing away on Kostya.

"Yeah, I don't see a giant glowing eyeball or anything, but that doesn't mean diddly so far as magic rings go. At least, I think that's true. I'm not absolutely certain since I can't remember squat. Ouch, that's gotta hurt." Jim flinched as one of the dragons tore off a piece of the picket fence and started beating Kostya with it.

"I just don't know what to do," I said, still twisting the ring, but at that moment, two more men emerged from the far side of the house. They, too, shifted into dragon form, but it was the long, silver sword that one of them held that decided me. "Stay here!" I told Jim, and ran forward a few steps, holding my hand out in a dramatic fashion while yelling, "I use this magic ring to stop you!"

For a moment, the dragons fought on as if nothing had happened, but then all of them, even the one moaning on the ground, turned to look at me.

"Oh, hell," I said, my eyes almost popping out of my head when the dragons sprang toward me. I backpedaled, waving my hand wildly in front of me, praying the magic in it would go off before the dragons reached me.

There was a rush of air, an oath snarled in a voice that seemed to come from the depths of the earth itself, and then Kostya was there in front of me, back in human form, one side of his body hitched higher than the other, with blood dripping down his arm. "Use it!" he demanded, snatching up a piece of driftwood and wielding it as if it were no different than the shiny sword. He turned to face the dragons, using his body to shield me.

"I don't know how!" I wailed.

"Focus on them. Harness the power of the ring. Use it on them!"

"You say harness the power as if I'm supposed to know how, but—"

The dragons leaped at that moment, all five of them

(the one guy on the ground had to be happy with crawling toward us in a menacing fashion). Kostya snarled something unintelligible, his legs apart, head down, clearly ready to sacrifice himself in order to give me a few seconds of time.

I knew with absolute certainty that he would not survive the attack. My fingers doubled into a fist, and clutching my hands together, I closed my eyes and bowed my own head, forming a mental image of the ring as a giant club. I swung it back, gathering my strength for one breathless moment before slamming it down before me, my eyes snapping open at the percussion blast that resulted.

Before us, all six dragons lay flat on the ground, each one surrounded by a ring of fire—dragon fire. Kostya staggered forward a step, then dropped to his knees, leaning heavily on the driftwood while he surveyed them.

"Well, what do you know about that?" I said, staring at the carnage before me. "I have a magic ring."

Seven

"So, let me recap for that part of my mind that's still high-fiving itself over the fact that I wasn't ever crazy and did actually see what I thought I saw two years ago. Curses are real."

"Yes." Kostya nodded toward my phone. "Make the call."

"Not until I get a few things straight in my mind. Curses are real, and they can affect more than one person."

"As I told you." His lips thinned in impatience. "All of dragonkin are subject to the curse."

I counted to eight to let my mind slide over the idea of the world being inhabited by a whole bunch of people who were in reality dragons. "And you guys are trying to break the curse, right?"

"Of course. It has pitted the septs against one another. Make the call."

I consulted the piece of paper he'd given me and slowly tapped in the numbers. "And this ring, the one Terrin gave

me two years ago, is the thing that can do that? Break this
curse that makes you dragons crazy?"

"Yes."

"Then I'll just give it to you—" I started to say, but
stopped when he made a sharp gesture, followed by some
swearing when his shoulder protested.

"It isn't that easy."

Before I could ask why, a voice spoke into my ear.

"Hello?" The voice was that of an American, which
really took me by surprise. "Hello? Is someone there?
You called me, so I assume you are, but if you're one of
those telemarketers—"

"Sorry, I'm here. Not a telemarketer. Um...are you
Aisling Grey?"

"Yes. I don't recognize your number. Who are you?"

"My name is Aoife, Aoife Ndakaaru. Well, actually,
I go by Aoife Dakar, because Dad always shortened his
name to that, but I don't suppose you want to hear about
my family name."

"Why wouldn't I? Dakar is a very interesting name. So
is Ndakaaru. Is it African?"

"Yes. Senegalese, to be exact. Dad was from there. My
mom was Irish."

"I hear you on that. My name is Aisling." She laughed.
"Oh, you know that, don't you? What can I do for you,
Aoife Dakar?"

"Kostya wants you to know that your demon is here
with us, and he's okay, although he does seem to have to
go walkies a lot. Also, he's lost his memory."

"What?" Aisling's shriek made my ear ring for a few
minutes. "Jim's with you? Wait a minute—Kostya told
you to tell me that? Drake! Oh my God, how is he?"

"Kostya or Jim? I'm sorry, Kostya said that I was supposed to call Jim an *it*, but he's a boy dog. I can't do it."

"Kostya! No, Jim. Oh, hell's bells, both of them—how
are they both? Pal, where's Drake? Well, go get him. Tell
him it's important. It's Kostya. At least, it's a friend of
Kostya's—I don't know. I can ask. Aoife, are you . . . uh . . .
Kostya's girlfriend?"

"What's she saying?" Kostya asked.

"She wants to know if I'm your girlfriend."

"Oh my God, is he there right now?" Aisling asked,
her voice going up half an octave with excitement.

"Yes, he is. Do you want to talk to him?"

"I can't. May and I tried, but mates can't talk to other
mates any more than dragons can talk to other dragons.
It's all part of the curse. There you are! Kostya's on the
phone. Well, Kostya's girlfriend. Her name is Aoife."

"I'm not his girlfriend," I corrected, looking over at
Kostya. He sat on the edge of the examination bed in Dr.
Ek's room, wincing when he moved his shoulders. Dr. Ek
had gone into a back storage area to find some elastic bandages, which he said would help Kostya with his broken
collarbone. "Drake is your brother, right?"

"Yes. Is he there?" Kostya got to his feet. I offered him
the phone, but he shook his head. "I can't hear or understand him. The septs haven't been able to communicate
since the weyr was destroyed by Asmodeus's curse."

"I didn't get to him yet." I gave Kostya a potent look.
"We'll get to just who this dude is who cursed you, and
why, just as soon as I'm done talking— What? Sorry, I was
distracted. Yes, Kostya is here, and he's fine, although beat
up a bit. He says the collarbone should heal up in a few
minutes. I guess dragons have some super-healing thing."

"She knows that," Kostya said, moving over to stand next to me. "Ask her why Jim was unbound. And tell her about the red dragons."

"I said I would, just give me a minute. And sit back down. You look like you're about to fall over."

That made him straighten his shoulders, which caused him to wince again. He snatched up his shirt and carefully inserted an arm into it. "Stop fussing over me, woman. I will be whole again shortly, and then you can resume ogling me and desiring my body."

"Oh, you wish," I muttered.

"He hurt his collarbone," I heard Aisling repeat to her husband. A low masculine rumble followed. "I don't know, Aoife hasn't told me yet. No, I don't know that either. Honest to Pete, Drake! The important thing is that he's okay, and Jim is there. I don't know—she hasn't told me that, although frankly, I'm amazed she's said as much as she has given that you and evidently Kostya are grilling us both to the point where we can't talk to each other." Her voice became stronger and louder as she returned to the phone. "Sorry about that, Aoife. Wyverns! Let me get the important details before Drake bursts."

There was a male protest in the background.

"I can't listen to her and you at the same time," Aisling said. "Now, Aoife—"

"What is she saying?" Kostya demanded, having gotten his shirt onto his back.

"Nothing. And if you don't stop distracting me, I'll never be able to ask the stuff you want me to ask. Go sit over there and stop flaunting your chest at me."

"I am not flaunting anything at you, least of all my chest!"

"You haven't buttoned up your shirt," I pointed out.

"Clearly you want me to admire your naked chest. Go on, admit it—as much as you make a fuss over me ogling you, you secretly love it!"

"And you love doing it," he countered. A tiny little curl of smoke emerged from one nostril. I suddenly felt very warm.

"Of course I do. I'm a perfectly normal woman with a perfectly normal libido, and you happen to be an incredibly handsome man." I took a step toward him at the same time he took one toward me. I could feel the heat in him, which I realized with a start was his dragon fire. It roared within him, but somehow he managed to keep control of it.

That didn't explain why it made me feel hot, though.

"Cease tempting me, woman," he growled, the tiny little silver lights in his black eyes glittering at me.

I turned around to face the door. "Fine, you want to be all chesty at me? I just won't look. Tempting you, my ass. Hello? Are you still there, Aisling?"

"Yes," she answered, laughter evident in her voice. "I was just waiting for you to be done looking at Kostya's chest. It is a very nice chest. Ow! Drake! There's no need to pinch me; Kostya is your brother, and he is a very handsome man. Honestly! Talk about jealous...Where were we, Aoife?"

"What is she saying now?" Kostya demanded. "Why are you laughing? Are you mocking me? Is she?"

"I'm not mocking you in the least, but I can say this— your brother is evidently just as big a pain in the butt as you are. Sorry, Aisling. I didn't mean to be rude about your husband."

"—can't possibly carry on a conversation with you

peppering me with questions like that. I know you're concerned about him—I'm just as worried—but he's evidently all right, because Aoife doesn't seem like the sort of person who would lie to me about that. *What*?"

Silence fell. I pulled the cell phone away from my ear to double-check that I hadn't dropped the connection. "Aisling?" I asked into it.

"Uh..." Her voice had an oddly strained quality to it. "Aoife, I've been requested to ask who you are."

"I told you who I was."

"Yes..." She hesitated. "Drake wishes to know if Kostya has named you as his mate."

"That again?"

"What?" Kostya asked, moving around so that he could see my face.

"Aisling wants to know if you called me your mate." I made a face.

To my surprise, a dull red tint flooded his face. "I have not named you as mate, and you can tell her that."

"He says to tell you that I'm not his mate."

"Hmm." She sounded thoughtful. "But you are romantically involved—Drake, I can't possibly ask that list of questions. It would take an hour or more. No. She says she's not. I don't know! How am I supposed to know the answer to that? I'm not there! Here, you want to ask her? You go right ahead."

There was a moment's silence; then a man's voice came on the phone, a voice similar to Kostya's but with a slightly different, more European accent. "This is Drake Vireo. You are the woman with my brother?"

"Yes." I eyed Kostya. His brother sounded just as officious.

"Where are you?"

"In a doctor's office."

"No, what country. You are American?"

"Yes, but we're in Sweden."

"What's the nearest large town?"

"Boden. Why?"

"Can you be in— One moment." A couple of muffled voices drifted through the phone. I held up my hand when Kostya opened his mouth to ask yet another question. Drake returned to the phone. "Can you be in Umeå in six hours?"

"Yes. It's about an hour's drive."

"Good. We will meet you at the airport. Bring Kostya and Jim."

He hung up the phone before I could respond. I tucked my phone away, giving Kostya a long look. "Wow. I can really tell he's your brother."

Kostya narrowed his eyes. "Why do you say that?"

"If I told you, you'd just deny it. Oh, thank you, Dr. Ek. I'm sure Kostya will be grateful to have that shoulder bandaged."

Kostya wasn't anything of the sort, but he did take his shirt off again (which allowed me some quality ogling time) and suffered Dr. Ek strapping his injured arm to his chest. The slash marks had long since healed, but evidently it took a bit longer for bones to fix themselves, because by the time we got Kostya's shirt back on him, and I'd thanked Dr. Ek again for his assistance, there were lines of pain around Kostya's mouth.

"Right, everyone into the car. Oh, sorry, Jim. You can talk now."

The demon, whom Kostya had recommended I order to silence while at the doctor's office, let out his breath as if he'd been holding it the entire time. "Fires of Abaddon, Eefs! I don't know what this other demon lord I'm supposed to have was like, but I can do with less of the ordering around and more of the providing of foodstuffs. Speaking of which—"

"Yes, yes, I'll feed you."

"I am desirous of food as well, but I wish to know what my brother said to you."

At first I thought Kostya was standing by the car waiting for me to give him the keys, but then he opened the driver's door for me. It was a strangely gallant gesture for a man who liked to scowl and protest as much as he did. "There's not a lot to tell, but first: is your broken bone healing up the way you think it will?" I asked when he got in the passenger side. Jim flopped onto the backseat, moaning to himself about starving to death and demon lords who took the word *cruel* to new heights.

Kostya tried moving his shoulder. He didn't flinch, but I got the feeling that it still hurt. "It's taking longer than I thought it would, but it appears to be better. What exactly did Drake say?"

"Hmm. You're sure you can self-heal? Oh, that's stupid. I watched two slash marks on your arm close up and disappear. Maybe it's because you've been through so much in the past twenty-four hours?" I started the car and headed to a restaurant that was about twenty minutes away. "He said to meet him in Umeå at four this afternoon. It's about an hour's drive, so we have time to get some food before I go back home and—"

"No."

I glanced at him from the corner of my eye. "—talk to the police and fire officials, and whoever else showed up—"

"You will not go back to your home."

"—when they noticed the fire. I assume there's a whole lot of people who wondered what happened, and who will want to talk to us—"

"We will go to this Umeå. And after that, Paris."

I ground off a few layers of teeth, making a concerted effort not to reach out and punch Kostya in the collarbone. "So, new rule: you stop interrupting me, and I don't pull the car over and shove you out of it."

The look he turned on me was downright comical. "You would push me from your car? I have been wounded saving you!"

"I also saved you," I pointed out, holding up my hand so he could see the ring. "Me and Wishy the Magic Ring. Jim, stop your bellyaching and take a nap until we get to the restaurant."

Kostya fumed silently to himself for a moment. "I did not intend to offend you by interrupting, but we cannot return to your home."

"Why? Not that there's anything left of it by now but rubble, but there may be things that weren't destroyed."

"You would not be safe there. The red dragons obviously know you are with me, or they would not have attacked. We will speak with Drake and go to his house in Paris. There you will be safe, and I will be able to ensure the ring is used to repair that which was destroyed."

"Do you always talk like you're straight out of a Tolkien book?" I asked in what I thought was a conversational tone of voice. "No, never mind, don't answer that. It doesn't matter. Look, I appreciate that you threw yourself in front of me when those red dragons attacked—it was, hands down, the most heroic thing I've ever witnessed—but I'm not a part of whatever it is that you're involved with, so there's no reason for those red dudes to come after me. Do all dragons have colors assigned to them?"

"Generally, yes. There is one sept that does not, but the wyvern of that is...special." Kostya rubbed his chin, rasping his thumb down his stubble while musing to himself. "The red dragons didn't know about you, that is true."

"And the ones who attacked us aren't going to be doing any talking," I pointed out, my brain shying away from the memory of the bodies of the red dragons who had attacked us. Part of me wanted to feel appalled by the fact that I had killed the dragons—or rather, the ring had via me—but they were so clearly intent on killing us that I couldn't summon up more than a sense of regret that we'd been pushed into that metaphorical corner.

"No, but if they traced me to your house, then they know about you. And thus you are at risk."

"But I'm not a dragon. Why would dragons want me dead if I'm not one of you?"

"This is not a simple war between septs—the curse has driven the septs apart, yes, but the red dragons are now different. They are part demon. They will not care if you are a dragon or not; they will simply want you destroyed because you hold the ring. You must come to Paris. There you will be safe."

I was touched that he was so concerned, a warm glow of happiness spreading out from my belly. "What a contrary man you are. Going by appearances, your favorite activity is scowling and being grumpy, but at the same time, you risked your own life to save me."

"I am a wyvern," he said, looking out the window. "It's what I do."

"But I'm not one of your dragons."

"No, but you are—" He stopped, his jaw tensing.

"I'm what?"

"How long will it take us to reach the place with food?"

"Another fifteen minutes. I'm what, Kostya? Your *mate*?" I gave the last word the emphasis that I felt was unspoken.

His fingers spasmed on his leg, but he didn't turn to look at me. "I have no mate."

"Not that I'm desperate for the job or anything—let alone getting involved with someone so pigheaded and arrogant—"

He turned at that, complete with a glare that probably would have singed the hair of someone who wasn't wearing a magic ring.

"But you have to admit that when you're not being annoying, the kissing part is a lot of fun." I smiled at him. He glowered.

"And speaking of the ring, why isn't it simple? Giving it to you, that is, and letting you break this curse."

His jaw tightened. "Traditionally, the breaking of a curse is done by someone not affected by it."

"Huh. You learn something new each day." I thought for a few minutes. "Traditionally? Do you mean you haven't tried to break it yourself?"

"I have not had the means." He looked pointedly at my hand.

"No," I said slowly. "But you would if I gave it to you. Why don't we do that, and then you can see if curse-breaking isn't easier than you think?"

He shook his head, saying simply, "It would not work."

I wanted to argue the point with him, but two things

stopped me: first, he was still obviously in pain, and the part of me that wanted to comfort him demanded that I stop picking on him, and second, all this business of dragons and curses and demon lords was new to me. Magically speaking, I probably had the wrong end of the stick.

The remaining hours passed quicker than I expected. I insisted on driving to my house to see what remained of it, but all that greeted us was a mass of smoky charred wood, with half of one wall still standing. Sadness gripped me at the sight of it, tears welling thickly in my eyes. I mourned the loss of the place of so many happy memories and came perilously close to breaking down and bawling when I felt Kostya standing behind me.

He didn't say anything, didn't even touch me, but just his nearness gave comfort. After a few minutes, I turned and walked to the car, Jim and Kostya silently flanking me.

I wanted to stop by the nearest fire station (about fifteen miles away) but made do with a phone call instead. After giving my information and promising to stop by in the next twenty-four hours to fill out the report of what we saw, I left messages for both my sister and brother briefly explaining that the house had been destroyed and that I would contact them later with information about where I would be staying.

"I don't know why you wouldn't let me tell them about you," I told Kostya when I finished with the voice mail for my brother. "Other than the dragon part, I mean. I could just tell them that you are a friend and you'd offered to let me stay with you—not that I have decided if I will, mind you—so they wouldn't worry."

"I do not know your siblings. They might pass along information that would lead the red dragons to you."

"You're really stubborn, you know that? No, to the left. We want the road that heads south."

Kostya was taking his turn at the wheel, his collarbone having finally healed. That, along with a meal and a stop by a store for some fresh clothing, had made us all feel better.

"I am a wyvern. I am not stubborn."

"Yeah, yeah." I watched the countryside slip past us as we headed south. "I don't suppose you'd like to answer some questions now?"

"No. I am driving. It would be unsafe for me to do so."

"A likely excuse. Okay, let's try this. Jim?"

"Huh?"

I turned around in my seat to see the demon, who had requested a copy of the local newspaper, look up from one of the pages. I had bought him the paper without making a single comment about the fact that he apparently not only spoke Swedish, but also could read it and was interested in the latest news.

"What do you know about dragon weirs?"

"Weyrs," Kostya corrected.

"Weyrs. What do you know about them? Oh, wait... I order you to tell me about weyrs."

The dog rolled his eyes. "You can ask me stuff without the bossy parts, you know."

"Sorry. Kostya said I had to order you."

"It's not very polite." Jim sniffed, and nosed the newspaper over to the next page. "I don't know anything about them other than it's some sort of a collective group. It's what the septs belong to."

"Oh, that's right. Terrin said something about that. It's like a United Nations thing?" I asked Kostya. "Your individual septs are members?"

"The weyr is made up of the dragon septs, yes." A muscle in his jaw flexed. "It *was* made up of the septs. It is no more."

"The curse had the power to do that? The guy who did that to you must be a humdinger of a bad dude."

Kostya was silent. I thought for a few minutes about picking at the question until I forced him to answer me, but the sunlight filtering in through the car window, combined with the lack of sleep and a full belly, all led me to simply say, "I'm going to find out, you know. If not now, then soon," before making a pillow of a sweater and snuggling into the car seat as best I could for a little snooze.

I woke up some time later at the sound of rain hitting the window.

"Ow," I said, sitting up from where I'd been slumped against the door. My neck twinged in protest from my odd position. I rubbed it and blinked as I peered around. I was alone in the car, the skies gray above, although the ground wasn't too wet, indicating it hadn't been raining for long. "Jim? Kostya? Hello?"

No one answered. I looked out at the rain but didn't see anyone. The car appeared to be at a small airport—not the large one with international arrivals, but a local one. A sign above a cluster of hangars announced balloon trips were available, as was pilot training. I got out of the car and scurried over to the door of the nearest hangar. Inside was a small plane, the kind crop dusters used, but no one was visible. "Hello? Anyone?"

It was as if the airport was a ghost town. I headed toward the big sign, assuming that's where the office was located, but movement from the side caught my eye. A plane had evidently just landed and was taxiing toward me. This was no crop duster—it was small but sleek and positively reeked of money. I paused, watching it as it came to a stop, and the steps slid down in a near-silent hiss.

A man appeared, stocky in build, with red hair and a wary look on his face. He didn't look to me like a dragon, but then, Kostya didn't look like a dragon when he was in man-form. I took a step toward the redhead but stopped when he was joined by a second man, also redheaded. Neither of them looked like Kostya.

I turned my feet toward the office, glancing up and down the rows of hangars for signs of Kostya or Jim.

A shout behind me had me stopping. The two men from the plane were now joined by others, including a woman with curly brown hair and a tall man with black hair. The woman pointed at me, and in a flash, I realized that I was looking at dragons—but not Kostya's family.

"Red dragons," I said aloud, clutching my hand to my chest. "They want the ring! Well, they can't have it!"

Feeling almost as brave as Kostya had been earlier (although with a lot more circumspection, given the situation), I spun around on my heel and ran back the way I'd come, hoping that Kostya had left the car keys in the ignition.

Almost immediately, there were sounds of running footsteps behind me. I dug deep for a burst of speed, but two years where the most vigorous exercise was a gentle stroll in the gardens had taken its toll, and before I was halfway to the car, I heard heavy breathing directly behind me. Ahead of me loomed the edge of one of the hangars. Behind it was my car, but I had serious doubts that I'd make it. I gathered every bit of energy I had and willed my legs to run faster, but just as I reached the end of the hangar, someone caught the back of my shirt and jerked me backward.

It was the taller of the two redheads. He said something in a language I didn't understand, pulling me toward him. Behind him, the stockier guy was approaching, as were the woman and dark-haired man.

"Let go of me," I snarled, my fingers curled into a fist. I swung at him, but he ducked. The second man reached us just as a large shape blurred past me, and then I was free. I ran a couple of steps forward, realized what the large shape must be, and spun around to see Kostya rolling on the ground with both redheads.

The dark-haired man checked his step for a moment; then with a roar of fury, he threw himself on the pile.

"Sweet sadistic salamanders!" I yelled, clutching my hand with the ring and trying to remember how I used it with the other red dragons. I tried to pull together power and directed it at them, bellowing, "Stop, stop, stop! I command you all to stop!"

Nothing happened. The men continued to fight.

Now what the devil was I supposed to do?

Eight

"Pal! Istvan!" The woman who had been with the three men reached us, yelling, "Stop, Drake! Aoife, get them apart! They'll kill each other."

I did a double take at the sound of a familiar female voice. "Aisling?" I asked.

The two redheaded men had dragged themselves out of the pile, but Kostya and the man who I assumed must be his brother still rolled around, thankfully in human form, but judging by the sounds, still beating the stuffing out of each other.

"I'm really getting tired of all the fighting," I told Kostya. "So you can just stop it right now, because I am not taking you to see Dr. Ek a third time!"

"Pull them apart," Aisling shouted, leaping forward and catching hold of Drake's arm, trying to pull him back.

He snarled something quite rude, his face black with fury. To my amazement, the two redheads did as she ordered, grabbing Drake and attempting to force him off his brother. Kostya lunged forward, taking advantage of the fact that Drake was temporarily unable to strike back, and nailed him with a solid blow to the face that, if the sound of the resulting crack was anything to go by, probably broke the latter's nose.

"Aoife, you're going to have to pull him off," Aisling ordered, trying to squeeze her way between the two men. "They won't stop until we get them separated!"

I looked around for something that I could use to help pry Kostya off Drake, but other than Jim, there was nothing at hand.

"Jim," I commanded, "find something to help me yank Kostya back."

"Seriously?" Jim pursed his lips. "Like what, a bulldozer?"

"You are *not* helping," I said in between grunts as I wrapped my arms around Kostya from the back and tried to pivot him over my hip.

"Aoife, babe, you've seen Slick go at it before. You gotta know that it's going to take something like a crowbar to remove him from the other dude, and realistically, that's only going to work if you knock him silly with the crowbar."

"Do as I order," I yelled, giving up on the pivoting idea. I decided Aisling had a better plan and tried to shove myself between the two men. "Grab the back of his shirt and pull!"

It worked, but only after I took an inadvertent blow to the jaw that made me see stars for a few minutes. I clung to Kostya, telling him to stop being such an idiot and other such words of wisdom, and with Aisling and her two friends pulling Drake back to a safe distance, at last we got the two men separated by thirty yards. Kostya stood panting, his shirt torn and sporting two black eyes. Drake didn't look much better, with blood dripping out of his nose, a fat lip, and a lump on his jaw that slowly faded away.

"What the hell?" I asked Kostya when the two men stood glaring at each other. "Why didn't you tell me you hated your brother?"

He shifted his gaze to me, the anger in it fading to puzzlement. "What are you talking about? I don't hate my brother."

I pointed to where Aisling was mopping up Drake's face. "You just tried to kill him. Don't tell me you didn't, because you most definitely did not pull that punch that I took instead of him."

Kostya's eyes sharpened on my face, a horrified look flashing in his eyes. He touched my jaw, his thumb stroking gently across the tender spot. "I struck you? Let me see."

"I'm fine." I batted his hand away, but he simply ignored that and turned my head until he could examine the bruised part of my jaw. His fingers were warm as he brushed his thumb again, sending an answering warmth down my neck, to where it pooled in my belly.

For a moment, it was as if time had stopped, and there was just Kostya and me, and a gossamer web of unspoken emotion between us.

And then the big oaf went and broke the spell.

"You did not tell me that I struck you. I will not have this! You will see a doctor," he pronounced.

I blinked a couple of times, already regretting the loss of the moment. "I will do no such thing."

"I won't have you hurt." He took my hand and started to stride around the back of the hangar. "We will go now."

"Like hell we will! Kostya, stop!" I dug in my heels and managed to get him to halt. "What about your brother?"

He turned around to look over at Drake, and instantly his body language changed. His teeth bared as he started forward. I leaped in front of him, blocking his way.

"Oh, you did not just do that," I snapped. "I don't know what's going on with you, or if this is how you normally greet family members, but I do know this: the next time you get in a knock-down, drag-out fight, I'm just going to let you get beat up."

"It's not his fault," Aisling called to me, starting across the gap between the two men. Drake snarled an order for her to stop, and started moving. The two redheads pounced and held him back.

"For the love of Pete!" Aisling said, gesturing at her husband. "I can talk to Aoife, can't I?"

Kostya growled, positively growled. I looked back at him, my hands still on his chest holding him back.

"Wow," Jim said, giving him a long look. "That's seriously feral-sounding, Slick. You may want to consult a vet about some rabies shots. I'd suggest a neutering, but I doubt if Eefster Island would let you."

"Do you want me to order you to silence again?" I asked the demon.

He sniffed and glanced away. "Man, censorship all over the place. 'Jim, don't pee on the doctor's flowers. Jim, don't sniff the waitress's crotch. Jim, don't make neutering jokes.' You're no fun, Eefers, absolutely no fun. I bet that Aisling woman would let me have fun."

"Don't you dare try to play her against me, because that isn't going to work one little bit."

Hurt darkened his eyes. "You don't want me. It's because I'm a demon, isn't it? Go on, you can tell me. You'll crush my spirits and destroy my heart and ruin what was turning out to be a perfectly nice relationship—"

"You just got done ranting to me about how I'm no fun," I interrupted.

"—and just when I was forming a bond with you," Jim continued, as if I hadn't spoken. "But that's okay. Oh, sure, I was learning to love you despite your quirky ways, and the fact that you starve me, and that you want to get it on with Slick, here, but none of that matters because I'm not human, right? Go ahead," he said, lying down on the ground. "Run me over again. Put me out of my misery. It won't matter because I'm just a demon."

"Oh, for the love of— Jim, get up. I'm not going to run you over. And you do matter to me, which is why I took you to the vet, and bought you a hamburger, and gave you my duvet to sleep with, so don't give me those big eyes full of martyrdom. Are you crying?"

"No," Jim sniffled, turning away from me. His voice was thick. "I just have something in my eye."

"I can't believe you're going drama queen on me right now. Kostya, are you seeing what he's doing? Don't you have something to say about it?"

Kostya's eyes narrowed on his brother until the little silver flecks in them glittered like sunlight on diamonds. "Wyvern," he drawled, his hands fisted, every muscle and sinew in his body as taut as a bowstring.

"You are absolutely no help, do you know that?" I told him.

I sighed and turned toward Jim, now rolling around on the ground in faux agony. But the second I took my hands off Kostya, he started moving forward. I shoved my shoulder against his chest, gave him a glare that he registered but didn't comment on, and said with as much good grace as I could, "Man, you are really pushing my buttons, aren't you? Well, I did not go through two years of deep psychological training to let someone mess with me that way. I do want you, Jim. If I didn't, I would have left you on the road when I ran you over."

He got up, still sniffling. "So you love me?"

"Yes," I snarled, wishing for what seemed to be the umpteenth time that day that it was over. "Yes, I love you to the ends of the earth and back again. Now get over here and help me hold Kostya back."

"Aoife. Meet me halfway," Aisling called. She'd gone back to her husband and evidently had been having a little chat with him. "Drake won't let me come to you, and I suspect that Kostya wouldn't appreciate you coming over here. Drake! Stay!"

"Okay, but only because you said you were sorry for treating me like I was dirt," Jim said, moving behind Kostya to take a big mouthful of his shirt and pulling backward as he did so.

I decided it was better if I didn't point out that no apology had been forthcoming and turned my attention back to Kostya. "Aisling wants to speak to me."

"Wyvern," he repeated.

"No, she's the wyvern's wife, and she wants to talk to me. I'm going to do so. You stay here."

"Drake," he snarled, his teeth grinding slightly.

I eyed him. "Don't make me give you orders like the dog there."

A muffled, "Hello, standing right here! I have a name. Plus, you said you love me. You can't refer to me like that if you love me, can you?" came from behind Kostya.

Kostya's eyes focused on me. "Are you insulting me?"

"No, but I will if it will make you stop fighting. Stay right here. I'm going to walk over there to talk to your sister-in-law, okay?"

He looked past me to Aisling, then to Drake, growled again, but nodded.

"Jim, I changed my mind; you can come with me. Since you used to belong to Aisling, she'll probably want to see you and make sure you're okay and possibly even ask for you back. Which I will be happy to do, since you don't seem to like the way I take care of you."

"Being run over kind of makes you lose a little faith in the quality of care you can expect," Jim answered in a dry tone, but he followed me as I met Aisling halfway between the two men.

"Hello, Aoife. As you guessed, I'm Aisling," she said, giving me a friendly smile before squealing softly, "Jim! I'm so happy to see you! Where have you been? Why are you in Sweden? Why aren't you with Magoth?"

The demon allowed her to hug him, snuffling her hair and her chest before answering. "Hiya. The Eefs says I used to hang with you. I don't know who Magoth is, but you seem nice enough. You wouldn't happen to have any food on you, would you? My current demon lord says she loves me, but the sad truth is that she's trying to starve me to death."

Aisling looked startled. "She is?"

"Yeah, she only let me have one hamburger for lunch. One! Like that is enough to sustain what is clearly an outstanding example of Newfiness."

"The vet said he could stand to lose a couple of pounds," I told Aisling, worried that she might think I was mistreating her dog. Demon. Whichever.

"Oh, that. Yes, my vet said the same thing. And Jim is the master of bitching about lack of food. Pay it no mind." A look of confusion crossed her face. "Wait—what do you mean you don't remember Magoth?"

Jim shrugged. "Memory's gone. Don't remember anything except Aoife mowing me down and then hauling me in to the vet."

"It was an accident!" I said quickly, panic filling me at the look that Aisling gave me when she stood up. "It was night, and he was standing in the middle of the road, just standing there, and of course, I took him to the vet, and she said he was fine, absolutely fine, not hurt at all, and I took him home, because I had no idea who he belonged to, but I assure you, I did not deliberately run him down."

"I see." Her voice was cold, but after a few seconds of giving me a tight-lipped look, she shook her head. "I'm sorry, I shouldn't be angry. I'm sure you didn't run Jim over on purpose." She stopped to run her hands along his body, obviously checking for signs of injury. Jim moaned happily and leaned into her. "But it's come as a shock to me that Jim doesn't even recognize me. I don't...I just don't have any idea what could have happened. I bound it to Magoth."

"Who's that?" I asked.

"A demon lord. Former demon lord, that is. He's by way of an acquaintance." She gave a wry smile. "In a nutshell, he has the hots for Drake and Kostya's mom, but she dumped him. Anyway, he was helping us smuggle Jim into Abaddon—that's hell to the common man—to find out what Asmodeus was doing and, if possible, to locate his ring."

I rubbed my forehead. "I feel like I should have a scorecard with everyone's name and stats. Is this the same Asmodeus of the curse?"

"One in the same, Mr. Head of Abaddon, the villain of the dragon and immortal worlds, what with this curse that's making a mess of all our lives." Aisling suddenly looked worried. "We've got to break the curse, Aoife. The war isn't just affecting the dragons; it's threatening to spill over to the mortal world, too."

"Now there's a *war* in addition to demon lords and a curse?"

I must have looked a bit wild-eyed because Aisling suddenly took my arm and called over her shoulder to her husband.

"We're taking a little walk. No, you do not need to accompany us. Don't kill your brother. We'll be right back."

"Where are you going?" Kostya asked, clearly torn between posturing at his brother and following us.

"Aisling's going to explain to me why there's a war and a demon lord curse."

"I could explain that to you," he yelled after me, his voice tinged with outrage.

"Yeah, but you never do, do you?" I turned my back to him and strolled with Aisling toward the main building, which was strangely unpopulated. "Getting a straight answer out of him is like finding a pearl in a clam."

"I thought pearls grew in oysters?" Aisling asked with a frown.

"That's my point. First things first—why is Kostya attacking his brother, and vice versa?"

She sighed. "It's part of the curse. Not only can the septs not talk to one another, which really makes it difficult to conduct any weyr business, but the curse also causes them to be overly antagonistic to dragons outside of their sept. And in this case—"

A roar of anger behind us had us both spinning. Drake and Kostya had evidently not been able to stand the strain any longer and were rolling around on the ground pummeling each other.

It was my turn to sigh, and I did, a long, martyred sigh. "Sweet salivating salamanders, that man does like to fight."

"Dragon," Aisling said, and to my complete surprise, turned her back on them.

"Um...shouldn't we stop them?" I asked when she took a few steps forward.

"I don't think it would do much good. They'd just interrupt us again. We might as well let them work off the worst of the curse while we get a few things straight. Where were we?"

I cast a glance back over my shoulder, part of me wanting to keep Kostya whole and unharmed, but the other part in agreement with Aisling. "They won't do any permanent damage, will they?"

"Not so long as they don't go into dragon form, no. Human form is much less effective, you see." She gave me a bright smile and paused in front of a cement bench next to a tiny control tower. The ground was littered with cigarette butts, indicating this was a favorite break spot of employees.

"I wonder where everyone is?" I asked, glancing around.

"Drake arranged for the airport crew to leave for an hour after we landed. He thought it was best that no one see us together. So, that's where we are: Jim was supposed to be with Magoth undercover in Abaddon, but it's here with you and Kostya. And we're no closer to bringing an end to the curse." She sat down, her shoulders slumping in defeat. "I wish Jim hadn't lost its memory. I'd like to know what it found out while it was skulking around Asmodeus's palace."

I let the idea of demon lords living in palaces slide by and focused on the important things. I sat down next to her and said, "I can't help you there, but I'm sure you'd like Jim back, yes? I'll just hand him over."

Aisling bit her bottom lip as she looked from Jim to me. "It may not be that easy. Jim, who are you bound to?"

Jim sat down with a put-upon look on his hairy black face. "I don't suppose I could have a burger first? Lunch was a long time ago."

I cocked an eyebrow at him.

"Fine! I'll just sit here and quietly starve to death. I'm bound to Aoife, not that I knew that until Slick over there told me who I was."

"Slick?" Aisling asked.

"That's what he calls Kostya. Mostly because it infuriates him." A little smile tugged at my mouth. We both looked over to where the fight was going on. Kostya and Drake were now on their feet, dancing around each other and making swinging jabs. The two redheads watched from the sidelines.

Aisling laughed and ruffled the top of the dog's head. "Well at least I'm happy to see that nothing else has changed, even if you did lose your memory. I'm going to have more than a few things to say to Magoth when I see him, but I suppose until I can get Jim back to where it belongs, I'll let that go. Can you please transfer Jim to me, Aoife?"

"Sure." I gestured at the dog. "Jim, you're now Aisling's demon."

He scratched his neck. "I'm not saying that I wouldn't like to do that, 'cause she has a nice smell and she knows how to scratch behind my ears just how I like it, but I don't think I can do that."

"Oh, I have to order you. Okay. Jim, I order you to be Aisling's demon."

Aisling was shaking her head before I could even finish. "It doesn't work that way, I'm afraid. First you have to disavow Jim first; then I can summon it and bind it to me."

I looked at Jim. "How do I do that?"

He shrugged. "No clue."

"You're the demon. You should know this sort of thing."

"You're the demon lord. You shouldn't go binding demons to you if you don't know how to give them back to their rightful, food-giving homes," he countered.

I turned back to Aisling. "I'm afraid I'm going to need a little help."

She frowned and shook her head. "Demons aren't bound to individuals by any set method. How you bound Jim to you determines how you unbind it."

I slid a glance over to where Kostya was battling his brother. Both men were now wielding what looked like two-by-fours.

"Um... maybe we can talk about passing Jim along later. I get the feeling if we don't do something pretty quick, those two are going to really start hurting each other. You may not think they will, but Kostya's kind of a badass."

"That's what comes from having too much testosterone," Jim commented. "That makes your balls big, right? Kostya's got quite the pair on him, so yeah, gotta be testosterone overload that's making him jump everyone in sight."

We both looked at the demon. Aisling appeared to be disconcerted for a moment. "I...you know, I really don't think I need to know about Kostya's testicles, thank you, Jim."

"Just trying to be helpful," he said, giving her hand a lick before wandering over to plop his butt down on my foot. "Eefs'll back me up on the ball thing, won'tcha, babe?"

A memory of Kostya standing in the doctor's office without the towel rushed front and center in my mind. "Um..."

"Moving on!" Aisling said brightly, and got to her feet. We both started forward, Jim following behind. "I suppose they've had long enough to fight. But we should make some plans. What exactly has Kostya told you about the curse?"

"Not much at all. I only met him yesterday."

She blinked at me a couple of times. "You *what?*"

I described briefly how Jim and I had found Kostya.

"That's...unexpected. I don't quite know...I assumed you were...Have you taken his fire?"

"Taken it where?"

She shook her head. "This is going to sound very impertinent, but you appear so much like a mate that I have to ask—have you been intimate with Kostya?"

I straightened my shoulders. "I realize that you dragon people are different from the rest of us, but that's seriously over the line."

"They played sucky face a couple of times," Jim said helpfully.

I ignored him. "Not to mention more than a little insulting that you think I'm the sort of woman who jumps into bed at the drop of a hat...er...dragon."

"And she keeps ordering me out of the room so she can touch his naked chest," Jim added, waggling his eyebrows. "They keep saying they aren't interested in each other, but you could steam broccoli with the looks they give each other when they think no one's looking."

"Oh, we do not," I said, feeling my face go hot nonetheless.

"You totes do, babe," Jim said, giving me a knowing look.

"Well, he's a handsome man," I snapped, feeling defensive. "You'd have to be dead not to want to kiss him. And touch his chest. And run your fingers through his hair, and feel those muscles in his back, and..." I realized what I was saying and stopped to clear my throat. "You'd have to be dead, and I'm not."

"I had a feeling that what I was going to say would come out wrong," Aisling said with a wry smile. "I didn't mean to imply anything. I simply wanted to know if you've taken his fire. Only mates are able to withstand a wyvern's fire, but if you've only kissed him a few times, then obviously you don't know what I'm talking about, so it's a moot point."

"Well," I said, wiggling my toes. "There was the thing with my feet this morning."

Jim gawked at my feet. "Ew! He has a foot fetish? Did he suck your toes? Because I'm a dog, and even I think that's wrong."

"No," I said, giving him a gentle whomp on the shoulder. "Of course I didn't let him suck my toes. And if I did, I wouldn't tell you. Oh, sorry, Aisling. I didn't mean to hit your dog."

Surprisingly, she gave me a cheery smile and stopped a few feet away from where Drake and Kostya were now fencing with the two-by-fours. "Don't think anything about it. I frequently have to banish it to the Akasha when it gets overly lippy with us. What happened with your feet?"

I glanced at Kostya, but he seemed to be fine, other than a stream of blood running from a cut on his forehead. "Kostya kissed me, and somehow that set them on fire. I thought they burned to horrible stumps, but they weren't touched at all."

Relief spread over her face, and suddenly she hugged me. "Oh, thank God, I was right after all. I wondered if he'd ever find anyone after Cyrene, but there you are, and you're perfect. You look absolutely perfect for him, and I'm sure you're just what he needs. Drake will be so happy. We've worried about Kostya, you know. Now, about the curse—"

"Whoa now, I didn't say I was his mate, if that's what you're implying with the hugs and such. I'm not exactly sure what a mate is, because Mr. Pigheaded won't tell me other than declaring that under no circumstances should I consider myself one, or that he is looking for one, or for that matter, does he even want me... Wait, what do you mean you're worried about him? Worried how?"

Aisling waved away the sudden worry I had that maybe Kostya wasn't all he seemed. "It's nothing to fret over. He's just... well, intense. I'm sure you've noticed that."

"Oh yes."

"A lot of that comes from the fact that he spent so long in captivity. In solitary confinement, actually, although he doesn't like to talk about it. He feels things deeply, but he doesn't want people to know that, so he puts on this brusque front and…and…really," she said with a little laugh, "I'm sure I'm preaching to the choir. You probably have figured all this out about him by now."

"Sure," I said blithely, hoping I looked like I was full of all sorts of Kostya-insights. And to be honest, I had gleaned much of what she told me. "It's just that he's very reticent to speak about himself. That whole thing about him not having a mate, or even wanting one. Mind you, he usually says that right before he kisses me, but that's neither here nor there. What does matter is that some dudes called the red dragons burned down my family home and tried to kill us, and now Kostya says I have to go to Paris with him in order to be safe. Why me? For that matter, why Paris?"

"She really is this clueless," Jim told Aisling. "You have no idea what a cross it is to bear."

"Quiet, demon." Aisling looked startled to find herself saying that, a look of sadness crossing her face, followed by obvious resignation. "It's so odd not to have Jim bound to me…but you're right. It's obviously fine with you, so I need to let that wait until we deal with the situation at hand. The curse is our primary focus—or at least, the breaking of it is. We need to find Asmodeus's ring and use it to end the curse and bring the weyr together again. Not to mention keep the mortal world from being affected by the dragons warring, but so far, the battle hasn't spilled over to them. And we'd like to keep it that way."

I shifted uncomfortably, part of me wanting to tell her

that I had the ring she was looking for but feeling too over my head to make that call on my own. I needed to talk with Kostya first.

"So where is this Asmodeus person?" I asked in an attempt to change the subject from that of the ring's location.

"Abaddon, so far as we know. Oh, I should probably give you a super-quick history lesson." She pursed her lips a moment while watching Drake block a sudden attack by Kostya. "The premiere prince is the demon lord who rules the other seven princes. Asmodeus is the current premiere prince. He took over from a truly evil man named Bael, and we thought that we were going to be fine with Asmodeus in place, but then two years ago he killed off most of the red dragon sept and kept a few to perform horrible experiments on, with the end result that now he has an army of red dragons who are partly demons."

"So those red dragons that attacked us are part demon? Ugh."

Aisling nodded. "As if a dragon isn't hard enough to kill, now they've got demonic strength added into the mix."

"Hmm." I thought about the red dragons left dead outside my home. Their corpses had disappeared into black curls of smoke before I had gotten Kostya to the doctor, which confirmed their demonic aspect. "Why?"

She gave me a curious look. "Why are we trying to kill them?"

"No, why would this head demon prince guy want you guys fighting with each other? I don't understand why he put a curse on you if he was just going to send his super-dragons to wipe you out."

"That is a very good question, and we don't know for certain what his motivation is in destroying all the dragons." She gave a little head shake, sliding a look back toward her husband. "We assume it's to destroy the dragons, but as to why...we just don't know. It kind of came out of the blue, to be honest. And worse, we worry that Asmodeus might be looking beyond the dragonkin to the rest of the Otherworld...and then to the mortal world."

"Eek!"

"Indeed." She glanced again behind her. "All we really know is that Asmodeus has declared war on the dragons by slapping us with the curse and turning the red dragons against us. I could speculate for hours as to the whys and wherefores, but I don't know how long Drake is going to be able to stand having Kostya so close, so we'd better deal with the important things right now. You said the red dragons burned down your house?"

"Yes. They attacked us when we escaped, which is where Kostya was injured the second time, but he appears to be back to normal now. Assuming beating up every dragon he comes into contact with is normal for him."

She gave a little laugh. "It's not far off." She gave me a long look before adding, "You know, most of the wyverns are really happy to find their mates. But Kostya...well, let's just say there's a good reason for him to be a little gun-shy. That doesn't mean that you have to put up with it, though. I'm a big believer in taking charge of situations, and clearly you're not the sort of person who lets people walk all over her."

I thought of how I'd spent the last two years and kept my mouth shut.

"So the next time Kostya's kissing you and telling you that you're not his mate, you might just turn his fire back on himself. That might show him a thing or two." At that moment, Drake smacked Kostya upside the head, which sent him flying.

Drake stood over him, his hands on his hips, and said loudly, "Are you done with your talk?"

"Just about," Aisling said, frowning. "That wasn't very nice, Drake. You might have given him a concuss— Oh, dear."

Kostya, who had been sitting up and shaking his head, suddenly lunged at his brother's legs, and nailed him on the chin in a way that left Drake limp on the ground, clearly knocked out.

"Very brotherly," I told Kostya when he staggered to his feet. Now his nose was bleeding, too.

"He started it," Kostya said, and lurched toward us. "What has Aisling told you?"

"Many things." I tsked at the sight of the way his shoulder was carried. "You've gone and broken your collarbone again, haven't you?"

"No," he said, touching it and wincing. "Possibly. But it will heal. What plans have Aisling and Drake made?"

"Er..." I looked at Aisling. "Kostya wants to know about any plans."

"We haven't really made any other than finding the ring, and we've had no luck there for the longest time." Aisling squatted next to Drake, dabbing at his head with her sleeve. "Drake's going to be furious when he wakes up. He hates it when Kostya bests him."

"What is she saying?" Kostya asked.

"Nothing your ego needs to hear. Kostya thinks we need to go to Paris, Aisling. I'm not quite sure why, but he seems to feel that's a safe place."

"Nowhere is safe from the red dragons," she said

slowly, rising when Drake, who had just come to, leaped to his feet with a snarl. He wobbled quite a bit, which is why Aisling was able to hold him back with just one arm. With her other, she handed me a card. "Here's my number. Call me in a bit and give me your number. Go to Paris with Kostya. Drake has a house there, and I'll arrange for us to head to France as well. Kostya must think the ring is there, else he wouldn't leave Sweden. Above all else, it's important that we find it, or the weyr is forever doomed. Jim, don't give Aoife any grief or be obnoxious, and do whatever she tells you to do."

I bit my lip, glancing at Kostya. Once again, I wanted to tell Aisling that I had the ring, but if Kostya hadn't instructed me to tell her I had it, then he most likely didn't want her to know. Although why escaped me. Perhaps he felt they would take it from us? It would be nice to hand off the responsibility of it to someone else, but on the other hand, it seemed like the ring had chosen me, and for some strange reason, I was loathe to give it up so easily.

While I was waffling over what to do, Jim tipped his head and looked at Aisling. "Can she tell me what to do, Eefster?"

"Hmm? Yes, she can."

"Oh, Jim, if only I had time...but I don't." Aisling leaned forward and gave the dog a hug, and kissed him on his head. "Just remember that you're a good demon, not a bad one. And for heaven's sake, stop standing around in the middle of roads!"

She and Drake began walking toward their plane, but Aisling paused to toss over her shoulder, "Remember what I said about Kostya's fire, Aoife. It's time he move past Cyrene and realize just how blessed he is to have you in his life! It wouldn't hurt to make him grovel just a little, but keep in mind that he's had a hard time lately. I'm sure you won't be cruel."

I looked at Kostya, wondering if my life would ever be the same again.

Nine

I watched Aisling and Drake's plane taxi away, then slowly turned back to Kostya, who instantly demanded to know what was said. "Did Aisling say what the green dragons were doing? Did you tell her about the ring? Is there news of the other septs?"

His eyes were as shiny as ever, the little silver flecks glinting dangerously in the surrounding onyx. I took a mental step back and looked at him, really looked at him. Aisling clearly thought that I was the person meant to be with Kostya, his life mate, or whatever dragons had, and that thought was both frightening and enticing.

I'd never had a serious relationship with a man but had long wanted one. I'd never felt like I was truly part of someone's life. There were my parents, and later my siblings, but they were family—stuck with me whether they liked it or not.

And when they don't like it, they stick you in an insane asylum, the small voice in my head said. I shook that thought away, eyeing Kostya even as he impatiently waited for me to answer his questions.

What was it about him that made me feel warm and fuzzy inside? Certainly not his gruff manner. Or his way of telling me that he didn't want me as a girlfriend, even while he risked life and limb to keep me safe.

I'd have to be dead not to feel the pull of his masculinity, but it wasn't just the cute cleft in his chin, or the six-pack, or even his fabulous butt that kept him uppermost in my thoughts; no, it was the sense of need surrounding him that struck such a chord within me, a sense of pain deep within him that I wanted desperately to lessen. He had scars that ran so deep, I wasn't sure anything I could do could ever heal them, but I knew that I very much wanted to try.

"Aoife?" Kostya almost tapped his foot with impatience.

I giggled to myself. What a man I'd picked to become obsessed with. "No, I didn't tell Aisling about the ring. I didn't know you wanted me to. Should I have? I can call her super quick if you think it's important they know this second."

Kostya shook his head before I even finished speaking. "No, we must go to Paris. We can't use the ring here."

"I thought you said we couldn't use the ring at all?"

"Dragons cannot." His gaze flittered away. "*We* are affected by the curse."

That sense of being an outsider, of not belonging, hit me again with his words. The meaning was quite clear—I was only a means to an end, a way to bring the ring to whoever or whatever would use it to break the curse.

Dammit, I was not going to fall in love with Kostya. Not when he kept pushing me away. To continue would leave me tragically heartsore.

"And then where would we be?" I asked aloud.

"We are in Sweden. You should know that. Are you having an episode of derangement?" He frowned, his two straight ebony brows pulling downward until I couldn't stand it any longer and reached up to smooth out the wrinkles between them. "You said that you were not deranged, but there is something wrong if you don't know where you are."

"I know exactly where I am." He caught my hand, his thumb rubbing across my pulse point in a way that had various parts of me tingling in pleasure despite my better intentions to not give in to his sexy, sexy ways. "What I don't know is *what* I am. I thought I was just me, a normal person who saw some pretty extraordinary things and was tossed in the nuthouse as a result. But now I don't know for sure. Why are you rubbing my hand?"

His expression was unreadable. "You were touching my face. I was simply stopping you."

"You are so messed up, Slick. Must have been that smack on the head that did it, because you're supposed to be encouraging hot babes like Aoife to touch you, not stop them. Although it was better earlier today when she had her hands on your ass, and you were grabbing booby— Hey! Ow! Make it stop, make it stop!"

Kostya set fire to Jim's tail with just a flicker of his eyes. Jim ran around in a circle for a few seconds before plopping down on his butt, extinguishing the fire. He glared at Kostya, who had turned back to me. "Man! Some people are just so sensitive."

"Do you not like to be touched?" I asked Kostya, wondering if he had a personal space issue that I hadn't picked up on before.

"What did Aisling say to you?"

"Ah, we're back to that game, are we? Let's see...I think I counter with why did someone hold you prisoner for seven years?"

"Did she say what the green dragons were doing? Why did you not show her the ring?"

"Why don't you ever answer a question?"

"I'm a dragon," he said with a little shrug. "We dislike answering questions, although I would point out I have just done so. Thus it is your turn. Why will you not answer *my* questions?"

"Kiss me," I demanded, deciding that I would start resisting him later, when I wasn't so confused about everything.

"Now that's what I'm talking about," Jim said, tipping his head to the side. "Don't mind me, I'm just sitting here. Boy, I wish I had a camera."

I didn't have a chance to tell Jim to stop watching us before Kostya, evidently deciding the questioning game wasn't going to go anywhere, obliged me by kissing all thoughts right out of my brain.

Instantly, my body was full of demands. My breasts wanted Kostya's hands and mouth on them, my fingers wanted to skim every reachable part of him, my hips wanted to rock against his, and that whole area in my body devoted to reproductive activities was evidently having a block party and insisted that Kostya join the fun.

I tried to quell my libido, but it was having none of it. Not while my body was all but mugging his, my hands entangled in his hair, his hands on my butt pulling me even closer, and between us, an inferno that grew hotter and hotter with each stroke of his tongue. Heat swamped me, his dragon fire, setting every atom inside me alight with need and desire and a wanting so great, it scared me. How could I have this sort of a reaction to a man I'd known for a day?

"You taste so good," he groaned into my mouth, moving me backward until I was pressed against the side of the hangar before he pulled me upward in order to delve deeper into my mouth. "You are spicy, like mulled wine, and just as heady."

"Too much talking, not enough kissing," I murmured before wrapping my legs around his hips, wanting to press him against all the needy parts of me—which was basically my entire body. Flames licked along my flesh, the heat inside building to the point where I was sure I couldn't stand it anymore, my body forced to cope with Kostya's fire or combust into an inferno.

Panic hit me hard for a moment, swamping me with a sudden desire to flee. But that would mean leaving Kostya, never seeing him again, never laughing at his scowls or soothing his hurts, never holding him tight, trying to ease the darkness inside him.

I couldn't do it. I knew I was making a choice in my life that I could never undo, but I just couldn't walk away from Kostya and everything he represented. He needed me, and I gloried in that, basked in the knowledge that I could help him, ease his pain, and along the way, perhaps find just what it was I was supposed to do with my life.

And at that moment, just when I was sure I was going to burn away to nothing, I accepted everything that had happened to me since that fateful day two years ago.

It was as if someone had flipped a switch, because suddenly the fire that threatened to consume me became part of me. I let it whip around me for a few seconds, enjoying the power and heat and thrilling in the fact that I could control it. I tugged on Kostya's hair, wordlessly asking for more, promising to give him everything I could.

Just what I expected him to do while we were standing outside, in clear view of anyone who happened to pass, I didn't know. I just wanted...*more*. I wanted Kostya and his fire and everything those two things comprised. I didn't care about convention or that it wasn't wise to leap into any relationship, let alone one with a man who was so obviously emotionally scarred. At that moment, I didn't even care that red dragons had destroyed my home and tried to kill us all.

I accepted that the world was a place where dragons were people, and Kostya was one of them.

I accepted the idea that there were demon lords and demons, and one of the latter was now bound to me.

I accepted that I was put on the earth to be paired up with Kostya and that I had suffered through two years of hell so I could help him overcome the pain he had lived through. More importantly, I understood that I was meant to bring his life back on track and surround us with the happiness that we both deserved, and with those epiphanies, my mind was free.

He jerked backward when I spun his fire around us both, then directed it back to him, pouring it into him with a joy that I hadn't felt since I was a child.

"What did you just do?" he asked, his eyes wonderfully misty with passion.

"That pole dance move? Looked to me like a cross

between trying to dry hump you and climbing a rope, but I can't see much from this angle," came an answer from Jim's direction.

"Jim, hush," I said, wanting to laugh with the sheer pleasure of my sudden insight. I was a dragon's mate! Me, boring old Aoife, who thought the most exciting thing in her life would be the time she went to a circus and became deranged. "You mean the fire thing? Aisling told me to give you your fire back, so I did just that. Still want to deny that I'm your mate? Because I've just realized that what she said was absolutely true, and it explains a whole lot about why I'm so attracted to you."

"You're attracted to me because all women are," he said in an offhand, dismissive manner that made me want to smack him.

So I did. Right on the chest. "Look, Buster Brown—"

"My name is Kostya."

"—you may think that you're the only one who's gone through hell in your life, but you're dead wrong, so you can take that God's-gift-to-women attitude and stuff it where the sun don't shine!"

"Oooh," Jim said, his eyes wide. "Hey, Slick, in case you don't know, she's talking about your—"

"And furthermore," I interrupted loudly, slapping my hand on his chest again, clutching his shirt to shake him a little. "I'd like a little acknowledgment of just how nice it is that I'm not fighting the whole idea that I'm a dragon's mate, especially given that twenty-four hours ago, I hadn't a clue that there even *were* dragons, let alone mates. And while we're on the subject, why is it that I have to get all the information about being your mate from Aisling? You should be the one telling me this stuff!"

He opened his mouth to protest, stopped, and then considered me for a moment. Slowly, gently, he disentangled my fingers from his shirt. "Aisling should know better than to interfere," was all he said before turning and striding off toward the main office.

"Oh, man, he did not just do that," Jim said, whistling softly. "Eefs, you are in for it now."

I patted the dog on his head and smiled. Jim was absolutely right; I was in for a hell of a ride, but at least I knew an important life-changing fact: I was a dragon's mate. "And if Kostya thinks he is going to get out of cherishing me the way Aisling says he should, then he can just bloody well think again."

"You tell him, girlfriend," Jim said, falling into place alongside me as we followed Kostya. "Although I kind of get the feeling that Slick isn't going to fall to his knees with gratitude, if you know what I mean. He seems kinda broken to me."

"Broken," I mused, nodding my head. "That's a good way of putting it. He does seem broken, and since I've been there and glued the bits of me back together—via the help of Dr. Barlind, although, again, I could have done without the electroshock torture—I'm the perfect person to help him piece his life into what it should be."

"And still get into his pants," Jim said with another bobble of his eyebrows.

"That goes without saying, although really, there's something almost borderline creepy about hearing a dog say it."

"Evidently I'm a student of human nature," he answered with a shrug.

"You're something all right." I was about to enter the

airport office when Kostya emerged, a slip of paper in his hand.

"We go to Stockholm," he said, taking my elbow and steering me back the way we came. "There's a pilot here who will fly us."

"Wait, you want to go to Paris right this second? Kostya, I can't leave Sweden yet."

He didn't stop marching me toward the hangars. "Why not?"

"Because my house burned down, remember? I have stuff to deal with concerning that, not to mention talking to my sister and brother so we can make some decisions about the house."

"Do they live elsewhere?"

"Yes. Bee has an apartment in Venice, and Rowan's job is in Malta, so he's there a lot of the time. But they come home a couple of times a year, so I'm going to have to tell them what happened. Oh gods, they aren't going to believe me!" I rubbed my forehead. "What if they have me committed again?"

"I would not allow that."

"Yes, well, the fact still remains that I have to deal with the situation of the house."

"I've told you that it isn't safe here. The red dragons know you are here—know we are both here—and they won't stop tracking us both down and attempting to destroy us. If they find out that you have the ring, they would launch an all-out onslaught." His jaw tightened. "I don't concern myself much with the mortal world, but I have seen the devastation that a war with Abaddon can wreak upon it, and I would not wish to have that unleashed again."

I thought of the looks on the red dragons' faces when they realized I had the ring, and blanched. Those dragons were dead, but if others found out . . .

"Eep," I said, my skin crawling at the thought. "I can only imagine that would be seriously bad. Wait—does that mean you're not mortal?"

"I am a dragon. We can be killed, but we do not die of illnesses or old age, as mortals do."

I looked at him with a new awareness, then pointed at Jim. "And demons?"

"They cannot be killed, although their forms can be destroyed. Do you notice that I am answering your questions even though I have much to do?"

"Yes, and you will receive a gold star at the end of the day for your willingness to play with others." I bit my lower lip in thought. "So what about me? Now that I'm your mate—"

"You are not my mate. I do not have a mate. I did have one, but she abused me horribly, so I disavowed her. I will never claim a mate again."

"—does that mean I get to be not-mortal, too? Is *immortal* the right word? That means 'can't be killed,' though, and you said dragons can be. Okay, now I'm just confused."

He stopped and gave me an irritated look. "Did you not hear what I just said?"

"Yes, but I decided to ignore it, because men who let their past experiences with ex-girlfriends screw up relationships that will be happy and healthy are just too irritating for words, so therefore, I'm ignoring any references you make to your ex. No, I take that back. I'll say this: I'm sorry that you got burned, Kostya. We all have. I had a boyfriend in high school who was using me so he could pass his classes and stay on the swim team. I know what it's like to be used, and I also know that it's possible to get over it. I'm willing to cut you a little slack if it was a recent event—"

"It was two years ago." He donned a noble yet martyred expression that made me smile to myself. "I will never forget the shame she brought to me."

"—but at the same time, I'm not going to ignore what's obviously right in front of us." I leaned forward and kissed him, willing him to share his dragon fire. To my amazement, little balls of fire formed in my hands. I spread them on his chest and stepped back with a smile. "So does that mean I'm a dragon, too? Will I die like a normal human, or will I just go on, like you?"

He made an annoyed noise, took my hand, and started forward again. "A wyvern's mate is not mortal, no. I will not discuss the matter any more with you—I have stated that you are not my mate, and that is final."

Jim snorted. I had to admit that I agreed with his sentiment. "I'll let that subject go for now because there is a more important issue, and that's your demand that I leave Sweden. My house—"

He sighed. "I will hire someone to take care of that for you. It is not safe for you to remain here. I have explained that numerous times now, and I grow weary of having to repeat that the red dragons will not stop until they find us."

I thought about that for a minute. "I suppose that would be all right, so long as I get the okay from Bee and Rowan. The three of us own the house together, and I'm sure they'll want in on the plans to rebuild. But I doubt if the fire officials and police are going to be happy with me taking off like this."

"I do not concern myself with mortal police," he said dismissively.

"Lucky you." I was silent for a moment before asking, "What's in Paris that's so important we go there right this minute?"

"We need help to use the ring, and we can likely find that help in Paris."

He released my arm to go talk to a man who emerged from a door, looking around hesitantly. Kostya showed him the paper, and the man nodded and gestured behind us.

"Ever been to Paris, Jim?" I asked, backing up as the man got into the plane and taxied slowly past all the hangars.

"No clue," he answered cheerfully. "But I expect the trip is going to be fun."

"Fun?"

"Yeah. They give you meals when you fly, right?"

"Sometimes."

"Like I said, fun."

"Famous last words," I muttered, and trotted forward when Kostya gestured for us to come.

The ride to Stockholm took less than an hour, but it was another couple of hours before Kostya could book us a plane to Paris, and then he had to go to the expense of a private jet rather than a commercial one.

"Isn't this kind of pricey?" I asked when he fetched Jim and me from the lounge. "It's nice and all, but I don't mind taking a normal flight. It's not like the dragons are going to implode if we don't get to Paris immediately."

"I have no passport, you have only the identity papers

that were in your car, and we don't have time to have documents made that would pass the mortals' security. Thus, we will take a private plane and bribe the pilots."

"Plus that means we get *all* the in-flight meals," Jim said as he marched up the short set of stairs that led to the interior of a sleek-looking jet. Judging from the exterior, it must have cost a small fortune to hire. "Can I have the chicken *and* the fish? Or both of whatever meal choices they offer?"

"Quiet," I ordered, catching sight of a flight attendant who hurried from the cockpit to greet us. "No talking around normal people. Hello. Yes, the dog is going to ride up here with us."

The woman looked a bit askance at Jim but got us settled quickly enough on some butter-colored leather captain's chairs. The plane was smaller inside than I imagined, although it had a long couch and four chairs that swiveled around to any position with small tables that could be popped up and adjusted to sit next to the chairs. I settled in one while Jim hopped up on the couch and proceeded to loll about like he was a pasha.

It didn't take long for us to get airborne. I waited until the woman was done pressing food and beverage upon us (Kostya accepted both, and after a moment's thought, I did as well. It goes without saying that Jim stared at me with huge eyes until I ordered a meal for him, too) before I said what was uppermost on my mind.

"About the ring—" I said around a mouthful of lemon-herb crusted chicken.

"Oh man, now I want onion rings," Jim said, looking up from his spaghetti and meatballs.

"Jim!" I shot a hasty glance toward the front of the plane,

but the attendant was busy chatting with one of the pilots through the open cockpit door. "Hush."

"You said I couldn't talk when someone could hear us. She's too busy hitting on that pilot dude. Are you going to eat those potatoes?"

"Yes," I said, scooting my plate closer to me. "Stop ogling my food and eat your pasta. And, no, you can't have onion rings."

"Meanie-head. I just know my coat is going to lose its glorious luster if you keep me on such a harsh diet." He returned to his meal with a pouting air.

I turned back to Kostya. "How's your steak?"

"It is food, nothing more," Kostya said, although I noticed he consumed his steak and mushrooms with an expression that hinted on blissful.

"Well, my food is excellent. If this is the sort of meal they serve on a private jet, then I'm all for traveling this way. Now, where was I in the important talk? Oh yeah, about the ring—"

"No," Kostya said, nodding toward the attendant. "We will not discuss that here."

"Oh, come on. We're in the air, and no one can overhear us. You can't seriously suspect that those people are baddies, can you?"

"They are not dragons, no, but that doesn't mean they aren't working for them."

"Isn't that a little paranoid?"

He shrugged. "I would rather be overly protective than be caught unawares again."

I don't know why I felt like I had to argue the point, but I did. "You told me that the red dragons have tried to kill you a number of times, yes?"

"They have."

"And yet you're still here," I pointed out. "If you managed to survive this long, I don't see that there's any reason you shouldn't continue."

"There's a very good reason why I cannot relax my guard."

"Oh, really? What's that?"

"You." He pushed his empty plate back and stood, nodding toward the back of the plane. "There is a bedroom back there. When you are finished eating, take the demon and sleep. You will have several hours before we get to Paris."

"What do you mean me? Wait, a bedroom? Really? Okay, that's like the most decadent thing ever, and I really have to see it, but don't even begin to think that I'm not going to pin you down about why you are so adamant that I'm not your mate, and yet you're doing the he-man protective thing with regards to my safety. Which I appreciate, in case I didn't say that, although I seriously doubt if it's necessary. Jim, are you done?"

Jim nosed aside a bit of parsley garnish. "Yeah. I'm not going to eat this green stuff. It smells funky."

"It's parsley, and it wouldn't hurt you to eat it. Since Kostya has that look on his face that says he's getting tired of answering questions—"

"I am *always* tired of answering questions."

"—then let's you and I go see how the rich people fly." I stood up and started for the door Kostya had indicated, but paused and glanced over my shoulder at him. "What are you going to do?"

"Plan," was all he said.

I thought about saying several things to that but decided

that none of them were going to be well received and, with Jim at my side, retired to the bedroom.

It was every bit as decadent as I expected, with its own bathroom en suite (complete with marble counters and a surprisingly large shower) and comfy bed. There was also a second, smaller room leading off the bedroom with another couch, a couple of captain's chairs, and a flat-screen TV.

"Oooh, DVDs," Jim said, nosing through them. "Hot damn, they have the original cast version of *Hair*. Put it on for me, would you?"

"All right, but I don't want you singing along with it," I warned, slipping the DVD into the player. "No freaking out the normal people, remember."

"Gotcha," the demon dog said, flopping down on the couch, his eyes on the screen. "Hoo baby, naked boobies. I love this movie!"

"I'd tell you that it is beyond strange for a dog to be ogling women's breasts, but you go so far beyond strange that it's not even possible to form that sentence. Besides, I thought you lost your memory—how do you know that you love *Hair*?"

"Beats me. I just do. Hubba hubba for boobies," he said, one paw tapping along with the opening music.

"I just…there are no words." I shook my head, dismissing the strangeness that was Jim. "Stay put and stay silent."

I closed the door to the room and turned around, wondering if I should take a shower first or climb into bed and catch up on some of the sleep I'd been missing. "Shower," I decided, and went into the bathroom to eyeball the facilities. There was a basket of sample toiletries and a stack of super-fluffy green-and-white towels, but there was one big issue that I didn't think the amenities covered. I thought for a moment, then went out to the main part of the plane, where Kostya was sitting with a tablet of paper and a pencil, making notes about something. He looked up as I approached. I eyed the flight attendant, judging that she was far enough away to speak.

"Can you magic up some new clothes for me?"

He just stared at me.

"I take it that's a no?"

The martyred look that I was coming to know very well took over his face. "I am a wyvern, Aoife. I have no magical abilities. I can't create clothing out of nothing."

"But you can shape-shift."

"That is not magic. That is what dragons are."

I let that point go, since I doubted if he'd understand that to everyone else in the world, dragons were magical beings. "I figured it was worth a try. I'm going to take a shower and thought it would be nice to have some clean clothes to change into, but if you can't do magic stuff like that, then I guess I'll just cope with what I have."

"I will get you new clothing in Paris," he said, looking back at his pad of paper.

I thought for a moment, decided that since the rules were different now, I could do things that I might not normally do, and then said, "It's too bad I'm not your mate, because if I was, I'd invite you to take a shower with me."

The pencil snapped in half. "We do not have to be mated to enjoy showers together," he said, standing, his eyes suddenly so full of heat I swear they started my blood boiling.

"No, but I've never been the sort of girl who'd throw

herself at a man she just met. Now, if you were my wyvern, then that could be excused," I said, and immediately was ashamed of myself. Kostya had taken a step toward me, obviously all eager anticipation, when my words hit him.

He froze, his face an unreadable mask.

"Oh, Kostya, I'm sorry. I should never have said that." I recognized the pain in his eyes: betrayal was in there, as were suspicion and self-doubt. I'd seen those very same emotions in the mirror, and I knew what pain accompanied them. Without considering what I was doing, I wrapped my arms around him, saying into his neck, "That was wrong of me to say. I'm not offering myself to you conditionally, and I'm not saying you can only join me in the shower if you say I'm your mate. I'm afraid the truth is much worse—I'm just shameless enough to want you to join me regardless of that, although I expect that now that I've put my foot in my mouth, you won't want to have anything to do with me, and honestly, I couldn't blame you—aieee!"

He scooped me up in his arms without regard to the flight attendant puttering around the cabin or the fact that he had a broken collarbone earlier that morning.

Ten

"Sweet salty balls, Kostya! You aren't doing this!"

"I am," he said calmly, entering the bedroom and using his foot to close the door behind him. "You desire me. You just stated that you do, and since I have no objection to fulfilling those desires, then yes, I am carrying you into the bedroom. Where is Jim?"

I wanted to smack him on the shoulder, but just in case his collarbone was still a bit ouchie, I contented myself with pinching his arm. "I never once said I desire you! I simply invited you to take a shower with me. Maybe you stink, and I wanted to get you clean—did you ever think of that?"

One eyebrow rose a quarter of an inch.

"Fine," I told him, annoyed that he'd called my bluff. "You don't smell, but that God's-gift-to-the-world attitude really rankles, Kostya. You could take a hit or two from the humility bat, you know that? Oh, all right, put me down. I don't want you hurting yourself by hauling me all over the place."

He set me down onto the bed and, having ignored most of what I said, announced, "We will have sex, and then when you are sated, I will return to making plans."

I squinted at him, refusing to allow my body to be distracted when he started to matter-of-factly remove his clothing. "You think so, huh? I sure hope you didn't talk to your ex-girlfriend in that condescending and arrogant way, because if you did, then I'm going to have to switch sides and sympathize with her."

He frowned, just as I knew he would. "Cyrene seldom let me speak, and she always lusted after my body."

I thought about it for a moment, decided I had asked for it by introducing the subject of his ex, and made a decision. "Right," I said, sliding off the bed. "New rules: one, no mention of ex-lovers immediately before, after, or during lovemaking. Yes, I realize that I brought her up, and I won't make that mistake again. Two: you may think that domineering attitude is going to fly, but it won't. I don't like pushy men, and I really don't like pushy lovers. Three: I'm going to take a shower. You can join me or not—at this point, I don't give a flying squirrel's butt."

He made an objecting sort of rumble when I pushed past him into the bathroom. I took off my clothes, noting some grubby dirt and soot marks from the fire that morning and wishing again that I had a fresh outfit to put on. By the time I was clad in nothing but a towel, Kostya entered the bathroom naked, complete with erection and frown.

"Silly me," I said, noting both. "I assumed that the act of physical pleasure would make you stop scowling."

"Scowling? I'm not scowling," he said, putting his hands on his hips and deepening his frown. "I never scowl. I am a wyvern—my feelings are hidden from all. That is the way of dragons."

"Seriously?" I turned him so he could see the mirror and pointed at his face. "That's a scowl. Or if you like, a really annoyed frown. Six of one, half a dozen of the other."

His frown shifted to a glare directed at me. "I am not frowning."

"Yes, you are. See how your eyebrows are pulled together? That's a scowl, pumpkin."

"I am not a pumpkin, and my eyebrows look normal."

"Well, they're not. That is to say, I've seen them locked into normal position, and what you have now isn't that."

He snorted. "I look as I always do, and since I know you will ask, no, I am unable to change my human form. If you find me unsightly, I will take reasonable steps to improve my appearance, but there is a limit to what I can do."

I couldn't help but laugh at both the fact that he seriously didn't realize he was frowning and at the notion that he was unsightly. "Kostya, you are *anything* but unsightly."

He glanced at the mirror. "I admit that I do not think of my human form much. It is what it is, although I did have a tooth replaced when the silver wyvern knocked it out." He pulled back his upper lip to show me a gold tooth along the side of his mouth. "It was a vanity, but one that makes eating easier, so I indulged myself."

"It's very nice, and completely understandable. All of you is nice, more than nice, really quite yummy, to be honest. That widow's peak is seriously sexy, and I love the cleft in your chin, although I have to admit I want to bite it more than I probably should. You have nice shoulders when they aren't broken, and I love your hands, but I've always had a thing for men with big hands. And your legs are good, and of course, your butt is really outstanding, and honestly, I can't ever say that I've seen a man with a six-pack before, but you definitely have one. All in all, you could quite easily grace the cover of *GQ* and not look out of place, so about that, at least, you can relax."

He stopped scowling, and instead looked pleased. "I am glad my form gives pleasure to you. Now that you have cataloged me, take off the towel so I can do the same."

I clutched the towel a little tighter. "I'm not even remotely comfortable with standing here stark naked and letting you examine me. For one, I could stand to drop a few pounds. And for another, I got horribly out of shape when I was at the crackpot center, and I lost a lot of muscle tone."

"You just invited me to shower with you," Kostya pointed out with maddening reason. "And yet now you do not wish for me to see you unclothed?"

I raised my chin. "I never said I made perfect sense all the time. Besides, there's a difference between soaping each other up in a steamy shower and standing around staring at someone while they stand awkwardly wishing they'd used the treadmill in the nuthouse gym."

"You stared at me. I simply wish to have my turn." He tried to tug the towel off me.

I slapped at his hands. "You are gorgeous. I mean, seriously, Kostya, just look at yourself. You're all muscles, and lovely bulges, and don't at all look like you need to join a Zumba class, whereas I do."

He frowned again. "What is—"

"Aerobics. Stop trying to take my towel, dammit!" I backed up toward the shower, still holding tight to it.

"You have no reason to be concerned that I won't like your body," he said loftily, which just made me want to pinch him. "Even if you were deformed in some manner, which I do not believe is the case, I would pay it no mind."

I stopped backing up to stare at him for a few seconds. "I...I don't...holy cranberries, Kostya, I don't know how to take that. It's flattering and yet at the same time condescending as hell. Honestly, I feel like your arrogance is showing, and I really don't like that."

He gave one of his martyred sighs, then marched forward and, before I could stop him, whipped the towel off me, pulling me up against his body when I started to protest. "No, no more stalling. You wish for me to make love to you, and I will do so happily, no matter what image you have of yourself. I find you...enticing. Your breasts are enjoyable. Not so large as to be ungainly and yet sufficient to tantalize. Your body pleases me. *You* please me. Tell me that you accept me as I am."

I stopped rubbing myself against him, feeling that I had to know the worst before I could commit myself any further. "I please you? Like...like a book pleases you? Or a nice meal? Or a gift from a loved one?"

"No one has ever given me a gift," he said, sidestepping the issue. His eyes were a combination of onyx with little molten flecks of silver.

I pinched his arm. "Kostya, I need to know what you're thinking. No, I need to know what you're feeling. Are we just giving in to perfectly ordinary lust, or is there something more going on here?"

"We are not, in any sense of the word, ordinary," he murmured, his hands suddenly busy with my behind, while he slowly pulled me against his chest, his mouth hot on my shoulder as he kissed a path toward my neck.

"You are seriously the most annoying man I've ever met. Also the sexiest, but the annoying is threatening to win out," I warned him.

He gave a little exaggerated sigh and gently bit my shoulder. "Do you think I would even consider intimacy with any woman who was not extraordinary?"

I smiled into his neck, arching my back when his hands slid around my hips and back up to my breasts. "Extraordinary. That's a start."

"You are also stubborn, do not appreciate the importance of my position, and are likely to drive me to the brink of my sanity, but I can't resist you. I must have you, Aoife."

I didn't know if he meant just in the sense of immediate sex or as a permanent fixture in his life. I curled my fingers into his chest hair, scraping him lightly with my fingernails. "Is this your way of saying that you think we have something serious going on?"

"I am always serious," he said, kissing a hot path across my collarbone. "You are the only woman I would consider doing this with, if that is what you are asking. I do not desire a woman in my life, but if I must have one, then you are the one I choose."

My toes curled into the plush bath mat at his words. I kissed his jaw and whispered, "I want to ease the darkness inside of you, Kostya. I want to show you what it is to be cherished. I want to bring you peace."

He froze for a moment, slowly lifting his head to look deep into my eyes. "You do not think I am at peace?"

"Are you?" I countered.

Silence wrapped around us for the count of twenty. "I wasn't," he finally said, his hands sliding up to take possession of my breasts just as his mouth closed upon mine.

Just the feel of my skin against his had sent my brain into overdrive. I danced my tongue around his, feeling the pull of his fire and wanting to bathe in it.

I pulled back, afraid I'd set the plane on fire, my breath ragged.

"Tell me," he growled. His head dipped as he lathed fire across my breasts.

"Oh, Lord, it's a good thing I'm not a spy, because at this moment, I'd tell you anything," I answered, moaning and doing a little dance of delight at the feel of his fire sinking into my flesh.

"Say that you want me." His tongue was as hot as his fire as it tormented my right breast.

"Holy Odin and all the little cherubs, I thought I'd made that pretty clear by now. Yes, yes, I want you. Now do the left one."

"Tell me you accept what I am." He obliged by turning his attention to my left breast. I stood on tiptoes and thought seriously that I might just expire at the sensation of his mouth on my aching breast.

"A dragon, you mean?" I wiggled my hips against him, dragging my nails gently up his sides and back. "So long as you don't expect me to have sex with you when you're in your other form, then yes, I accept that you're really a dragon in a super-hot man package. And speaking of package..."

He pried my hands off his genitals, saying as he did so, "If you touch me now, I will not be able to last, and I would like to look at your thighs and hips and legs and all the rest of you, and then taste you, and finally, claim you." His eyes were like deep pools of water with light glinting off the surface. Heat emanated from him—his dragon fire—leaving me wanting to dance in the inferno that only Kostya could create.

"C'mon," I said, backing up toward the shower, pulling him with me. "Let's take a fast shower, and then we can address the issue of my hips and thighs and all of your really marvelous parts that I desperately want to touch and taste and possibly rub myself on."

Just as I reached the shower door, he asked, "Why do you wish to take a shower now? I want to make love to you."

"Well," I said, waggling my eyebrows just a little, "who's to say we can't accomplish both things at the same time?" I entered the shower and turned on the tap, adjusting the water until it was warm but not too hot. I expected Kostya to heat things up.

He stood outside the shower, frowning as I grabbed the complimentary body shampoo and spread it across my breasts, lathering them up with a thoroughness I'd never before thought necessary. "It is more comfortable on the bed."

"Yeah, but way more slick in here." I soaped up one leg and cocked an eyebrow at him. "Why don't you come and soap up my other leg, hmm? Then I'll return the favor."

He hesitated, an amusing array of expressions crossing his face. First lust danced past, followed by regret, desire, and uncertainty.

I stopped doing my version of an enticing "come shower

with me" dance and faced him dead-on. "All right, what's going on? Even with the flabby lack of muscles and few extra pounds, I shouldn't disgust you to the point where you don't want to take a shower with me, especially since you keep looking at me like I'm a bit of roast beef and you're a starving dragon."

He made a face and said slowly, "Water is not...Black dragons do not like it. It is not our element."

"Your *what*?"

"Each sept has an element with which they are sympathetic. The green dragons like water—we do not."

I turned off the water and reached for a towel. "Are you saying you don't ever bathe?"

A look of distaste flitted across his face. "Of course we bathe—we are not animals! It is a necessary evil, one that must be borne so that we are clean. But we do not enjoy the experience, and we do not linger in water."

"That's a shame, because there's nothing I like more than a good long soak in a bath, but I guess that means I just get all the hot water to myself. All right, you win, the bed it is, although I want to point out that it's more romantic to romp in the shower than the plain ole everyday bed."

"No," he said, wrapping an arm around my waist as I was about to leave. "Not the bed. I have changed my mind. We will remain in this room."

"It's...uh...not terribly suited to such activities."

"Nonetheless, it has one benefit to the other room." His head dipped, and he took the tip of one of my breasts in his mouth, his hands sliding down my back to dig into my behind. I clutched his shoulders and saw stars for a moment, relishing the flash of heat as it swept through my body.

"What ... sweet sweating sailors, I'm never going to get tired of that ... what benefit?"

He lifted his head, his eyes like molten onyx, if there was such a thing, a little smile making the corners of his mouth curl. "It has lots of marble, and marble does not burn. You, however, will."

"Oooh," I said, wiggling my hips against him in blatant invitation. I was a bit shocked at my behavior, but the sane part of my mind got shouted down by the rest of me, which said that I was exactly where I was supposed to be—in Kostya's arms. I bit his lower lip, sucking on it to take the sting away before saying, "We should probably be responsible and discuss things like disease and birth control before we get carried away."

"I am a dragon," he murmured, kissing a hot trail down my neck to my chest, and thankfully attending to my second (and very needy) breast. "We do not have human diseases."

"Oh good. I'm not on birth control right now, because there was just no need for it at the crazy castle, and frankly, if I had to stop right now in order to find you a condom, I think I'd die of sexual frustration. I take it that it's not possible for dragons and humans to have a baby?"

"It is possible," he murmured against my breastbone as he dropped to his knees. He proceeded to kiss along my belly, stopping to nibble on my hips. "But the conception rate is much lower than it is for dragons."

I thought for a moment. "It's been three days since ... yeah, I should be okay. But if we're going to go on like this, one or both of us is going to have to take precautions. Not that I don't like kids and all, and I'd like to have them someday, but I'd rather not be surprised. Oh my God, you aren't going to do what I think you're going to do, are you?" I looked down at his head. He had slid his hands up my thighs, shifting my feet wider. A little whiff of smoke drifted out of his nose as he glanced up at me, the corners of his lips curling even more.

"I am going to blow fire on your woman's part."

"Yes, please," I said, my fingers clutching his shoulders hard without any consideration for his previous injury. I yelped when he breathed fire on me, but it wasn't from pain. The heat sank into me, making my own personal inferno go into overdrive. But when he put his mouth on me, his fingers doing a fiery little dance of their own, I knew I was a goner. "*Herregud*, Kostya! I'm not going to be able to last if you do that again."

He pulled me down to the floor, his mouth literally trailing fire across my flesh. "I like how you taste, Aoife. You are spicy and sweet, and you inflame my senses." He buried his nose in my neck and breathed deeply. "Your scent intoxicates me. It drives me insane with the need to possess you and to claim you for my own. I must mate with you now."

"I hope so, because I really am going to die of frustration if you don't." I tried pulling him down onto me, but he hesitated, his face twisted for a moment with pain.

"I must... I cannot—" With a low growl, he flipped me over onto my belly, one arm beneath me pulling me upward. "You are mine now, Aoife. Tell me you understand."

"I understand. Honestly, I don't give a damn what position we do it in, just so we do it right now!" I yelled, clutching the bath mat that was beneath me.

He moved, and suddenly I was invaded, but oh, what a welcome invasion it was. He was as hard and hot as

I imagined he would be, moving within me with a rhythm that, impossibly, made the fire inside me burn even hotter. And then his dragon fire was there, inside me, around me, coating us in a cocoon of want and need and sexual ecstasy manifested in fiery form. I caught at it with my mind, twisting it around first me, then Kostya, my back arching when an orgasm claimed me. The fire slid out of my control for a moment, but even as Kostya growled his own climax, I spun the fire back into him.

Pain blossomed to life for a moment on my hip, hot and searing, but just as that sensation registered in my brain, it was gone, leaving me with a warm, tingling spot. I fell forward, gasping for air that apparently was consumed by Kostya's fire, my intimate muscles still clutching Kostya in a grip that surprised even me. I shook with little tremors of pleasure and wondered, with the tiny part of my brain that was still working after the orgasm to end all orgasms, just how I was going to survive sex with Kostya on a regular basis.

He rolled off me, his broad chest heaving as he attempted to get air into his lungs, his eyes closed, one hand flung over his head. His skin was damp and shiny with the effort, and after observing him for a moment— which was really an excuse for me to try to get my brain working again—I leaned over and bit his arm.

The look he gave me was filled with disbelief.

"Now you have to take a shower," I said with a grin.

He made a face, then to my utter delight, answered my smile with a rueful one of his own. "It was worth such a sacrifice."

"Oh, definitely." I rolled over onto my side, intending on saying more, but a little pinch of pain had me sitting up and examining my hip. "What did you do to me? I've got some sort of a burn."

I touched the shape that was high on my left hip. It looked like a faded henna tattoo of a vaguely phoenix-like dark tan beast with wings curving overhead and a barbed tail.

Kostya looked away, but I could see that his scowl was back in place. "I don't know what you are speaking of."

"Like hell you don't." I slid my fingers across it. It was smooth, just like a tattoo. "I felt you do it. My hip was all hurty for a couple of seconds; then it faded away."

His jaw worked for a moment; then he shook his head. "The mark is unimportant. Do not speak of it to others."

"Unimportant? You burn a mark onto my hip and act like I did something wrong—no, sir! I told you that I'm not a doormat, and I'm not going to let you get away with that. Nor am I going to let you spoil what was a wonderful—if incredibly intense—intimate experience. Okay, so you suck at pillow talk, but that doesn't mean you have to snap my head off when I point out that making love to you left me physically scarred."

"It is not a scar. It is a mark of the black dragons." He got to his feet and stepped into the shower, quickly and efficiently cleansing himself before taking a towel and going to the bedroom.

"Really?" I looked at it again. "Is that going to happen every time we have sex?"

"It will not happen again."

Whether he meant the marking or the lovemaking, I had no idea, and he didn't say anything more. I sat on the floor for a few minutes, caught between the desire to rail at him for ruining what had been profoundly wonderful lovemaking and the need to understand just why it was that he was so desperate to deny the connection between us.

"I'm not a saint," I told the now-empty bathroom. "So I'm going to have to say a few things to him about proper après-sex behavior, but I'm also going to get to the bottom of this whole dragon-mate thing. Because if that mark is what I think it is, then he's going to have to spill with a whole lot more than a few facts and details."

Which is just exactly what he doesn't want to do, my inner self pointed out somewhat smugly.

"There are times I really hate the fact that Dr. Barlind made me get so in touch with myself that I can't shut you up," I told my reflection, then got to my feet and took a fast shower. When I was dry again, I rolled up the bath mat and tossed it into the tiny trash bin that sat alongside the toilet.

The mat was scorched black. I couldn't help but give the female shape burned onto it a little smile. I just hoped I had the stamina to keep up with Kostya's lovemaking.

Eleven

I returned to the main cabin and sat down on the couch next to Kostya. He had a new pencil and was writing on his pad of paper in a language I didn't understand. "That mark you put on my hip—it's something to do with me being your mate, isn't it?"

He didn't answer me, but I noticed his jaw tightened.

"I thought so. Did you put the same thing on your ex's hip?"

The muscles in his jaw worked a couple of times but finally gave when he answered, "No. I told you that she was not my mate. She just forced me to name her as such."

I wanted to point out that he'd told me repeatedly that I wasn't his mate either, but figured that was petty. "How'd she force you? I don't think I could make you do anything you didn't want to do, certainly not without some serious leverage, and even then, you don't strike me as the sort of man who can be forced into doing things against your will."

"She used her woman's body against me," he snarled, careful to avoid my gaze.

Well, now. There was a lot to be said about that, but I remembered the pain hidden deep in Kostya's eyes, a sign that he, like me, was one of those people who felt things deeply but who'd been burned for wearing their heart on their sleeves.

"When I was seventeen," I said carefully, tucking my legs underneath me as I scooted over until my thigh pressed against his, "I fell madly in love with the mail boy in my dad's office. His name was Thor, and he was everything a seventeen-year-old gawky girl with braces on her teeth could dream of—tall and blond and wore a Thor's hammer necklace, and man, was he built—and the day he managed to recognize that I was a living, breathing human being and said hello to me, I thought I would die of happiness. I started going to my dad's office every day, ostensibly to have lunch with him, but the reality was that I just wanted to hang around and hope that Thor would notice me again."

Kostya muttered something so softly I didn't catch it, but it had an edge to it that could sever concrete.

"After what seemed like weeks of mooning around the office, one day I was casually posed in the hallway in a spot that I knew Thor would have to pass. As I waited, I heard laughter coming from a nearby office. I edged close to the door so I could hear what was so funny and heard one of the junior executives telling Thor that he needed to go ahead and bang me so that I'd stop mooning around the office."

Kostya's frown grew to an epic level of blackness. The pencil snapped in half.

"I was so mortified that evidently everyone in the office knew what I thought I was hiding so well that I almost missed what Thor said in response. *Almost*."

"What?" Kostya snapped, the word emerging with the velocity of a fiery bullet. His eyes were black as night, the little silver bits in them glowing. "What did he say?"

The old memory hurt but was no longer crippling. I'll say that for Dr. Barlind—she helped me lay a few ghosts to rest, this one in particular. "He said that he had no use for a mongrel half-breed, not even for casual sex. He didn't use the phrase 'casual sex,' but my mother raised me to not have a potty mouth, and other than occasional swearing, I try not to."

"Half-breed," Kostya said on a hot breath of fury. I thought for a moment that his fire was going to get away from him, but he had better control than I gave him credit for, so the papers in front of him didn't actually burst into flame. They smoked a little, though. "Mongrel! He dared to damn you because of something so trivial?"

"You know, if I didn't want to already kiss you just because you're so kissable, I'd want to even more simply because you're so incensed on my behalf."

"Of course I'm incensed!" Kostya's hands were fisted on his thighs. I put my hand over one of them, nudging him in the side with my elbow so he'd stop glaring. "This man you desired, this unworthy mortal, devalues you— you who are so far above him that he should be on his knees with gratitude that you would even consider look- ing at him, let alone allowing him to touch your body… This is intolerable. Give me his surname. I will find him and lesson him."

I laughed and kissed him, allowing my lips to linger in

a way that I hoped told him just how much I appreciated the outrage. His fire immediately kicked into high gear, but mindful that we were in an airplane, I tamped it down and pulled my mouth from his in order to say, "When you stop to think about what you said, you'll realize just how less than brilliant jealousy has made you."

"Are you calling me stupid?" he demanded, pulling me closer, his eyes all outraged and yet soft with desire.

"Of course not. Except where old boyfriends who weren't even real boyfriends are concerned, and that just makes you more adorable than ever." I tucked a strand of hair behind his ear. "Thor doesn't matter, Kostya."

"He insulted you—he matters!"

"Only because you are very sweet."

"I am not sweet!" He looked even more outraged, if that was possible. "I am a wyvern! I am the stuff of nightmares!"

"Oh, I'm sure you're very nightmarish when you want to be, but that's not what I'm talking about. And don't think I can't see that you're trying to Google men named Thor in Sweden on your phone, because I can."

He slid his hand, which had indeed gone to the cell phone sitting on the couch next to him, back onto his lap.

"I told you about Thor to show you that we all have painful experiences in our past. The thing with Thor— that was painful, yes. Did it make me shy away from all guys for a while? Of course. At the time, I thought I was going to die of embarrassment. But Thor's attitude was *his* problem, not mine. I don't mind that my parents fell in love and had my siblings and me, and I don't mind my appearance at all. To be honest, I get a lot of envy about my curly hair, which makes me all shades of smug, so that more than makes up for the occasional bigoted insult that comes my way. So stop looking like you want to turn the plane around to find Thor—who is probably going bald and has a beer belly by now—and instead appreciate the fact that although you had a bad experience with a woman, it doesn't mean I'm going to treat you the same way."

The emotional shutters fell over his face. He released me and reached for his tablet of paper again, along with a fresh unbroken pencil. "I do not wish to talk about Cyrene."

"That's fine with me. I don't particularly want to know about you and your ex, anyway, other than to point out yet again that I'm not her. Have I made my point?"

"There is no point to be made," he said, clearly refusing to understand, his attention focused on his work.

I sighed in frustration. "Boy, I don't know how Dr. Barlind did it. I sure don't seem to have the patience to deal with blatant denial. Okay, how about this as a conversational subject: the mark you put on me has wings. Why is that so, when you dragons don't have them?"

Kostya growled something under his breath.

"Is it going to stay there forever? Or will it fade away with time? And does something special happen to me now that I'm your mate?"

He growled some more.

"Not even going to deny it?" I asked, knowing that he needed to confront his emotions in order to be free of the pain that bound him.

"Christ's blood!" he yelled, slamming down his pencil. It broke into three pieces. "What do you want from me? You say you are not like Cyrene, and yet you obviously expect me to name you as mate in front of the weyr. You are doomed to disappointment! The weyr is no more! You can't receive recognition if there is no one to recognize you!"

His voice reverberated around the small cabin. The flight attendant, who had taken one look at us when we emerged from the bedroom, had murmured something about providing a restorative and taken herself off to the galley, which meant Kostya had only me to rage at.

And he was most definitely in a rage. I couldn't help but wonder what his ex had done to him—or whether it was even her that was at the bottom of his refusal to accept the obvious.

"By rights," I said slowly, picking through words to get the ones I really wanted, "I should be offended by the implication that I'm using you for my own purposes, when in reality, I'm trying to help you. For one, I have this badass magic ring, although to be honest, if you asked me nicely, I'd give it to you. And for another, I genuinely want to help you, Kostya. I don't need to be named as your mate in front of anyone other than you. If you don't want to acknowledge it, then there's nothing I can do to make you see the truth."

"The truth," he snorted, glaring so hard at the broken pencil collection on the table in front of him that one of them caught fire. I patted it out quickly before the flight attendant could see it. "The truth no longer matters."

"Of course it matters. We have a bond, you and I, whether or not you want to admit it, and let me tell you, if there's one thing I learned from my time at Casa de Crazy, it's that lying to yourself never ends well."

He eyed me for a moment, then held out his hand.

I looked at it. "What?"

"The ring."

"Oh. You really want it?" Hesitantly, I pulled it off my finger. I was a bit surprised just how reluctant I was to do that—it felt so right on my hand, but the thought occurred to me that in itself might be a bad thing. "Okay, but only because I feel really close to purring 'my precioussss' if I keep it on much longer."

I dropped the ring onto his palm. He looked at it for a moment, then slipped it on his little finger. He pursed his lips and held out his hand, examining it.

"Well?" I asked, glancing toward the galley. The flight attendant was still out of sight. "Do something magic with it."

He shook his head, then pulled it off and gave it back to me. "It is as I thought. The ring has chosen you. It will not yield to my will, whether due to the curse or some other reason. The result is the same. Put it on again, and keep it safe."

With a sense of profound relief, I slid it back onto the middle finger of my left hand. "Terrin said something about it having a mind of its own, but I didn't really understand what it was he meant, because really, how many sentient rings do you run across in your lifetime?"

"One," Kostya answered, picking up the writeable end of his broken pencil.

I smacked him on the arm. "You made a funny!"

"I did not."

"Yes, you did. And you smiled earlier. That's two points for Team Aoife and nothing for Team Kostya."

He looked outraged for a moment. "You are on *my* team!"

"I stand corrected," I said with a laugh, leaning over to kiss his cheek. "I'm very much on your team, even though you've got to be the most obstinate, annoying man in the universe. The question of our relationship aside—for the moment—what do you expect me to do with the ring in Paris? Aisling said that Drake hoped to use it to break the curse, but I can tell you right here and now that I have no idea how to go about doing that."

"You will not break it—we will find a Charmer."

"A what?"

"Someone who can break the curse. You will give the ring to the Charmer, and she will do the work."

"She? You have someone in mind?" I told the little spurt of jealousy that threatened to rise to knock it off.

"I know of no Charmers, but there are bound to be some in Paris. The Venediger is known to favor them."

"Someday," I said, looking out the window, "I'm going to be able to have a conversation with you and actually understand *every* word you say."

He smiled. It didn't last long, just a couple of seconds, but it was there and I saw it, and I rejoiced at the fact that his emotions weren't so devastated that he couldn't be brought around. He smoothed his hand across my hair. "Now go to bed and sleep. I must make plans."

"I'm not a doormat," I told Kostya. "I just want you to know that. My first inclination is to brain you with something bulky, but because I'm a nice, civilized person who has a goodly amount of empathy, I'm going to let your comment slide and instead ask you what a Venediger is."

His lips tightened for a moment, and then he gave another of his martyred sighs and tossed the pencil stub onto the table. "You are doing this to enrage me, aren't you?"

"No." I shook my head. "But I was raised to ask questions if I didn't understand something, and you are not going to make me feel bad for doing just that."

"The Venediger is a mage who lives in Paris. She controls the Otherworld in Europe." A slightly amused look came into his eyes.

"The Otherworld being, what? The part of the world with dragons and mages with funny names?"

"Among others, yes . . . What are you doing?"

"Snuggling with you." I scooted over on the couch until I was pressed up against him, running my finger along his eyebrows until the frown smoothed out. "I like it when you smile, Kostya. It makes me happy . . . and a little aroused, to the point where I want to touch you and kiss you and do wicked things to you with my tongue. I don't, however, like it when you frown. That just makes me want to pinch you. Now, which mood would you like me in?" I kissed a little path along his jaw to his ear, sucking on his earlobe.

If anything, he looked grumpier than normal. He gave me a sidelong glance, then said sourly, "Drake was right."

"About women who think you're sexy when you smile?" I asked, nibbling my way back to his chin, where I swirled my tongue around the cleft in it. At the same time, I unbuttoned a few of his buttons and slid my hand inside his shirt, delighting at the sensation of his soft chest hairs.

"No. He has said many times that Aisling has made his life a living hell and that a mate would do the same to me. Later he said that he enjoyed her brand of hell and would die rather than give her up, but I believe that to be a statement of pride. She has certainly put him through much that I would never tolerate."

I leaned back to look at him.

He accurately read the question in my eyes. "I will not have a mate."

I held my breath for a moment. Did he really bring the subject up so soon after shutting me out? I had to tread carefully here, I knew. I tipped my head and, beneath his shirt, stroked his pectoral muscle. "Why?"

"I've already spoken to you about this. Repeatedly."

"That's because you haven't really told me why you are so hurt. I won't judge you, Kostya—surely you can see that I was devastated by the whole Thor thing. I can empathize with the pain from the loss of misplaced love."

He sighed a huge sigh that could have filled a hot-air balloon. "Very well, I will explain to you this once, and then we will speak of it no more. I told you that Cyrene forced me to declare her as my mate."

"Yes, but she wasn't really your mate, and I am. So despite that, you're going to spurn me, spurn everything we could have together—and again, I want bonus points for going from a perfectly normal human being to someone who accepts that there are dragons and Venedimages and demon lords marching around—"

"Venediger, not Venedimage."

Gently, I pinched his side. "You want to turn all that down just because you had a bad experience with a girlfriend? One who didn't even throw racial and sexual slurs at you like some people I could name? Really, Kostya? You're that dense?"

And in a flash, he was back to enraged. "A proper mate does not refer to her wyvern as dense!"

"I bet she does when he acts that way!"

He narrowed his eyes at me. "It's Aisling, isn't it? She

told you to say these things to me. She's not going to be happy until you have me as deranged as she has Drake."

I laughed and leaned forward to kiss him again, very sweetly this time, before biting his lower lip. "She didn't, but I can see I'm going to have to have a long, long talk with her. Am I your mate or not?"

His lips tightened for a moment; then suddenly we were both on our feet. "If you do not wish to sleep, then I will," he said, heading for the bedroom.

"Coward!"

His shoulder jerked. He paused a moment, half turning toward me. "To retreat when you cannot win a battle is not cowardly. It is self-preservation."

"Hmm," I said aloud after he disappeared into the bedroom. "Now what am I going to do about that?"

I had no answer, but I was fairly confident that something would occur to me before too long.

Three hours later, I was no wiser, although I did put the problem aside to appreciate the fact that I was in Paris. "You're sure it's okay to talk in front of this guy?" I asked Kostya as we got to a taxi. The driver was a middle-aged man with a nice face, brown hair, and a lovely French accent.

"Rene is a friend of Aisling," Kostya answered.

"And that makes him okay?"

Kostya just gave me one of his "I dislike answering questions" faces and proceeded to pay off the bribe to the pilot for getting us into the country without having to go through customs.

"Hi," I said to the taxi driver. "I'm Aoife, and this dog is—"

"Jim!" Rene said in a delighted tone, bending down to

hug the dog and kiss him on both furry cheeks. "It has been too long, my old friend, much too long, yes?"

"Hiya," Jim said, giving the man a friendly swipe of his tongue. "I take it you knew me before my memory got the eraso-matic, huh? I'm here with the Eefenator, not Kostya. She's my boss now."

Rene shot me a startled look. "She is? Aisling will be very upset by this news. She thinks the world of you. Eraso-matic? What is this?"

"It's okay—you don't have to be worried I'm trying to steal Jim from Aisling," I said in a soothing voice. Honestly, the man looked worried to death over the idea that Jim wasn't with his former boss. "It was an accident, and we've already met with Aisling, so it'll be all straightened out in a bit."

"Ah," Rene said, absently patting Jim on the head. "It is not ideal, though, is it? Jim and Aisling made a strong team together. And then there is Jim's beloved Cecile. What will become of her if he is not there to molest her ears?"

"Ew!" I looked at Jim. "You molested some poor woman's ears?"

"I did?" Jim looked as horrified as I felt.

"No, no, Cecile, she is the small dog from Wales. She has no tail and snaps most vigorously if one attempts to pet her, but for Jim, she is all that is amiable. It is true love between them, *hein*?"

"Jim the demon has a Welsh corgi girlfriend?"

"Cool!" Jim said. "Are there pictures of her?"

"Alas, I do not possess any, although Cecile's owner might. She lives here in Paris."

"Gotcha." I thought about making a comment regarding

the size difference between a corgi and Jim but decided there were some things best left unsaid. "Well, at least that makes the ear molesting a little less creepy, Jim."

"A corgi, huh?" Jim said thoughtfully. "They have those cute little stubby legs, don't they? Yeah, I can totally see why a hot corgi babe wants me."

"And we just crossed over the line back into ew-ness. No more comments about hot corgis and yourself, please. Rene, do you happen to know if Aisling is back in Paris yet? I tried calling her en route, but her voice mail was on, and she hasn't called back."

"That I do not know, I'm afraid. Will you enter?" He held open the taxi door for me.

"Shotgun!" Jim said, and leaped in through the open driver's door to take up a spot in the front seat.

"Thanks. What...er...what are you? I take it you're not a dragon because you can talk to Kostya."

He smiled. "What I am is not so important as the fact that I am the very great friend of Aisling and thus will be delighted to help you and Kostya while you are in Paris. One cannot have too many friends in a time of war, can one not?"

I bit back the urge to press him for more information, but Kostya had finished his business and got into the backseat alongside me.

"Greetings, Rene."

"And to you, Kostya Fekete. You are well, I see."

"No thanks to the red dragons. Have there been any sightings of them in Paris?"

"Not that I have heard." Rene started up the car and swung in a big arc on the tarmac to exit the small airport on the outskirts of a Paris suburb. "The Venediger is most adamant that the war not spill over onto her domain. She already warned Drake and Aisling that she would not tolerate any dissonance from dragonkin."

Kostya said nothing, but looked thoughtful for a few minutes.

"The Venediger again," I said softly, not entirely sure that I wanted Rene to hear all of our business. Jim was chatting up a blue streak in the front seat, keeping Rene laughing and answering his questions about Cecile the corgi, so I felt it was a good time to ask my question. "She doesn't like dragons?"

He made a face. "She fears us because she has no power to call us to heel. But she won't stop from harming us if we are to bring the battle for the weyr onto her territory. She all but threw me out of Paris the last time I was here. Do not expect a welcome reception from her, Aoife."

"I wasn't expecting much of anything, to be honest. Although that statement kind of indicates that you view me as being on par with a dragon, such as, oh, I don't know, a wyvern's mate?"

"You are a mate?" Rene asked, jerking the steering wheel when he was about to plow into oncoming traffic. He eyed Kostya with speculation in the rearview mirror until I squawked and pointed out the front window. "Pfft. I was not even close to that lorry. There was at least three inches of distance between us. So, Kostya has found his mate? Again?"

Kostya looked irritated. "There is no *again*. Cyrene was *never* my mate."

"And yet you declared her such, or so Aisling told me," Rene commented, deftly avoiding mowing down a family that was crossing at an intersection.

Kostya glared into the mirror. "Trust Aisling to tell everyone about that unfortunate episode."

"Ah, my friend," Rene laughed, "it is the way of women to keep us humble, is it not?"

Kostya said nothing but studiously avoided meeting my eye. I couldn't help but smile to myself, but by then, we were reaching Paris proper, and my attention was drawn by the magnificence of the city itself. "I haven't been here since I was a little kid, when my parents moved to Sweden. Oooh, Jim, look: Eiffel Tower!"

"Huh," Jim said, sticking his head out the window. "Can we go up to the top and spit off it?"

"Whereabouts is your place?" I asked Kostya, ignoring Jim as he speculated how much impact his drool would have falling from the topmost platform on the Eiffel Tower. "And don't think I didn't notice that you didn't deny I was your mate, because I did. But obviously, now is not the time to continue that discussion. You may thank me later."

Kostya started out by looking annoyed, but to my amusement, chagrin immediately followed and changed into resignation. "I have an apartment in the Latin Quarter, but I seldom spend time there since it is not very well protected. That is not where we are going, however."

"Oh?"

"No. Despite the Venediger's dictates, I do not doubt that the red dragons would attempt an attack upon us, and my residence is known to dragonkin. We will stay with Drake and Aisling."

I clicked my tongue in irritation. "Aisling said something about that, but I didn't think you'd agree. Kostya, you can't be in the same house as Drake! Hell—"

"Abaddon," Jim said, then looked surprised at himself for making the correction.

"You could barely stand to be in the same airport as him. How on earth do you expect to keep from killing each other if you're in the same house?"

"Drake's house is equipped to handle attacks; mine is not. The curse notwithstanding, it is there that you will be safe, and that is where we will go."

"Me?" I looked at him, but when he refused to stop staring moodily out the window, I put my hand on his thigh. That startled him enough into glancing at me. "Are you saying that if I wasn't around, you'd go to your apartment by yourself even though it wasn't safe?"

"I am not afraid of the red dragons," he said stiffly, although he put his hand on mine and caressed the back of my fingers.

"So you're doing this just to protect me?" I shook my head, turned my hand over, and twined my fingers around his. It was an oddly intimate gesture, but I marked that down to the fascination I had with men's hands. Kostya's were almost perfect, with long, sensitive fingers that reminded me of my harpist mother's hands. Like hers, Kostya's were those of an artist. "That is so incredibly touching...and annoying at the same time. Oh, don't get that look on your face—I meant it as a compliment. I do appreciate that you are sacrificing your peace of mind, and possibly a tooth or two if your brother gets to you, because you have this idea that you have to protect me, but I assure you that I'm no slouch when it comes to self-defense. I've had training, you know. My dad insisted that both Bee and I know how to take down a boyfriend who goes over the line. And then there's this." I nodded toward the ring on my left hand.

"It is for that object we are going to Drake's home. He has many security measures in place because of his children, and it is that which I count on to keep you safe when the red dragons attack."

"*When*?"

"Yes." His jaw tightened and he looked away, but his fingers gripped mine with a strength that was almost painful. "They will not be content to allow the ring to exist so close to dragons. Asmodeus covets it above all else."

"Holy jalapeños," I said softly, rubbing my thumb over the back of his hand. "But, Kostya, even if we get Drake to agree to us staying with them, and although I don't know him at all, he doesn't seem to be any too happy to see you. Yeah, I know it's the curse, but still—even if he agreed to that, we can't endanger children."

"What children? Drake's?"

I nodded. "You seem to be pretty confident that the red dragons are going to track us down and try to attack. If we're in Drake's house with his kids, then we'd be putting them in grave danger. I can't imagine any parent would want that, and I certainly wouldn't risk the chance that they'd be harmed."

"The children aren't in Paris."

"They aren't?" I nudged him when he didn't answer the obvious question. "Where are they?"

"Safe. Drake would not risk the lives of his children any more than he would risk Aisling." A funny little twist came to his mouth, not quite a smile, but still indicating amusement. "He does not like for others to know that she is far more powerful than she appears, but he has always been proud of her abilities."

I thought of making a comment about it running in the

family but decided that there was no need to goad him, not when he was opening up to me. Instead I snuggled into his side, my body sending up a cheer of happiness when, without thinking, he put his arm around me and pulled me closer.

"We will be safe at Drake's house. I admit the curse will make things...difficult...but it is the only answer for the situation. We must have an interpreter, though."

"What? Why?"

"Because we will not be able to speak to them."

"We could use Jim," I said, indicating the dog.

"No. Demons are unreliable at best, especially one who has forgotten loyalties and relationships. Rene, are you available?"

"Eh?" Rene, who had been having a conversation with Jim about restaurants and the best way to prepare a steak, turned to look back at us, sending the taxi hurtling straight into an intersection despite a red light. Horns blared, tires screeched, and the sound of crumpling metal and breaking glass followed as Rene, with a casual flip of his wrist, straightened our path and sailed through the intersection. "Am I available for what?"

"Interpreting."

"Ah, that." His gaze in the reflection of the mirror considered me for a moment or two before answering. "Yes, that is possible. You understand that I am a bachelor for the next week—my wife, she has taken the little ones to Spain so that they may paddle in the water. I told her that we have water in France, but pfft. She insists. So I will be available for one week only, and after that, my family will return, and my time shall not be my own."

"I don't understand why you think I won't be able to

talk to Aisling. I did just fine in Sweden. She said the only people who couldn't talk to each other were dragons and their mates— Oh!" I slid him a glance. He was back to looking stoically martyred. I reviewed our conversations of the past five hours, decided he'd had about as much soul-searching as was going to benefit him, and said nothing.

But I was confident that if Kostya would just get with the program and stop trying to reject me, all would be well ... which just goes to show you how misplaced confidence can bring down even the best intentions.

Twelve

My confidence was short-lived, but it was Kostya's plan to stay at his brother's house that gave me pause. The taxi stopped in front of one of those expensive houses that sits in fashionable areas of Paris, taking up at least half a block and costing the earth. Just stopping in front of it made me feel very aware that my clothes were wrinkled and less than fresh, that my hair hadn't been combed in several hours, and that I was nowhere near comfortable with the sort of affluence required to maintain that home.

"Are you sure this is going to be safe?" I asked Kostya when we emerged from the taxi. Rene had gone to the door and was chatting with a woman who answered it before being invited in. She didn't even glance our way.

I examined the front of the house. It didn't look any different from the other houses on the street—surely the little black wrought-iron railing in the front wasn't going to keep murderous demonic dragons out? Not if they could burn down my family home so easily.

"Yes. It would take a concerted effort to bring down Drake's house again," Kostya answered, his eyes narrowed.

"Lovely. And this is supposed to be a good spot to stay?"

"There is nowhere safer." His words were more abrupt than normal, and I realized with surprise that he was tense and ready to spring, his fire riding high inside him. His gaze was constantly moving, flicking up and down the street. I was reminded of a film I'd seen of a knight protecting some damsel in distress.

"What you need is a big old sword, the kind those guys in the Middle Ages used," I told him, giving him a smile in hopes of lightening the tension that he was exuding.

"I wish I had my old longsword," he said, looking wistful. "I separated many silver dragons from their heads with it."

"You're kidding." I stared at him for a moment, decided that he wasn't joking at all, and shook my head. "You had a sword you used to fight with? A real sword?"

"Of course. I wouldn't have survived long without it." He didn't stop his vigilance, keeping an eye on every bird that twittered in the trees, every car that passed, every person strolling by.

"Just how old are you?" I asked, wondering if people still used swords as far back as the First World War. I had a feeling they did.

"I was born in 1584."

"Sweet scuppering salamanders!" I said on a gasp.

He looked surprised at the fact that I was clearly gobsmacked. "You thought I was older?"

"Younger! Much, much younger. I know you said that you guys were not mortal, but..." I did a quick calculation in my head. "Four hundred and thirty-one is a whole heck of a lot of immortality."

He said nothing. I was about to ask him what it was like living through history when my thoughts were drawn elsewhere.

"We going to go in or stay out here where the sun is going to ruin my nice coat?" Jim asked, wandering up. I gave him a look when I noticed the wet marks on a pretty planter full of red flowers. He noticed the look and gave me one in return. "Hey, when you gotta go, you gotta go, and no one asked me if I had to go walkies. You're supposed to do that, you know. Matter of fact, I may have to indulge in a number two pretty quick. You got a bag or something to pick it up?"

I grimaced at the thought. "You can just hold it until we get our accommodations settled. And hopefully someone will have some sort of hygienic method of poop removal that I can use."

Jim screwed up his furry black face. "Okay, but I don't think I'm going to be able to last long. That popcorn you made me with the second DVD is acting like roughage. Hey, there's that French dude again."

I turned to see Rene back at the door. "Oh good. Apparently he's explained the situation to Drake's people."

Rene stood on the steps and called out, "You may come inside. Suzanne—she acts as a cook and housekeeper for Aisling and Drake—has cleared her things from her room."

"Oh no, that sounds like a lot of trouble," I said as Jim and I hurried over to him, Kostya bringing up the rear.

Rene held the door open for us, waving us into a small antechamber. He closed the door, and the sound of several electronic locks clicking into place was plainly obvious. "This will take one little moment," Rene explained as a couple of lights flashed on the ceiling. Ahead of us, a substantial-looking door clicked open. "Ah, good, the scan is completed. And here is the hall."

"I hope those weren't X-rays," Jim said as he looked around the hallway. "Those things are bad for your noogies. Leaves you sterile. Hey, something smells good." He lifted his head and sniffed. "Cinnamon toast!"

"Suzanne was making it for Aisling, evidently," Rene said, gesturing us toward the back of the hall. I got a few seconds to admire the paneled walls, antique furniture, and what looked like original old masters on the walls before we entered a short passage. "Suzanne's room is off the kitchen and has its own entrance at the rear of the house, which will be most comfortable for you, yes? Come, I will show you. The others are upstairs until I tell them that you are settled."

"I feel horrible that we ran someone out of their room," I said, fretting about discommoding Aisling's household. "I'm sure we could find some hotel or somewhere that the red dragons don't know about—"

"No, no, Aisling and Drake agreed that you would be safest here," Rene said quickly, escorting us through the kitchen. I had to stop and grab Jim by his collar in order to keep him from moving through that tantalizing room and into a small suite beyond. "Suzanne has moved her things up to Istvan's room. They are companionable, you know? Not mated, but together, so it is no hardship. Aisling has commanded that I tell you that she will bring extra towels and blankets down later and that you are to make free use of the kitchen, although if Kostya is to be in the room, please close the door leading to the hallway so the other dragons will not stumble upon him."

I sighed and looked at Kostya, who was examining the room we'd been given. It was a standard-sized bedroom but had a nice bathroom attached. Kostya gave close scrutiny to each window before turning to the door. It opened onto a narrow passage, evidently belonging to servants of centuries gone by. Kostya went over them while Rene chatted with me about how Aisling had planned to go out to the country where her children were housed but would now delay that visit for a couple of days in order to see that all was well here.

"Does it pass muster?" I asked Kostya when he closed the bedroom door on the passage.

"Yes. I had no doubt that it would—as I said, Drake frequently has his children here, and he has a passion for security systems. There are several spells bound into the surface of the door as well, which, coupled with the wards Aisling has drawn on the windows, should keep us from invasion."

I pursed my lips at the mention of spells and wards but didn't want to appear ignorant in front of Rene, so I just said, "Good."

"I have a plan I wish to discuss with Drake," he told Rene, pulling out the paper he'd peeled off from the tablet. "You will read this to him and report back to me on his thoughts."

"Ah, the plan of masters, eh?" Rene said, taking the sheets. "Is he to write his responses for you?"

"No. I would not be able to read them. You must take notes of what he thinks and read them to me."

"Very well. I shall be back momentarily with your answers." Rene bustled off, the door closing soundly behind him.

"Sounds like a lot of trouble," I said, eyeing the bed. I had to admit that the lack of sleep was catching up with me and wondered if Kostya would be all right if I went to bed early.

"It is, but until the curse is lifted, there is little we can do."

"Think I'm about to hit critical mass," Jim said with a scrunched-up thoughtful look.

I stopped picturing myself snuggled into the bed. "Fine, I'll take you out for a walk. But we are going to have a long talk about you taking yourself next time."

Frowning, Kostya blocked my way when I was about to go out the back door. "You cannot go out."

"It's not my idea, trust me." I pointed at Jim. "He needs to go for a walk, and no, evidently it can't wait. Besides, it's going to be dark soon, so better I get this over with now."

"It's not safe," Kostya said, giving Jim a look that would have scared off a few years on anyone else. "The demon will just have to wait."

"I'm gonna blow soon, Slick," Jim said, doing an impatient little dance. "I have like maybe a minute at best, then *blammo*! You're all going to be seriously sorry you didn't get me outside."

"The red dragons could have heard of our flight from Sweden," Kostya told me when I pushed past him to the door leading into the kitchen and immediately began rustling through the drawers in search of a garbage bag, or plastic grocery sack, or something of that ilk. "They will know soon enough that we are in Paris, and they will follow."

"Yeah, well, they can't possibly know where we are this soon, and unless you'd like to show Jim how to use the toilet, or clean up that very nice room, one of us is going to have to walk Jim."

"Very well," Kostya said, grabbing Jim by the collar and dragging him to the door. "I will do so."

"Help!" Jim yelped, and immediately started retching. Kostya released him, stepping back when the dog hacked up a spitball. "Fires of Abaddon, you can't *choke* the poop out of me! Well, okay, you probably *can*, but it's not going to be fun for either of us."

"Kostya, stop!" I said at the same time, letting him see my exasperation. "There's no need to strangle him. You stay here and deal with Rene and your brother, and I'll pop over to the park that Rene said is a block away."

"No," Kostya said. "You cannot go out without protection. You are too valuable."

I wanted to ask him if he meant me, personally, or the ring, but decided that my ego didn't need the boost if it was the former or the blow if it was the latter. But before I could argue with him any more, there was a tap at the kitchen door as it opened, and the woman I'd seen out front put her head into the room and said something.

Her words sounded familiar but were garbled. A little chill ran down my back at the realization that I was seeing the effects of the curse in person. Which proved that I was really and truly Kostya's mate, but like almost everything else, that wasn't something I had time to think about.

The woman, who I assumed was Suzanne, gave us a wry smile, walked into the room, giving Kostya a wide berth, and pulled open a drawer that held a number of plastic bags. She set some on the counter and turned to call out a word.

Kostya tensed when one of the redheaded men who was at the airport in Sweden entered the room. The two of them watched each other warily, but I was relieved to see that neither of them leaped into immediate attack mode.

"That is Istvan, one of Drake's elite guards," Kostya said, his body language showing contained energy.

"Ah. Gotcha. Hi, Istvan," I said, giving him a little wave.

Istvan bowed in return, then gestured toward Jim, before pointing behind him.

"Is he offering to take Jim for walkies?"

"It would appear so," Kostya said, his stance relaxing slightly. "That would solve our problem."

"What? You want me to go with some strange dragon? I don't know him! I can't poop with him watching me!"

"It doesn't really matter who takes you, Jim," I said, feeling slightly guilty at passing off the responsibility of Jim onto Istvan.

The demon gave me a hurt look. "It may not matter to you, but I have tender sensibilities. You're my demon lord—if anyone has to be with me when I unload, it should be you."

I rolled my eyes but said, "Fine, although really, I could do without the scatological honor."

"Aoife, I just told you that it was dangerous—Rene, you are back already?" Kostya interrupted himself when Rene appeared, his manner excited. "You were not gone long. Did you not read my plans to Drake?"

"Yes, yes, and he has many things to say, not all of which I would repeat in front of Aoife, you understand, but I did as you said and made notes of the most important. Here, let me show you—"

Kostya slid a glance toward me.

"I'll take Istvan with me for the walkies, okay?" I said, shooing Jim out the door. "We shouldn't be gone long, since Jim is evidently about to explode."

"Do not stray from Istvan's side," Kostya said, giving me a worried look, but evidently he realized that he was being overly cautious, for he accompanied Rene into the bedroom, where I could hear Rene explaining some objection or other that Drake had.

"We're down to about thirty seconds before Poopocalypse rains down upon us," Jim warned, his expression now pained. "Say your prayers and make your amends, because it ain't gonna be pretty when it hits."

"Right, let's get you to the park," I said, snatching the plastic bags from Suzanne's hand and rushing Jim past Istvan, who must have realized what was up because he had the front door open even before we reached it.

Luckily, we made it to the park before Jim excused himself into a long line of rhododendron bushes.

Istvan—who stood next to me, and was doing a fairly good impression of Kostya with the way he was scanning everything and everyone around us—said something, pointed in a circle, and then gestured to the ground, which I assumed meant he wanted me to stay in the area.

"You're going to patrol the area, gotcha," I told him, even though he couldn't understand me. I nodded to let him know I was with the program, and he took off at a fast walk.

I realized Jim had disappeared from view and called out to him. "Don't go into the bushes. I have to pick up your offerings, remember, and I don't fancy crawling around inside of a bush to do so."

Jim stuck his head out of the rhodie. "I'm not going to do this right out there in the open where anyone can see me! That's unnatural!"

"A talking dog who is really a demon is unnatural," I pointed out, shaking the plastic bags at him. "Now, get with the program and poop."

"You're looking at me again!" he said, emerging from the rhododendron. "I can't poop when people look at me, and while we're on that subject, what does it say about you that you *want* to watch me?"

"Sweet Samarian sandals, I don't want to watch you! I'm simply trying to keep track of where you are so I can pick up your ploppies. Now, stop arguing and get down to business."

He squinted his eyes at me. "You sure you don't have some sort of dog pooping fetish?"

"Argh!" I yelled, slapping the plastic bags on my thighs. "I don't have any fetishes whatsoever. Why the hell aren't you pooping? You said you were about to explode!"

"It's Abaddon, not hell," Jim corrected with a sniff, and turned his back to me, strolling over to a patch of grass near the fence line.

"Well?" I asked after a couple of minutes and still no action. "Come on, Jim. We don't have all day; I'm tired and I want to curl up in bed."

"I can't go with the sort of performance pressure you're putting on me!" Jim snapped, glaring at me.

I looked pointedly at my watch. "Honestly, I had no idea demons were this fussy about bodily functions."

"Me being a demon has nothing to do with it," Jim

answered, moving to another spot. I cast a look around, but Istvan had evidently just completed his check along the perimeter of the fence and was heading back our way. "It's because I picked this magnificent form, and you can't rush things like internal functions if you want to keep your form in nice shape."

I stopped dead next to a small azalea. "Wait a minute—you *picked* your form?"

"Of course." Jim snuffled a couple of leaves on the ground and moved on down to the next shrub.

"You wanted to be a dog? You didn't just end up that way?"

"Demons don't work like that. We get to pick our forms unless our demon lords order us to a different one." He struck a pose for a few seconds. "Could you imagine anything more fabulous than this? There isn't anything. I've got the pinnacle of demon forms, let me tell you."

I followed after him deeper into the shadows as a line of trees marching alongside the fence cast inky fingers that the streetlights didn't disperse. "Wait a second—how come you're suddenly an expert on being a demon when a few days ago you thought you were nothing more than a dog?"

"It's called asking questions, babe. Turns out Rene knows a lot of stuff."

I shrugged off his explanation. "So, you could be anything you wanted, anything at all? Like a horse? Or an elephant?"

He laughed and headed for a bench that sat firmly in the shadows of a tall line of elms. "Yeah, but you really would not want to take me walkies if I was an elephant. Talk about ploppies! Hey, that spot over there smells pretty good. This area has been peed on a lot." He set off at a fast walk across the corner of the park toward a clump of trees where a small groundskeeper's shed sat. I stood for a minute in thought before I realized that he was almost out of view. I dashed after him, hearing Istvan shout something behind me, no doubt chastising me for getting so far from his protection.

"You annoying demon!" I said as I ran up to where Jim was smelling the door of the shed, an odd look on his face. "Right, this is ending here and now. As your demon lord, I command you to stop being a dog and instead change into a human being, the kind who can take himself to the bathroom and who doesn't slobber all over everything, including my shoes and Kostya's pants legs."

"Hey, you know what this smells li—" Jim's eyes bugged out the second the words left my lips. He spun around, his body elongating and changing as he moved. There was a little ripple in the air, and Jim the dog was gone, replaced by a man a little shorter but stockier than Kostya, with a broad chest, dark hair and eyes, and an expression of absolute astonishment. "Fires of Abaddon, Eefies! What did you do to me?"

I stared openmouthed for a second until I realized what I was doing. "You don't have any clothes on!" I said, pointing at his crotch. "Jim, put some clothes on!"

"You made me human," he said, putting his hands on his hips, an annoyed expression on his face as he examined himself. "Man, I can't tell you how much this sucks. Look at my package! It's not nearly as good as it was, and I don't have that cute white spot on my chest anymore, and crapballs, I don't have a tail! How am I supposed to express my emotions without a proper tail? I'm ugly and awkward, and look, I can't even lift my leg properly."

I spun around at the sight of Jim trying to lift his leg on the side of the shed, and rubbed my forehead, hoping the dull throb there was going to go away. "Holy testicles, Jim! You can't do that now. And stop whining—being human isn't that bad."

"Yeah?" He marched around to stand in front of me. "You're saying I can't pee on whatever I want? Or take a dump behind that shed, like I was going to do before you got all demon lord on my butt?" He glanced over his shoulder to his backside. "Aw, man! My butt is huge now, too! There isn't anything good about human form! I bet I can't even lick my own—"

"Okay, new ground rules. When we are in human form, we do not mimic the behavior of dogs. We also don't talk about the things that we can no longer do. Got that? Good. Let's go home and you can use the bathroom there, or if you can't make it that far, we'll stop at the café on the corner and use their facilities."

"Right, because the café won't have an issue at all with me showing up starkers because you forgot to order me to have some clothes when you forced me into a new form." Jim's expression was oddly the same now that he was human—and a tiny little voice in my head pointed out that I actually missed Jim's doggy form—and right now, it read sour discontent.

"Oh no, you aren't going to make this my fault." I turned toward the entrance of the park. "You coming naked is all ... uh .... Jim?"

"Yeah, that's a red dragon," Jim said, turning to look with interest at the two men and one woman who stood blocking the way. "I was going to tell you that the shed smelled like some dragons had been around the area, and they didn't smell like the dudes in the house we're at. Oh, and now thanks to you being Hasty McDemonlord, I can't even bite them."

I eyed the three people before me. The woman said something, gesturing toward me. The two men with her stepped forward, obviously intending to grab us. I wanted very much to avoid that, just as I wanted to avoid having any contact with the swords all three wore strapped to their respective hips. I looked around for Istvan, but he had disappeared. "Jim, I'm going to give you an order, and I want you to follow it to the letter."

"Attack the dragons?" he asked, watching as the men suddenly rushed forward.

I stepped back, clutching my hands together, very aware of the ring sitting heavily on one of them. There wasn't any way to escape them, no place I could run to, and no Istvan to help me. I did the only thing I could think of. "No. Go to Kostya. Right now. RUN!"

I tried to reach for that whoosh of power I'd felt back in Sweden when the dragons attacked Kostya, but there was nothing there, just a faint sense of anticipation, as if the ring were cocking its head at me and waiting for me to do something. There was no time to stop and consider what the hell the ring wanted from me—I simply yelled a Viking battle cry and threw myself at them, praying the ring would give me the oomph to get past them.

"Well, hell!" I said a few minutes later. The two dragon men didn't topple over from the combination of myself and the awesome power that was held by my magical ring. Instead, one caught me and twisted me around while the other wrenched my right arm behind me and up into a painful hold.

"Abaddon," came a now-familiar correction.

"Oh no, Jim, not you, too." I peered over my shoulder, and sure enough, another man and woman emerged from around a clump of trees with the naked Jim in tow. I fisted my left hand and held it close to my stomach, praying that the dragons wouldn't notice the ring on my finger. If I could just get a moment where they wouldn't see me doing so, I'd tuck the ring into the pocket of my jeans.

The dragons said something in harsh voices that made my skin itch and shoved us forward, toward the entrance of the park. I saw no signs of Istvan, which gave me hope that he'd gone for help.

"Sorry. I would've been much faster as a dog." The look of accusation in Jim's eyes was all too clear.

"You know what? I've had it trying to be nice, especially when you don't understand that I was simply trying to make both our lives easier."

"Nice? You call forcing me into a naked human form nice?" Jim shook his head. "Why don't you use that badass magic ring of yours to lay out these dragons the way you did in Sweden, so we can go home and I can use the unsanitary toilet that all the dragons put their butts on."

"A toilet is far more sanitary than...oh, never mind. Where's Istvan?" I clutched my hand to my stomach even harder, at the same time casting a glance over at the nearest dragon. "And stop mentioning the you-know-what. There's a good chance these guys grabbed us because they know we're connected with Kostya, not because I have the thing in question. And frankly, I'd like to keep them from finding that out."

"They can't understand us," Jim said with a shrug. "That curse thing works for them as well as the other dragons."

"We don't know that for certain, and I'm not going to risk calling attention to it just in case they can understand us."

"In which case you just told them that you have an object of great importance," he pointed out.

"Stop using your logic on me!" I commanded, and was about to continue when a sudden shout from the dragon to my right had my heart sinking. As we moved around a small fountain, the sight of Istvan trying to fend off three other red dragons had me leaping forward. They were all in human form (I assume there was some unwritten rule about appearing as a dragon in public), but Istvan was outnumbered. Two of the dragons had swords, one of which was raised high in the air as a dragon was clearly about to decapitate poor Istvan.

The dragon behind me jerked back on my arm so painfully that I saw stars for a second or two, but that just seemed to make something inside of me snap. With a roar that I was astonished came from my mouth, I summoned a ball of Kostya's fire and slammed it into the dragon with the sword. It splashed against his chest but didn't stop the downswing of the sword.

"NO!" I bellowed, and shoved my free hand forward in an instinctive attempt to block the attack. The dragon with the sword flew backward about twenty feet, slamming into a group of people that had come running at the noise. Istvan, who had been forced to his knees, struggled to his feet, taking advantage of the distraction to kick at the knees of the other sword-wielder, bringing her down before he snatched up the weapon and turned to the others.

They were all staring at me. Or more precisely, at my still-outstretched hand.

"Way to not let them know about the ring," Jim said, giving me a wry look.

"Oh, shite," I swore, pulling my hand back against my body.

"You said it, babe."

The dragons left Istvan and circled around Jim and me. "I have a very bad feeling about thi—aieee!"

As I spoke, the woman nearest me made some sort of intricate gesture, almost as if she was drawing on the air. Out of the corner of my eye, I saw a faint black image glowing in the middle of nothing and decided that drawing on air wasn't such a bad metaphor at that. But it was what happened after the symbol dissolved into nothing that had me squawking. First of all, there was the matter of the woman reaching up and pulling back something—what, I have no idea, since there was nothing in front of her, but whatever it is she did left a big black gaping hole. And into that the two dragons holding me leaped, taking me with them.

Thirteen

I felt like someone had taken a two-by-four, wrapped it in velvet, and bashed me in the gut.

"You going to ralph? You look like you're going to ralph. Doesn't it hurt being on your hands and knees like that? Oh, man, that looks bad."

I retched up nothing, gasping with both the taste of bile in my mouth and the pain from the walloping that my stomach had taken. Groggily, I turned my head to see Jim's legs next to me. He was leaning down, his hands on his knees, sympathy mingling with wry amusement in his dark eyes.

"Urgh."

Jim nodded his head. "I heard that it's not easy being dragged to Abaddon if you're not a demon."

"Abaddon?" Wincing at the pain in my hands and knees, I managed to get to my feet, looking around as I did so. "We're in hell? It looks like a ballroom. Except for the lava rocks. Who carpets their ballroom floor with nasty little lava rocks?"

"Someone who likes to cause people pain, I'm guessing."

That's when I noticed that Jim was standing on a small piece of cloth. A familiar-looking small piece of cloth. "Hey! That's my shirt!"

"Just the back of it. You weren't using the back, and you couldn't expect me to stand on the sharp pointy rocks in my bare, vulnerable human feet, could you?"

"Ack!" I said, slapping my hands on my legs. "Jim, we're in hell!"

"Abaddon."

"And the dragons know I have the ring! Is your discomfort really the only thing you can think of at this moment?"

He raised an eyebrow. "*You* have shoes."

"I give up," I said, exasperated beyond words. "Fine, you want an apology? I'm sorry that I changed you into a human. I thought it would be easier for us both, but evidently I was wrong. Very, very wrong."

"You said it, sister."

"So you want to be a dog again? Go ahead and change yourself."

"I can't do that once a demon lord has picked a form for me." The look he gave me was as sour as a lemon.

"This demon lord business is really just a pain in the butt, you know that? Fine, you have my permission to be a dog again, if only so I don't have to keep seeing your naughty bits every time I turn around."

"My other package is much, much better," Jim said, doing a little dance of anticipation, which had the unfortunate result of making the aforementioned naughty bits jiggle around.

"Jim!" Hastily, I averted my gaze. "For the love of all that isn't genitalia, stop dancing."

"You have to command me! And don't forget my white spot, and the three white toes. Those are stylin', let me tell you."

I rolled my eyes for a moment, praying to whatever deity was handy for a little patience, and said, "Jim, I command you as your demon lord to change back into a dog."

"What? No, you can't— Aw, crapballs."

I eyed the Dalmatian that stood before me, complete with spots and little red collar. "Why are you a Dalmatian?"

"Because you didn't order me properly. Man, I sure hope that Aisling chick is a better demon lord than you, because this is terrible." Jim bent double to look at his undercarriage. "Yup, terrible. Change me back!"

"I told you to change into a dog!"

"Yeah, but you didn't give me parameters. Instead I had to go with *your* idea of a dog."

I blinked for a moment in thought, then suddenly remembered a Dalmatian stuffed toy that I had loved dearly as a child. "Oh. Sorry. Okay, let's try this: Jim, I command you as your temporary demon lord to change into a dog that isn't one I remember from my childhood, or that I particularly like."

A heavy, martyred sigh that could rival one of Kostya's followed immediately.

"Well, now, that's just silly," I told Jim the now-Chihuahua.

"Parameters," he said, his deep voice at odds with his tiny little body. "You didn't do them right. *Again*. Great, now I fit in your pocket. I don't even wanna see what this did to my package."

A door at the far end of the ballroom (as I continued to think of it, although who would give a ball in hell?) opened, and a man strolled into the room, accompanied by two women who were several inches taller than him and probably a good fifty pounds heavier. They looked like bouncers of a particularly hard-core New York City club.

"My pocket sounds like a pretty good place for you right now," I said, scooping up Jim and tucking him into the crook of my arm. He was probably five or six pounds, one of those Chihuahuas that rich girls and Hollywood starlets dress up and carry around in their bags, but my main concern at the moment was to keep Jim safe.

"This is beyond humiliating," Jim said, his voice muffled from where I had him pressed against my side. "Wait, is that your boobie? It is, isn't it?"

"Hush," I told him as the man and his two bouncers approached. The man wasn't much to look at—just a normal-looking middle-aged man with brown hair and eyes, of medium height and build, but with every step forward, a sense of dread grew until it weighed down heavily on top of me. It was like being smothered with a lead blanket, and I struggled to breathe by the time he came to a stop in front of me.

He stood examining first me, then Jim, who scooted even deeper into the crook of my arm.

"Your name?" the man said with no preamble.

A squeak was all I could utter. I cleared my throat, remembered I was now a dragon's mate, and tried again. "Hi, I'm Aoife. And you are?"

The man ignored my question. "What is the name of the demon?"

"Jim. Er... Effrijim is his full name, I think. At least that's what Kostya says, and he would know."

"Effrijim." The man frowned. One of the two bouncers moved forward to whisper in his ear. "Ah. The Guardian's demon. Why is it bound to you?"

"That's kind of a long story. I'm sorry, I didn't catch your name." I was trying to be polite, but at the same time, I really disliked the idea that I had been hauled forcibly to hell and was now at the mercy of who-knew-what.

"Oh, man," Jim moaned into my side. I glanced down to find him trying to bury his head in my shirt. "We're gonna get squashed now for sure. That's the premiere prince, Eefums. The head honcho. Mr. Big himself."

"How do you know?" I asked in a whisper. "You lost your memory, and I doubt if Rene had time to show you pictures of demon lords."

"I don't have to remember him to feel the power coming off him."

That was true enough. The power seemed to snap and spark around him, like it was a living thing embracing him.

"Er... my apologies, Your... uh... Highness, is it?" I gave the man a little smile, even though that was the last thing in the world I wanted to do.

He just stared at me, a dead look in his eyes that increased the feeling of dread until I thought I was going to be pushed down into the ground by it. His dark gaze crawled over me again for a few seconds. "You are a wyvern's mate."

I filed away that statement to trot out to Kostya at a later date. If even the head of hell knew I was his mate, Kostya could just get over his emotional baggage and embrace the fact. "Yes, I am."

"That is satisfactory." He gestured toward me. "Take my ring from her."

"What?" I clutched my hand, ignoring the squawk from Jim as I smooshed him against my side, backing up as one of the bouncers came forward. "I don't think you can do that, can you? It picked me, evidently, so it's kind of mine now."

"If you do not give it willingly," the bouncer said, her voice as harsh as the lava rocks underneath my feet, "I will simply take your hand to present to Lord Asmodeus."

I stared at her in horror, not just because of the appalling things she was saying, but because her teeth were pointed. All of them, and she seemed to have an extraordinary number of them.

"Sweet suffering sycophants," I whispered, getting ready to turn and run, although I had no idea where I was going to escape to. But at that moment, there was a rustle in my arms, and Jim leaped down to stand in front of me, his spindly little legs vibrating, his hackles up all the way down his back.

"You're going to have to go through me first," he growled at the bouncer.

She lifted one heavily booted foot as if to stomp him into nothing, but I shrieked and scooped him up, clutching him to my chest as I backpedaled madly, stumbling over the lava rocks. "Jim, what the hell do you think you're doing?"

"Protecting you. I'm a demon and you're my demon lord; as you can see by Hans and Franz there, that's what we do. It would have been more effective in proper form, but you won't let me have that."

I turned and ran to the other end of the room, looking desperately for a door or some means of escape, but there

was none, of course. That would have been far too con-
venient. I spun around and watched as the two bouncers
stalked forward, neither of them in a hurry and both with
expressions that I swear took off at least ten years from
my life span.

Hastily, I set Jim down. "I order you to go back to your
old form."

He turned into a Dalmatian. "Criminy dutch, Eefsters!
I thought we had this discussion."

The two women got closer, the one with the smile now
holding a wicked-looking dagger.

"Crap! The dog form, the dog form!"

A Chihuahua faced me with an extremely bitter look
on his tiny little face. "Fires of—"

The second woman started smiling now, and hard to
believe, it was even worse than the first bouncer. Panic
filled me, along with a desperate need to be anywhere
but that exact spot. "No, the other one! The big one that
comes from that place in Canada. Crap, I can't remember
the name of it. Nova Scotia?"

"Eefs, how hard is it to—"

My mind shut down at that point, unwilling to deal
with the fact that two horrible women were about to hack
off my hand in order to give a ring to the prince of hell
and unable to think of the name of Jim's preferred form.
"For the love of all that's not canine, just change back to
human form! Now, take down Shark Teeth there while I
tackle her buddy."

Naked human Jim stared at me in disbelief. "You're
kidding, right?"

"Attack!" I screeched, and threw myself onto the sharp-
toothed woman.

The scuffle that followed was anticlimactic at best, due in part to the fact that Jim didn't even make it to his assigned bouncer before they both grabbed me.

"Get her hand," one of them said, which just made me try to punch her in the face. I didn't connect, of course, because evidently I'm doomed to never land a blow.

Jim leaped at the first one when she twirled her knife around her fingers, but the woman just slashed at him, leaving two long bloody marks across his bare chest. Jim looked down in stupefaction, touching one of the gashes and holding up the red-stained fingers to show me. "Um. Ow?"

"Gods of the woodlands and fields," I shouted, fighting the woman who held me in order to get to Jim.

Asmodeus, who had strolled nonchalantly across the ballroom while his bouncers were stalking me, now arrived and said something that caused his bouncer to release me.

"Are you okay, Jim? That looks terrible! I need to get you to a doctor." I grabbed the hem of the front of my shirt and ripped it off, which more or less evened the garment, since Jim had poached part of the back. "Stand still. Try not to breathe hard. I'll wrap this around you now, in order to put pressure on the owies. Stop looking like you're going to faint. It'll be okay, I promise."

"I feel woozy," he said, weaving a little. "There's a bright light. Is there supposed to be a light? Should I go into it? It looks warm and happy, and I want to go into it."

"If your comedy act has finished," Asmodeus said, holding out his hand, "I would like my ring returned."

"Stop being so dramatic," I hissed to Jim out of the side of my mouth. "You're not cut up that badly. And as for you, Prince Asmodeus, or however you prefer to be addressed, I don't think this ring is what you think it is. Kostya—he's the dragon that I'm evidently a mate to—he tried to use the ring, but it was dead to him. The ring seems to like me, so I don't think it's going to work the way you expect it to." I was bluffing, true, which might not have been the brightest idea since the man I was trying to fool was the head of hell itself, not to mention the fact that I had no idea of whether what I said was true, but really, I didn't feel there was much other choice given that situation.

After all, the bouncers were quite willing to lop off my hand to get the ring to Asmodeus. I suspected that even if I handed it over willingly, they wouldn't throw me a "thank you for being so cooperative" party and send me on my way. It behooved me, therefore, to find a way to stalemate his attempt to acquire the ring.

Asmodeus just looked at me, his hand still outstretched. "It is my ring. I created it, and it was taken from me. Return it to me, now."

Jim suddenly started humming under his breath. I shot him a curious look and was interested to see that he looked thoughtful, not terrified or worried, as I expected. And that got my own mind working—why was Asmodeus *asking* me to give him the ring? Why did he stop his bouncers from taking the ring (and my hand) for him? If I were the boss of hell, you can be sure that I'd be throwing my weight around wherever and whenever possible, including bypassing all the trouble it took in order to reason with someone who had an item I wanted.

"Huh." I smiled and held my hand close to my chest. "You know, I don't think I will give it to you. As I said, it kind of likes me, and I have a feeling that it's not going to like being forcibly taken from me."

Asmodeus didn't react; at least there was no expression that clued me in to what he was thinking. His bouncers, however, looked at him with surprise, which verified my speculation.

"I will take it from you if I must," he finally said, in a manner that implied I was too boring for words. "If you insist on destroying yourself in the process, then it is no concern of mine."

Huge leap of faith time, I told myself, and held out my hand. "Okay. Go ahead and take it. *If you can.*"

Asmodeus looked at my hand, his own fingers twitching a little, little black tendrils of electricity snapping around him. Even as he looked, the ring grew warm on my finger and started to glow with a blue-white light. He narrowed his eyes at that; then suddenly he turned around and stomped off in the opposite direction.

"Take them to a cell," he ordered as he left.

"Ha!" I gloated, relief swamping me as he left the ballroom. A tiny fraction of the doom that his presence had caused to squash me lifted, enough so I felt like I could take a deep breath. "I knew it! You can't take it from me, can you?"

The nearest bouncer growled at me, a low, ugly, feral sound that had me shivering despite my newfound confidence. The second grabbed me painfully by the arm and commenced to haul me out of the ballroom, Jim following behind with his own bouncer.

He bitched the entire time it took for the two demons to take us down a couple of flights of stairs and lock us into a small windowless room. It wasn't, as I assumed, a dungeon, but more like an unused room in the cellar.

"Well," I said, examining the situation. The room had a dirt floor, wood walls, and a lone naked lightbulb that swung from a cobwebby wire from the ceiling. There was also the faint smell of mice that left me jumping at every shadow. "Now what do we do?"

"First of all, you change me back to my proper form. Then you use your magic ring to get us out of here," Jim said, giving me the king of all disgruntled looks. "Unless, of course, you get your jollies out of seeing me starkers."

I averted my eyes from his nakedness. "In your dreams. I just couldn't remember the name of the breed you like."

He glared at me. "Newfoundland. It's not that hard."

"I know, I know, but I was under stress, and I suffer from test anxiety." I took a deep breath, fixed my eyes on his, and said loudly, "Jim—"

"Effrijim."

"Sorry, Effrijim, as your official demon lord, I order you to change back into the Newfoundland dog form that you like. The one with the white spot on the chest."

"And the big noogies."

"And the big..." I stopped, giving him a look. "Just resume the form you like best."

Naked man shimmied into the shape of a large black dog, at which point Jim sighed a happy, happy sigh and plopped his butt down onto the floor. "At last! Sheesh, beginner demon lords are harder to deal with than I thought."

"I don't need any lip out of you," I told him sternly, then considered my hand. "Just how am I supposed to use the ring to get us out of here? Is it like a transporter on *Star Trek*? Can I just zap us somewhere else?"

"Dunno. It's your ring."

"Fat lot of help you are," I said, giving him a little frown before holding out my hand and saying, "Ring, please take Jim and me somewhere safe. Preferably Aisling's house."

Nothing happened. The ring didn't even so much as glow; it just sat there on my finger being a ring.

"Well, that's disappointing," I said, and gnawed my lower lip a bit while I thought.

"Anticlimactic," Jim agreed, nodding.

"Okay, maybe the transporter request was too much for it. I'll try this instead." I placed my palm on the flat, cold surface of the door. "Open sesame!"

Jim rolled his eyes. "Seriously?"

I slapped my hand on the door. "It has to be the intent behind the words that powers it, right? So it shouldn't matter what I say. Dammit, door, open up!"

The door, like the ring, remained annoyingly inanimate. I tried everything I could think of for three straight hours, from vaguely remembered incantations used in popular movies and TV shows, to suggestions from Jim of archaic Latin commands. None of it did anything but leave me hoarse, frustrated, and more than a little worried.

We dozed for a bit and lost track of time. I had no idea how many hours had passed when I gave in to the dark thoughts that had been growing ever more persistent as each minute passed. It could have been the following morning, or a week later, for all I knew. Time seemed to blur in Abaddon, which left me feeling even more at sea.

"What if Asmodeus finds a way to get the ring off me?" I said, slumped into a corner, my knees to my chest, with Jim pressed against me for comfort. "What if the way he does that is to leave me here to starve to death so he can just pluck the ring off my cold, lifeless fingers? What if I spend the rest of my life trapped in this dank, dark hell-hole, kind of a modern-day man in the iron mask, only without the mask. I'll end up an old, old lady with crazy hair and crazier eyes until one day, I'll just topple over and die."

"You're a wyvern's mate, babe. That means you can't die unless someone lops off your head, or cuts out your heart, or something like that," Jim said in an obnoxiously cheerful voice.

I lifted my head from where my cheek lay on my knee and gave him a look that I felt he deserved. "Great. So now I just get to be perpetually old crazy lady in a cell that no one remembers."

"You got me, chicky," Jim said, rubbing his head on my leg. Unfortunately, that also meant the drool tendrils that swung from his furry lips had a landing zone. I shifted my look to the long, slimy ropes on my pant leg before cocking an eyebrow at him. "Heh. Sorry. Afraid that's one of the downsides to having such a stunning form. I'm sure it'll dry quickly."

I sighed, fully engulfed in martyr mode. "It doesn't matter now. I'm doomed, doomed, doomed."

"Emo much?"

"Doomed with a smart-aleck demon. This just gets better."

"Man, you are a Debbie Downer today."

I straightened up and glared at him. "I am not! And if I was, I have every right to be one. I mean, look at the situation!"

"I am. It's not so bad."

"Are you insane? How can being locked in a cell in hell not be bad?"

"Abaddon, and you're not thinking right."

I squinted at him with suspicion. "What are you trying to say?"

"I told you what you were, right?" Jim stood up and stretched, then ambled over to the door to give it a sniff.

I thought. "You said I was emo and a Debbie Downer, which I'm absolutely not."

"Not that, the other thing."

I dug around in my memory. "Wyvern's mate?"

Jim snuffled the bottom of the door. "And what does that mean?"

I chewed my lower lip again. "It means that Kostya and I are a couple, even if he doesn't want to admit it. Don't give me that look—I know full well that you're implying that Kostya will somehow feel obligated to rescue me, but that's not very realistic. For one, he has stated more times than I can count that I'm not his mate, and he doesn't want me even if I am. And unless I'm missing something, hell—fine, Abaddon—isn't a place that's likely to be easy to conduct a jailbreak. So even if Kostya did feel inclined to rescue us, I don't see how he's going to do it."

"Dragons don't like being parted from their mates," Jim said with a little shrug, sitting down just out of range of the door. "And judging by the way that Slick goes for your boobies, I don't see him washing his hands of you and going on his merry way."

"I do have the ring," I said thoughtfully, my spirits rising. "He can't want that to fall into Asmodeus's hands. Hmm. You might be right, Jim."

"'Bout time someone finally admitted that," Jim said, tipping his head to the side and looking back at the door.

I was about to ask him what he so obviously heard

when the door suddenly burst into flame. I leaped to my feet and pulled Jim backward.

"Dragon fire!" I said excitedly, hope blossoming again within me. "You were right! Kostya is rescuing me!"

"Us." He nudged my hand with his head.

"Yes, sorry, us, both of us." I patted his head and almost did a dance of joy as the door, now burning merrily, started going black around the edges. If the door had been set alight with normal fire, Jim and I would have likely choked to death on the smoke, but with dragon fire, there was less smoke and more flames. "I wonder how long it's going to take. I'd like to get out of here before Asmodeus realizes— Holy shish kebabs!"

As I spoke, a sudden whumping noise shook the door. A second followed, and on the third, the door collapsed inward, revealing Kostya.

With a half sob, half laugh, I flung myself at him, my heart filled with happiness at the sight and scent and feel of him. He caught me before I could topple him, spinning me around once and wrapping his arms around me with a muttered, "Aoife. You are not harmed?" before kissing the answer right off my tongue.

"When I heard you were taken, it was as if my heart were ripped from my chest," he murmured against my lips, then suddenly pushed me back to examine me, the silver in his black irises glittering dangerously. "The red dragons did not hurt you, did they?"

"No, they didn't. I'm fine," I said shakily a moment later, when I could think again.

"I'm fine, too, although I'm more than a little weirded out that Eefs likes to see me in naked human form," Jim said, sauntering through the still-burning door frame.

"Jim!"

"Just sayin'." Jim turned his attention to Kostya. "Nice shiner, Slick. We going to get out of here, or what?"

"Shiner?" I pulled back enough to frown at Kostya's face. "You have a black eye. Was that from Drake—"

"Yes," he interrupted, pulling me down the hallway, not toward the stairs as I expected, but deeper into the cellar. "It matters not, however. We must leave now. The distractions will keep Asmodeus and his minions only so long."

"What sort of distractions? The green dragons? They helped you?" Kostya was moving so fast, I had to trot to keep up with him. "That was nice of them."

Kostya snorted. "I paid for that service, I assure you."

"Drake charged you? Well, I have to say, that's kind of mercenary. I mean, he is family— Whoa, what's that?"

We had entered another cell, a slightly larger room, this one holding rusted pieces of what looked like medieval torture implements. I averted my gaze and instead gawked at a black, jagged rent that appeared to be floating in midair next to a thin man with slicked-back blond hair.

"It's a tear in the fabric of space. Aisling ordered the demon to keep it open for us. Jim, you go first."

"I have a name," the blond man said with a sniff. "I am Amy, lord of twenty-six legions and servant to Ashtorath. Effrijim, I see you still insist on clinging to that motley form."

"Motley?" Jim said, about ready to jump through the inky tear into nothingness. "Dude, you are clearly suffering from form envy. Get with the program. Let me walk you through a tour of all my magnificent points—"

Jim likely would have continued, but Kostya, with

an annoyed click of his tongue, hefted Jim and tossed him through the gaping black tear in the fabric of space. Behind us, a horrible keening sound started, one that set my teeth on edge and made the skin on my arms crawl in horror.

"Go!" Kostya ordered, shoving me toward the black rent.

"All right, but I'm not leaving you here." I grabbed his wrist and jumped, pulling him into the abyss with me.

Fourteen

"So, this is the delicious Eva, hmm?"

Groggily, I shook my head and got to my knees, looking upward at the man who stood next to me. He was about my height, with black hair that was slicked back and a face that looked strangely familiar. He also had a leer that instinctively had me reaching for Kostya. "It's Aoife, not Eva. Kostya, are you all right? Where are we?"

Kostya lay facedown next to me on asphalt. Judging by the debris, water-stained cardboard boxes, looming large trash receptacles, general smell, and dimness of light, I judged us to be in an alley of some sort. I scooted over to him, ignoring the pain as small pebbles and a plastic bottle cap dug into my knee, and rolled Kostya over.

His eyes opened, but they were unfocused.

"Holy crapballs, what did you do to him?" I snarled in the direction of the black-haired letch. "Kostya, my darling, are you all right? It's me, Aoife. Do you recognize me? Did you hit your head? Is anything broken?"

Quickly I felt my way down his body, but nothing seemed harmed.

He said something I didn't understand and blinked at me. His hair, normally swept back from his brow, looked rumpled, as if someone had ruffled his hair and left it standing on end. His black eye was already fading, allowing him to squint at me and say, "Aoife?"

"Yes, it's me." I smoothed his hair down. "Did you hurt yourself? I think I blacked out going through that tear thingie, but I didn't feel sick like I did when Jim and I got dragged into hell."

"Abaddon," corrected the man next to us. "Wyvern, the Guardian told me to instruct you to return to her home. You will tell her that I have completed the tasks she has given me, and thus you are to give me the location of your mother, as agreed."

Kostya sat up, shaking his head a little, obviously to clear it. He frowned, then glared up at the man. "Who... oh, it's you. I forgot Aisling had to use you."

"*Use me*! I am used by no woman, unless she has a donkey rig and several small, barbed whips." Even as I helped Kostya get to his feet, the man hitched his leer up a notch and waggled his eyebrows at me. "I don't suppose you care for barbed whips, my delectable little wyvern's mate?"

"Who the hell—"

"Abaddon."

"—are you?" I asked, brushing off first Kostya, then my own jeans.

"Magoth, former prince of Abaddon and ruler of more legions than you could count, demon lord extraordinaire, and star of stage, screen, and soon a highly anticipated series of erotic webisodes. I believe that's the correct word. My people would know." He waved a hand in a vague manner. "You may call me 'my lord.' Or perhaps 'master,' although that tends to be overused these days."

"How about neither," I grumbled, glancing up and down the alley. "Where's Jim?"

"The demon went off to find transport." Magoth pulled out a cell phone and read some messages. "The location of the wickedly inventive Dona Catalina?"

Kostya straightened up, finally getting himself together. He gave Magoth a long, long look before shaking his head. "She is well able to take care of herself, so I don't know why I hesitate to tell you. She is in Aruba. Recently, she began a bondage club there and has expressed her intent to stay on until it bores her."

"Oooh, bondage club," Magoth said, a little ripple of pleasure visibly affecting him. "What a delightful notion. City and address?"

Kostya told him.

"I shall look forward to offering her my expert advice on the best way to add a little extra sado to her masochism." Magoth gave us a little bow, tried to catch a look down my shirt, and when I crossed my arms, heaved a huge mock sigh and toddled off.

"That was a former demon lord?" I asked Kostya when he, without even a glance my way, turned and headed in the opposite direction. "Why does he want to know where your mom is? And while we're on the subject: you have a mom?"

"Of course I have a mother. Everyone does."

I glared after him for a moment, then broke into a trot to catch up, taking his hand when I did so. "Yes, but not all of them are alive, especially not if you're several hundred years old. Aren't you a little bit worried about sending a demon lord her way? One who clearly has some sexual deviancy issues?"

His fingers weren't at all their usual pleasant selves. He didn't so much as rub his thumb over the back of my hand. Nor did he look at me. Rather than being a man who, according to Jim, had missed me greatly, he had the appearance of one who couldn't bear to have me around.

I was far more hurt than I wanted to admit, but I was unsure of whether I should just ask him what was wrong or give him the space he was so obviously signaling that he needed.

"Unfortunately, my mother spent some time enjoying Magoth's company. It drove Drake mad, but our mother has long made her own choices, and she little heeds our advice. Besides, the last time she and Magoth got together, he was out of commission for a good three days." Suddenly, he smiled, a hint of pride in his eyes. "There are few who can best Mother, especially when it comes to dubious sexual practices."

"Great. I'm marrying into a family of bondage fans," I said lightly, giving his hand an encouraging squeeze.

He dropped my hand, striding across a narrow street into another alley.

I stopped, wanting to cry, and hit him, and run away and hide for a few years. I did none of them.

Kostya must have realized I wasn't with him, for halfway down the alley he stopped and turned to gesture me forward.

"This is not the time or place," I told myself, hesitating a few seconds before I crossed the street and entered the alley. "There are better times to deal with whatever bee is up his butt." As I approached him, he turned, obviously not even able to stand looking at me. "To hell with the right time—what is the matter with you?"

He had started to walk on, but when I didn't follow, he half turned back toward me. "What?"

"That's what I want to know—what's wrong with you? Have I suddenly turned into something repulsive that you can't even brace yourself to look me in the eye? Do I smell like something horrible? Are you pissed at me?"

He blinked for a couple of seconds, then shook his head. "We must hurry."

"No, sir." I crossed my arms. "I'm not going anywhere with a man who obviously can't stand being with me."

A low, primal growl was ripped out of him as he moved, quicker than I could follow, down the alley. One moment I was standing there thinking how much I'd like to punch him in the arm, and the next I was smashed up against something hard, cold stone at my back and hot dragon at my front.

"You think I cannot bear to be with you?" The silver flecks in his eyes glittered a warning, but I could sense his fire riding high and knew just how close he was to losing control. "I cannot bear to be without you, woman. You are life to me. There's not a breath I take that does not need you to complete it. The sun rises, and the moon sets, and without you, it would all be meaningless. Do you understand now?"

"No," I said softly, putting my hands on his chest, melting at the romance of the moment despite the setting and the fact that the words sounded as if he were chiseling each one out of granite. "But that's beautiful, Kostya. I'm touched, I really am. But if you feel that way about me, why are you treating me like I'm a leper?"

He growled again; this time it was a sexy sound, one that had my internal engine humming. "Dragons do not like to be parted from their women. When they do, they must join. It is an urgent need, one basic to our beings, that can't be dismissed. We must reclaim that which is ours."

I squinted at him, confused by his declarations. "You wouldn't even let me hold your hand, you idiot. How is that the sun rising and moon setting?"

He heaved a sigh, and his lips hovered over mine, but despite me tipping up my head in welcome, he pushed away with a snarl. "You have no idea how you tempt me. How I want to hold you and possess you. How I wish to breathe in your scent and feel the warm satin of your skin against mine. I need all this with a desperation that is almost making me insane, but I cannot have it. If I was to so much as kiss you, I would not be able to maintain control."

"Oh?" I followed when he turned and continued down the alley, the penny finally dropping. "Oh! You mean you're giving me the cold shoulder because..."

His jaw was so tight, it's a wonder he got any words out. "You would not like me taking you here in the street. Besides, it would be unsafe. The red dragons are clearly on the hunt for us. Above all else, I must protect you."

"I think that's the sweetest thing you've said to me yet," I said, smiling. His shoulders twitched. "And here I was worried that you were freaking out because I mentioned marriage."

Kostya didn't touch me as we reached the end of the

alley, but he gestured for me to stay back while he peered up and down the street, obviously looking for signs of danger. With a short nod at me, we continued down the street.

"You expect to marry me?" he asked conversationally. Or as conversationally as you could while keeping a vigilant eye on everything and everyone surrounding you.

"Am I your mate?" I asked.

"Tch."

"Uh-huh. Well, if you expect me to spend the rest of my life with you, then yes, we're going to get married. I was brought up to believe that people who spend their lives together should be married, if only because it makes things nicer, legally."

"It is a mortal convention. I am a dragon."

"You look human, and I am human, so guess what? We're getting married. I'm not saying we'll have a big ceremony or anything, just—"

He held up a hand as we rounded a corner onto a busy street.

"Red dragons?" I whispered.

"No. Mimes." We hurried onward, pausing only when Jim came barreling down the street, slobber flying.

He skidded to a stop in front of me, and said sotto voce, "Called Rene. He'll meet us in the Tuileries. Gotta go walkies anyway." He dashed off again, but not before confusing a little old lady in black with a tiny pug who stared first at Jim, then at me, and finally fainted dead away.

By the time we entered Aisling and Drake's house, some half an hour later, I was just about done with the lecture. "And if you ever do that to me again—"

"I had to go! I can't help it if you didn't have any bags

with you. I told you I was about to explode earlier, and I never did get to go because the red dragons dragged us to Abaddon and you wouldn't let me go in the cell."

"I'm not talking about the pooping incident, although goodness knows you didn't have to do it right where everyone walks. I'm referring to you speaking where innocent old ladies hear you and almost keel over because they're so freaked out at a talking dog. Hi, Suzanne. Rene, can you tell her hi for us? Oh, and Aisling, too."

I waved as Aisling emerged from one of the downstairs rooms and was about to give Rene a message of thanks to pass along to her when Kostya suddenly scooped me up in his arms and, without a glance at anyone, stalked off to the door leading to the kitchen.

I looked at Kostya. His eyes were glittering with what I was coming to recognize as sexual interest, his jaw tight and his scowl firmly fixed in place. In other words, he looked like the Kostya version of a man who badly wanted to get it on with me.

"I guess your control isn't going to stand a few minutes more while we make some plans with the ring?"

"No. I told you this is the way of dragons. I must claim you now."

He nudged open the door to Suzanne's bedroom, set me down, and closed the door, taking care to lock it before turning toward me and pulling off his shirt. "Undress."

"Just like that? No foreplay? Not even a kiss and a quick fondle? Just take off your— Oooh."

He dropped his pants and kicked them off, standing naked before me. I let my eyes do a little enjoyable wandering, my fingers already working on the buttons of my shirt.

"Do you need assistance?" he inquired politely, his fingers spasming slightly.

I was about to say no, when it occurred to me that there could be much fun in having him help me. I gave up on my buttons halfway down my shirt and fluttered my hands at the same time I offered a coy smile. "Why, yes, I think I do need some help. How very generous of you to offer. There are so many buttons on this shirt—"

The ripping noise that followed took me by surprise, but not as much as the fact that Kostya could get me out of my shirt and jeans and onto the bed without so much as ruffling my hair.

"Hey! That was one of my favorite shirts." I eyed the remains of it as it fluttered to the floor. At least my jeans hadn't been shredded off of me. "You could have simply unbuttoned it, you know."

"No time," he said, moving over me on the bed, the urgency in his eyes confirming his words. His hands and mouth seemed to be everywhere at once, little fires starting at the slightest touch—literal fires, ones that danced merrily along my skin until Kostya kissed his way past them. "I must claim you now."

"I appreciate the fact that you're so driven to sexual madness by my allure, but—just a little to left, please. Oh, yes, that's it right there—but honestly, I think you could have let me have Rene thank Aisling first."

He lifted his head from where he was kissing a fiery path across my belly. "Too much talking and not enough writhing in ecstasy. You will commence writhing now."

"I don't really like being commanded to—"

His fingers pulled aside my underwear and dove inside me.

I writhed in ecstasy.

"Holy cats in pajamas, Kostya!" Stars seemed to explode behind my eyes when he dipped his head down and breathed fire on all those sensitive, tingly parts of me that were even now clamoring for him. My underwear went flying, along with my bra, and as his fire twined around us, I gave myself up to the pleasure that I was ready to swear only he could bring.

He stopped just short of sending me over the edge, moving up my body, but gave way when I pushed on his shoulders until he yielded. The expression of surprise almost made me laugh when I quickly took advantage of the situation and straddled his hips.

"What are you doing?" he demanded, his eyes straying to my breasts. Both of his hands immediately took possession of them, an act that my breasts and I both commended.

"Being on top. I thought it would make a nice change."

"I am wyvern!"

"That doesn't mean you can't be on the bottom once in a while. Besides, it's your turn to writhe in ecstasy."

His expression turned smug. "It is unnatural for a wyvern to give up control like this. You may wish to please me, but you will not be success—"

I slid back to his knees and bent down to that part of him that had been poking me in the thigh.

"I feel obligated to point out," I said after two minutes of laving him with my tongue, "that you are not only writhing in ecstasy, but you're also moaning and you've shredded Suzanne's sheets."

He looked up, his eyes uncrossing. "You're stopping? Now? Why are you stopping? You should continue."

"Really?" I traced the long length of his penis, gently drawing my fingernails up the length of it. He bucked beneath me. "It seems to me that you're pretty close to losing control, Mr. Wyvern. For one, your claws are out."

He lifted a hand and looked at it. Sure enough, his fingers were black, with long, ivory claws. "That happens sometimes."

"That's why I asked if you really want me to continue— you seem perilously close to losing control. You sure you want me to go on?"

"Yes," he said without thinking, then made an annoyed sound. "No. Perhaps. No, it is best if you do not use your mouth anymore. If you insist on being on top, then impale yourself on me. Then I will maintain control and can give you pleasure."

"Bossy, bossy, bossy," I said, moving up, making sure to rub his hard length between my breasts as I did so. "And for the record, you always give me pleasure."

He moaned again, and he tried to pull me where he wanted me, which luckily was exactly where I wanted to be as well.

"How about you just lie back and let me set the pace?" I murmured, biting gently on one of his nipples.

"Wyverns do not give up control. It is in our natures to dominate. To the left just a little, Aoife."

I shifted to the side, and bit his hip, licking away the sting. "Tell me what you like, Kostya."

His eyes, which had been closed while he writhed around beneath me, opened to show irritated arousal. "You're questioning me? Now? When you insist on pleasuring me with your hands and your mouth and those breasts that should, by right, be in *my* mouth and hands? Now you insist on asking questions?"

"It's called sharing, and yes, I'm asking you what you are thinking and feeling and what you enjoy me doing to your delicious body. Before you tell me that wyverns never answer questions, let me point out that you've driven me to this. Most men are quite happy to vocalize what they like and dislike, but I have to pry every feeling out of you. I blame PTSD."

He stopped in mid-reach for my breasts. "What is that?"

"Post-traumatic stress disorder."

His face went all outraged on me. "You think I have a disorder?"

"Calm down, it's not like I'm calling you mental or anything. It just means that you suffered a lot at some traumatic event, and it's shaped who you are today. Now, getting back to what you like, does this do anything for you?"

I swirled my tongue around his other nipple at the same time I reached down and fondled his noogies.

Both of his hands clutched at the sheets and his eyes flared with an unnatural light. I smiled to myself. "You know, it really is odd, but if you had told me that I wouldn't be bothered at all by a man who goes all dragony when he's sexually excited, I'd have told you that you were nutso-cuckoo. I mean, it's just not normal, is it? And yet, it's you, so it's okay."

Kostya cracked open one eye to glare at me. "Are you going to narrate this?"

"Yes, yes, I am. And you're going to tell me what you like. It's called sharing. Do you like it when I noogie-fondle?"

His brow wrinkled. "Noogie?"

I gave his testicles a gentle tug. "It's my polite term. Do you find it quirky and charming?"

"No," he said abruptly.

A little pang of pain shot through me.

He pulled me down until I lay flush on his chest, his hands warm on my butt. "I find you quirky and charming. Why are you not impaled upon me yet? You ask me what I like, and I like to be inside of you."

"See? That wasn't so hard to open up, was it?" I shifted, positioning him so that I could sink down and give us both the pleasure my body wept for. "All you had to do was just tell me— Oh, holy hallucinations, you're bigger than before!"

I swear as I sank down on him that he was larger… and hotter. I did a little moaning of my own as he invaded me, pushing his way in to where my muscles could ripple around him.

"I am just the same as I have always been." His eyes widened when I made a little swiveling move in order to accommodate his girth. "That!"

"Hmm? Seriously, did you get bigger when I wasn't looking?"

"Do that again. You asked what I liked. I like that." Little pricks of pain touched my hips as he urged me into repeating the movement. "Christos, yes!" I looked down. "Claws, Kostya. Oh, never mind, you can leave them out. It's kind of arousing, to be honest."

I sank down the last little bit until he was wholly enveloped in my heated embrace, and looked down at him. His eyes were a field of onyx with brilliant little flecks of mercury.

"Wow," I said, my mind and body focused on his invasion. "You're really there, aren't you?"

"It is good," he agreed. "You may be on top more often. But only if you begin to move. Do you need help? I will help."

He urged me upward.

"I don't need help, but I have to say, I like it when you do that. Oooh, and that, too."

His hands had moved around to my back, leaving little trails of fire as he stroked a path up my spine. "I'm sorry I'm not bouncing up and down on you, but I swear you inflated. All right, I'm going to try a downward swoop. Are you ready?"

"I may well expire if you don't, so yes," he said, his entire body as taut as a bowstring, his eyes glittering, and his claws pricking softly on the flesh of my behind.

I sank back down on him, my back arching when he pulled me down enough that he could catch one of my breasts in his mouth.

And that was all it took. The second he blew fire on my breasts, my brain just seemed to kick into high gear, and I found myself riding him like a rented mule, his hips bucking beneath me when I found a rhythm that had us both mindless with pleasure. My muscles tightened around him when he gave a hoarse shout of purest joy. At that moment, I didn't care that the others might hear us, didn't care that I had bound myself to a man who carried more emotional scars than me, and wasn't thinking at all of the wisdom of falling in love with a dragon in human form... I just knew that I was meant to be there, at that exact moment, and that Kostya was my future.

You said the L-word, my mind pointed out some time later, when Kostya had rolled us over so that I lay tucked partially beneath him, one of his legs thrown over mine, his even breath ruffling my hair. *Are you so sure it's not just an infatuation?*

I smiled to myself even as those thoughts rattled around in my head. I loved the fact that Kostya was always grumpy, defensive, and had a secret vulnerable self that called to me.

I just loved him.

Fifteen

The détente, as I thought of it, was held in the hall of Aisling's house.

"Aisling says that you have brought the payment that Drake demanded of Kostya for his help in freeing you?" Rene asked when Aisling came out of one of the ground-floor rooms. She smiled at me.

I waved and smiled back. She patted Jim on his head before he returned to my side and sat down.

"Payment?" I glanced back to the open door of the kitchen. Kostya lurked just inside of the door, out of the line of sight of the room where Drake likewise stood watching us through an open door. We had discovered that if the two men couldn't see each other, they didn't seem to mind relatively close proximity. "There is so much I could say about a brother that makes you pay for helping you . . . but I'll save it for another time. I don't have much money, Kostya. Do you have a check or something for me to give to your brother?"

An odd look passed over his face. "Oh. That. Er..."

"Why are you looking guilty? What's happened?"

He straightened his shoulders and looked down his nose at me. "I am a wyvern. Whatever choices I make are best for my sept."

"I'm not in your sept," I couldn't help but point out. Much as I wanted to force him to admit the obvious—that I was his mate and that he needed me—I knew that wasn't going to be the way to start our life together.

He waved a dismissive hand. "That applies to all my decisions. I do whatever is for the best of all concerned."

"Uh-huh." I tipped my head to the side. "What did you promise Drake? My house that is no more? Jim? *Me*?"

He gave me a look that clearly said I should know better. "You tried to give Jim back already and cannot."

"That's just because I don't know how, and Aisling couldn't really explain what I needed to do. So if it's not any of those, what did you off— Oh no, Kostya, you didn't."

He looked away, suddenly absorbed in a kitchen cabinet.

"Really? You told Drake you'd give him my magic ring?" I marched over to him and poked him twice on the chest. "It's not yours to give away!"

"It is of great value, priceless to be exact. It would naturally appeal to Drake."

"Whereas something trivial like me wouldn't, you mean?" Now I was irritated with both Kostya and Drake. "Gee, talk about treating family like crap."

The look Kostya gave me was priceless. "You are angry with me because I did not offer you to my brother?"

"Of course I'm not," I snapped. "And stop being reasonable when I've got hurt feelings."

"Aoife." Kostya pulled me against his chest, rubbing

his hips against me in an attempt to distract me that was pretty darned obvious. "That implies that you are not worthy of his high esteem, and you are. Even if I shared women, and I do not, Drake knows I value you more than the ring, and thus when he asked for payment, he demanded only what I was willing to give up."

I bit his chin. "All right, given that and the sentiments you expressed in the alley, I'm willing to move past hurt and into acceptance of the fact that you offered Drake something that isn't really yours."

"The ring is not yours either—it simply is content for you to be its caretaker for the moment," Kostya warned.

"Right, but there's one big problem with your plan that seems to have escaped you: Drake is just as much a cursed dragon as you are, which means that he won't be able to use it."

"We are both well aware of that fact." Kostya looked up when Jim entered the room. "The possession he speaks of will occur once the ring has been used to break the curse. Until that time, it will be used for the purpose we most need it."

"Hey, Eefs! Aisling says to ask you what's the holdup, and if you and Slick are going to get busy, then to please take it to the bedroom, because she's gonna be hungry and she can't face the kitchen table if you guys are doing the nasty on it."

"I really don't like the idea of giving it up permanently," I told Kostya, ignoring Jim. "Helping to end the curse is one thing, but to just hand it over to Drake...I suppose if that's what it takes to get Jim and me out of hell—no, don't say it, Abaddon—then I'm going to have to. But I don't have to like it."

"What?" Jim, sitting in the middle of the doorway, looked over his shoulder. "No, he's got his hands on her boobs, though. I think they were playing sucky-face, but now Aoife is yammering at Slick about not sharing with others."

"Jim, please stop—" I stopped, suddenly realizing something. "Are you talking to Aisling?"

"Yeah. She's getting impatient with you taking so long."

"Are you tattling to her about us?"

"Just keeping her up to date. She asked me to. She seems nice. Kinda emotional, but at least she's not a space cadet like some people I could name."

"I'm new to this!" I said in exasperation. "I'd like to see you be poised and hip if you just suddenly learned that the world wasn't what you thought!"

"Hello! Memory wipe! I didn't know I was a demon until Slick pointed it out. So we've had the same amount of time to get up to speed, and one of us is lacking."

"Please tell me I have the time to talk to Aisling right now to give him back," I asked Kostya. "I know you want to get out and about to find this charming person—"

"Charmer, babe. You'd think she could retain that longer than a few hours, huh, Slick?"

Kostya set fire to Jim's head. He yelped and ran into the bedroom. Sounds of splashing from the adjacent bathroom followed.

"If your head is in the toilet, you're going to get a bath before I pet you again," I called out, giving Kostya a gimlet eye. He still held me, but he looked thoughtful now, as if he was plotting. I put my hand on his chest and stroked the heavy muscle there until he glanced down at me, a question in his eyes. "Part of telling me what you're thinking about applies to non-sex times, too. Do you have an idea of something we can offer Drake instead of the ring?"

"No. I was considering your request. It makes sense. I will leave you here to work with Aisling while I speak to the Venediger about a Charmer."

"Oh no, you don't. Not with those red dragons just waiting to pounce on you."

He stiffened. "You do not think I can handle a few red dragons?"

"I know you can. I've seen you do just that. I've also seen your almost-dead body washed up on a beach because the red dragons did something to you—what, exactly, did they do?"

"It matters not," he said dismissively. "I am not a child to cower behind doors. I have been attacked many times in the past and survived. I will not let fear of what might be keep me from that which must be done."

"It's always amusing when you talk like something out of a Tolkien book, but as entertaining as that is, I'm more concerned with keeping you in one piece. Besides, if the red baddies catch you and take you to hell—"

"Abaddon," Kostya and Jim said in unison, the latter having emerged from the bedroom with a sopping wet head.

"—then who am I going to get to save you? Evidently Drake isn't inclined to help out without charging, and I have nothing with which to barter. Besides, I kind of want to see this Venediger person. After all, I faced the head honcho of Abaddon and she can't be any worse than that."

"Dunno, babe. Asmo was pretty bad. I think someone who's even half as bad is still going to be dangerous,"

Jim piped up, shaking himself so that the fur on his head stood out in spiky clumps. "Man alive, Slick. Next time just yell at me or something. You could have burnt my fabulous fur!"

After a moment of thought, Kostya gave a quick nod. "Very well. I will make some phone calls to rally the black dragons to Paris."

"How many people do you have in your sept?" I couldn't help but ask. The thought of Kostya leading a group of dragons to war had a heroic quality that I had to admit was highly enticing. I didn't cherish the thought of violence, or the possibility of Kostya and his people being harmed, but it was undeniable that there was just something ruggedly masculine about the thought of a man who was willing to fight for what was important to him.

"Seven."

"I think she's coming, Aisling," Jim said as he padded his way out of the kitchen. "Kostya set fire to my head. Dude seriously needs some anger management counseling. Hey, what time is lunch, 'cause Aoife didn't give me much of a breffy, and I can't maintain this level of gorgeousness on crumbs..."

Jim's voice trailed off as he wandered back to the hall.

I admired Kostya's thick eyelashes and handsome eyes and thought to myself that he really was the sexiest man I'd ever seen. "Really? For some reason, I assumed there were more dragons around than that. I mean, we must have seen at least ten red dragons. How many more of them are there?"

"Legions." He was silent a moment, his jaw working; then he added, "The black dragons were almost entirely destroyed. A few escaped and went into hiding. We have only returned to the weyr recently."

"Gotcha." I patted him on the arm and gave him a quick kiss. "I'll leave you in peace to make your phone calls while I figure out how to give Jim back to Aisling. Let's just hope it doesn't involve me having to run him down again."

I repeated that sentiment a minute later when I stood with Aisling, Rene, and Jim in the hall, while Drake leaned against the door frame watching silently. Rene dutifully passed that on to Aisling and Drake, and the former made a face and said something long that involved much hand waving.

Rene listened and nodded his head several times, then turned to me and said simply, "Aisling says no, do not run Jim over again."

"All that for just no?" I asked.

Jim answered. "There was a lot about what she was going to do to Magoth when she got him in a sound-proofed room and some references to knowing your heart is in the right place but not exactly trusting you with continued care of me, and then she said no, I couldn't have a second breakfast because evidently there's some vet who said I was fat. Me! As if!" Jim looked down at himself and waved a paw. "Like that's even possible. I'm ninety percent fur and the rest is a lean, mean demon machine."

"In your version of reality, maybe, but the rest of us see something different. All right, Rene, let's get this shindig under way. What should I be doing first?"

The next half hour was filled with various flavors of frustration. For one, there was the whole language barrier thing—or rather, the curse creating the language barrier—and for another, Aisling kept insisting that the key to the situation was within my grasp.

"But I don't know what I did that night," I repeated for

the third time when she—through Rene—told me that
I had to recall what words I spoke to bind Jim to me in
order to undo that, "much less what I said."

"Aisling says that you must try harder."

"That is so not helping. I'm trying as hard as I can."

"I guess I'd better get used to being bound to you," Jim
said, rolling over onto his back. "Belly scritches?"

"Jim!" I said loudly as Aisling squawked and waved
her hands at him. "No one wants to see that. I'll scratch
your belly later, but right now, I have to figure out what I
said that stuck me with you."

"Stuck." He sniffed. "More like granted you the extreme
pleasure."

"Roll over onto your side, you deranged demon." I
waited until he did so before shaking my head at Rene.
"Tell Aisling that I'm sorry, but I just don't remember
what I said that could have bound a demon to me. We're
going to have to find another way to unhook Jim."

He repeated the words to Aisling. She answered, and
Rene translated simultaneously. "She says you are not
considering... What is that? Ah, yes. All the possibilities.
You must consider all the possibilities."

I just stared at him.

"She says that you must open— Are you sure that is the
word? It makes no sense, though. Ah? Very well. She says
you must open the little door in your brain." He tapped his
head. "The one that makes you see things."

"Okay, I don't..." I paused and shook my head. "You
know, I went to the nuthouse because of what I thought
I saw, so I'm not sure that I'm the best person to be saying
that to, although now, of course, I know that I saw exactly
what I thought I saw. A door, huh?"

"That is what she said, although myself, I do not see it." He shrugged. "But Aisling is quite firm that is what you must do."

I sighed but closed my eyes and envisioned a door in my head opening. It didn't do much for me other than make me want to giggle.

"Nothing?" Rene asked, his face hopeful.

I shook my head. "Sorry."

"My wife," he said slowly, giving me a look of consideration, "she does the yoga in order to remain supple, you know? The teachers also do meditation, which my wife has sometimes tried, and she said that it once helped her remember where she put the car keys. Perhaps it could help you? It is worth a try, yes?"

"Yes," I agreed somewhat hesitantly. "It's better than wanting to beat my head against the wall. I've never meditated, though. Dr. Barlind didn't approve, saying it had too much of a New Age smell to it. What do I do?"

Ten minutes later I was sitting on the floor with my legs crossed, palms upturned on my knees, and Jim snoring next to me. "Om," I said. "Zen. I am Zen. I am the om. Hare hare, hallelujah."

"Now you must think back to that night. Aisling says that opening the door in your head is important, so you must add that as well. But mostly, relax, and allow the memories to return."

"I'll try," I said, more than a little doubtful, but I kept those thoughts to myself. It took me a little bit to slow down the mad rush of thoughts, but after about ten minutes, I found myself slumped against the wall, the morning sun warming me and the gentle rhythm of Jim's snores soothing my frazzled nerves. I sank into a form of reverie that Dr. Barlind said was a crutch and to be avoided on the path to emotional stability. I disregarded that and tried to let the memories wash over me.

Little fragments of memory started flitting through my mind, bouncing off each other and repeating in a seemingly endless loop.

At least you're not dead. That's the important thing. At least you're not dead. Damn, houses here can be a mile or more apart. Looks like you're my responsibility now. Ack, don't howl again! I'll take care of you, I promise...

I sat up straight, my eyes snapping open as those last few phrases drifted past my awareness. *You're my responsibility now. I'll take care of you, I promise.* I looked up at Rene. "That must be it. I promised to take care of Jim."

"Ah, yes, that sounds very much like a binding. Let me tell Aisling."

I shook Jim's shoulder and got to my feet while he was doing so. "Ask her how I go about reversing it. Do I just tell him I'm not going to take care of him anymore?"

"Huh? What?" Jim looked hurt. "You woke me up to tell me that you and Daddy don't love me anymore?"

"Kostya would do more than set your head on fire if he heard you call him Daddy," I told the demon, turning when Rene, listening intently to Aisling, nodded and then came over to Jim and me.

"She says that is the binding. You must disclaim responsibility for Jim and tell it that you will no longer take care of it and that you release it from whence it came."

"Hey, now!" Jim protested. "I thought you were going to switch me over to the nice-smelling Aisling, not just throw me back in the demonic fish pond!"

"Rene?" I asked, worried now.

Aisling was talking, striding over to us, her hands gesturing as she spoke.

"Oh, good," Jim said, then nudged my hand with his nose. "She says she'll summon me as soon as you release me. She also said that Suzanne is a great cook and that she has a liver recipe that I evidently used to love. So if you don't mind, I'd appreciate it if you'd let me go so I can have some liver."

I patted the demon on his head. "I'm so glad to know you won't miss me."

"I didn't say that." He gave me a wink and bumped my thigh. "But you gotta admit that a good cook who is willing to make me liver stacked up against you and Slick is going to be no contest."

I laughed and bent down to hug him. "True, but I'll still miss having to be responsible for you. Kind of. I won't miss the potty walks. Are you ready?"

He sat and nodded. "Yeah. Unbind me, baby!"

"Jim, I absolve myself of responsibility for you. I will no longer take care of you and protect you and take you for walkies. I won't rescue you from Kostya when you annoy him, and I won't change you into a human again, even though you weren't bad-looking once you got past the part where you were stark naked. I release you back to the demon holding area and disclaim any and all ties and binds thereto."

Jim opened his mouth to say something but suddenly disappeared in a wisp of black smoke.

Aisling clapped her hands and cheered, then immediately began drawing a circle on the ground and doing some sort of ceremony where she faced in four different directions.

"Ah," Rene said, moving over to stand next to me as

we watched her. "She is calling the quarters. It is exciting this, no?"

"Very." I took a look over my shoulder but saw no sign of Kostya in the kitchen. He must've still been making his phone calls. "While she's doing that, can you help me with Drake?"

"But of course."

We skirted Aisling's circle and went over to where Drake was keeping guard from the depths of his doorway. "Please tell him that I know Kostya promised him a certain something I have in my possession for rescuing me, but we've changed our minds, and now he can't have it."

Rene gave me a curious look but repeated the words.

Drake stopped leaning against the door and frowned at me. I wanted to smile at the frown—it was nearly identical to Kostya's.

"He says that is not acceptable, and that Kostya agreed to a price, and that you must uphold that agreement."

"Cow cookies," I said calmly. "Tell him that instead of the item in question, I'm giving him Jim."

Drake sputtered and spoke quickly, quite obviously arguing the point. I held up my hand and said simply, "He can't have what Kostya said he could have. End of story. And if Drake wants to get snotty about it, then he can't come to the wedding."

A twinkle appeared in Rene's eyes as he dutifully repeated my words.

Drake was about to protest, but he checked himself and repeated one word.

"Married?" Rene translated.

"Yup." I smiled at Drake. "I'm going to marry Kostya just as soon as this business with the red dragons is taken care of."

An odd look passed over Drake's face, part amusement and part something that looked a whole lot like pity.

"Hey!" I said, pointing at his face. "I can only hope I'm reading that expression incorrectly, because otherwise, I might have to deck you, and that would be a shame. I want us all to get along. So you can start with the congratulations and the acceptance of Jim as your fee for helping get me out of hell—"

"Abaddon," came a familiar voice. We turned to see Jim standing in the circle, tongue lolling and tail wagging.

"So get with the program and stop being a dick," I finished up, following which I surprised myself and Drake by leaning forward and hugging him.

"Heya," Jim said, sitting and eyeing Aisling. "You know, you're right. This does feel different. Comfortable, almost. You're not going to order me to do stuff like Aoife did, are you? 'Cause she was always, 'Effrijim, do this,' and, 'Effrijim, be a naked man that,' and I tell you, a demon can only take so much. Besides, she never fed me as I should be fed. When will Suzanne be making me the liver, and can I get some fried onion straws with that?"

Rene and I looked at each other. "All is well with the world," he said.

I laughed. "At least he's no longer my problem. I've got enough going on to be thankful Jim is back where he belongs. I don't suppose you happen to know of any Charmers who are hanging around Paris, do you?"

"A Charmer?" he thought for a moment, then shook his head. "No, but I am not very conversant with who is in town. You would do better to speak with the Venediger."

"Kostya's planning on doing that. I just thought you

might know of someone. Where is the Venediger? Does she have some...I dunno...big palace or something?"

"No, she has G&T."

I looked askance at him. "A gin and tonic?"

"No, no," he laughed, waving a hand. "Goety and Theurgy. It is the bar in Paris, the center of all things Otherworld, and the business belonging to the Venediger. Aisling owned it at one point, when she was acting Venediger, but she did not seek that job and passed it on to the current Venediger."

"Gotcha. I'll go tell Kostya and see if he's done gathering his people." I looked over to where Drake was now standing with Aisling while Jim announced that he had to pee. Aisling looked pleased as punch. Drake looked a little weary, and Jim...I felt a little pang of sadness at the thought that Jim was no longer my problem, but the truth was that he was where he should be.

Without another word, I left them to their reunion and returned to my room to tell Kostya about the proceedings.

"I told Drake he couldn't come to the wedding unless he backed down with regards to his demand for the ring," I finished, watching Kostya as he typed on a small laptop. I wanted badly to sit on his lap, run my fingers through that silky black hair, and kiss the tongue right out of his mouth.

"My brother will not be moved by a human convention like marriage," he said without even glancing at me. "If he allowed you to substitute Jim for the ring, it is because he values Aisling's desires more than his own. He has always been foolish that way."

"So not the thing to say to the woman who is the breath in your lungs and the sun in your sky," I said, pinching his arm.

To my delight, he shot me a fast grin that was full of humor. I settled down beside him, feeling happier than I had in... well, ever. "I was thinking about the ring now that I've told Drake he can't have it. What if I'm wrong? What if, despite the curse, the ring did like Drake?"

"It is doubtful. It does not simply hop from individual to individual. It has chosen you for a reason, and until you have fulfilled that purpose, it is unlikely to allow itself to be given to another." He closed the laptop and stood up. "We must hope the Charmer is that person, or we will all be in trouble. Now we must go to the G&T."

"You know about that place, huh? How fancy is it? I mean, I know it's a nightclub and we're in the middle of a day, so it shouldn't be open, but is it a really nice place? Should I try on that dress that Suzanne said I could wear if I needed to? I hate to, because I already had to confiscate this nice linen tunic and pants after you shredded my clothes, but I also don't want to stand out."

"Your clothing is sufficient. Come. We will see if the Venediger is present." He rose and took my hand, which made my inner girl give happy little squeals.

"Can't we just call her and ask her about Charmers?"

"The Venediger handles requests in person only." He made a wry face. "It is easier for her to exact payment that way. Also, she has forbidden dragonkin from entering G&T. Naturally, we will disregard that, but until—" He froze in the doorway and snarled. I dropped his hand and hustled around in front of him, blocking him from lunging into the hall where Drake was still standing with Aisling, Rene, and Jim.

"We're off to G&T," I called over my shoulder to them, trying to shove Kostya back but doing no more than keeping him from moving forward. "Can we get through, please?"

"Of course. Aisling apologizes and says that they will accompany you."

Drake tried to shoo Aisling into a room.

Rene, thoughtful of our situation, continued to narrate. "Ah, I am mistaken. Drake says she will stay at home, and he will go to G&T to make sure that you are not attacked."

Aisling gave Drake's shoulder a shove and sauntered past him.

"And now Aisling has told him that he is insane if he thinks that she will allow him to treat her as if she is made of glass simply because she is *enceinte* again."

"Oh, I didn't know she was expecting. Please pass along my congratulations."

Rene did so, watching with interest as Drake intercepted Aisling on the way to the door, pointing to the stairs.

"Drake now informs Aisling that she will remain home if he has to lock her in a room."

Aisling gasped and began speaking extremely quickly. Drake's face had the same scowl that Kostya so often wore. I leaned against the latter. "This feels vaguely voyeuristic, and yet, it's as fascinating as a soap opera."

"Aisling has now threatened to set Drake on fire while he is next sleeping. He is now attempting to use reason on her, but she is having none of it."

"Heh," Jim said, grinning when Drake tried to pick up Aisling. "You left out the part where she threatened to nip his noogies if he ever spoke to her again like that. Now he's trying to tell her that he just wants to protect the baby and that he has full confidence in her abilities, yadda yadda yadda. Oh man, this isn't going to end well."

Aisling, obviously furious, snarled something at her husband, made a symbol over his chest, and escaped his hold in order to stride up the stairs to the floor above.

Drake tried to go after her, couldn't move, and began yelling at Aisling's back.

"What on earth?" I asked.

"Binding ward," Jim said, snickering as he got up to follow Aisling. "He went too far. Heh heh. I'm going to like being bound to her."

"Right," I said, slapping my hands over Kostya's eyes. "It's time for us to give them a little privacy to work out their issues. You're going to walk forward and not try to remove my hands, okay?"

"I don't need to be blinkered!" Kostya protested, pulling down my wrists. The second his eyes settled on Drake, he snarled and spat fire.

I raised one eyebrow at him.

"Fine," he said through his teeth. "But only until I am past Drake."

Between us, Rene and I managed to get Kostya by Drake (who lunged and tried to grab his brother) and out the door. Luckily, Rene's cab wasn't parked far, so in no time we were zipping through Paris, on the way to Goety and Theurgy, infamous Otherworld nightspot.

Sixteen

"This is ridiculous." I tried to get through the open doorway that led into the G&T club. "There's nothing here, and yet it feels like there's an invisible sheet of rubber stretched across the opening that just will...not...let... me in. Gah! Kostya, what is this?"

Kostya, ever vigilant, was busily scanning up and down the street. There wasn't much to look at—the club was located on a short avenue lined with small, dark shops that looked like they had been there forever. There weren't a great many people out and about, just one or two ladies with string shopping bags who hurried past, their minds obviously on the tasks of the day.

I waited until the nearest one passed us before prodding Kostya on the arm. "Earth to Kostya. Do you read me?"

"Read what?" he asked, still watching the ladies with bags.

"I was being funny. Or rather, trying to."

He gave me the one-eyebrow-up look. I made a face at him. "All right, it wasn't a big success, but at least I tried, and you can't complain because you weren't even listening to me when I was telling you about the invisible rubber thing across the door."

He frowned at the door. "You cannot enter?"

"No. It's like something's there stopping me, but I don't see anything." I waved a hand through the doorway. "See? There's nothing there when it's just my hand, but when I try to step through..."

I smooshed up against an invisible barrier that distorted my body when I tried to enter the building.

Kostya squinted at the door for a moment, then breathed fire on it. For three seconds, a symbol lit up gold in the doorway, an intricate design that looked somewhat like a Celtic knot, but with a few extra twiddly bits. "Protection ward. She's keeping out the dragonkin."

I waggled both arms through it. There was nothing there, not until I tried to lean in with my torso. Through the open door, I could see chairs stacked neatly on tables, evidently waiting for the club to open.

"Why doesn't she want you going inside?"

"She believes we'll bring the war to her patrons. That is foolish, because she has enough power to keep G&T neutral. We could not war inside without the most extreme of repercussions."

"Extreme, how?" I couldn't help but ask, my curiosity piqued by the idea of a woman who had enough power to keep the dragons from attacking each other.

"Death," he answered succinctly, turning to look behind me. "Rene should have parked his car by now. I will have him call the Venediger and ask her to allow us in."

I eyed the door again. "You said Aisling used to be a Venediger. Could she help us get through it?"

"Yes, but I will not ask her to risk the welfare of her child to help us." His eyes scanned the street, clearly looking for Rene.

I looked down at my hand. "I wonder," I said softly to myself. The ring had protected me against Asmodeus... would it do so against the bit of magic keeping us out? I made a fist and held it out to the door.

Nothing happened.

Well, obviously, I told myself. *You have to will it to do things.* Accordingly, I closed my eyes and thought about what I wanted. I thought about Kostya, and how he filled my thoughts, and how my life was now bound to his. That didn't seem to do much for the ring, so I thought about how nice it would be to have the curse taken off so the dragons could talk to one another without murderous thoughts, but again, the ring didn't seem to be impressed. I moved on to the altruistic intention of keeping it out of the hands of Asmodeus and his demon horde.

Still nothing.

"Oh, screw this!" I snapped, my patience at an end. "Let me in the damned place so we can talk to this chick and find a stupid Charmer. NOW!" I bellowed the last word at the same time I charged forward, and evidently, the ring decided to cooperate, because the next thing I knew I was running into the wall across from the door.

Kostya whirled around and stared at me. "How did you do that?"

I held up my hand. "I got pissed, and the ring listened to me. Let's see if it works for you."

It took a good five minutes for me to figure out that it

wasn't so much getting angry that triggered the ring to heed me, but any strong emotion.

"Arouse me," I demanded, having gone through the door to where Kostya stood and wrapped my arms around him.

His surprise almost made me laugh, but I licked the tip of his nose instead and wiggled my hips against his. Instantly, his eyes adopted that look that I thought of as smoldering, and he grabbed my butt, his fire twisting itself around us. I slid my hands into his hair and kissed him, allowing the fire to burn deep within me.

He was just getting into the kiss, his tongue going all bossy on mine, when I started moving backward, pulling him with me. He was about to break the kiss, no doubt to ask me what I was doing, but I bit his lower lip and sucked it into my mouth while continuing to back up. By the time I was out of breath, we were inside the club.

"Emotion," I breathed onto his lips, giving him one last kiss before stepping away from him. I knew I had to put a little distance between us or else I'd simply wrestle him to the ground right then and there and have my way with him. "That's what the ring responds to. It likes me emotional."

He blinked a couple of times, then tamped down on his fire and looked around. "Ah. Just so."

"What is the meaning of this?" A woman strode out from what must be the back room of the club, a seriously pissed look on her face as she moved around the tables with the upturned chairs. She wore a beige power suit, had sun-streaked blond hair done in a short bob, and was followed by a nondescript middle-aged man who held a tablet computer. "Guillaume, examine the ward. It must be weak in order to allow dragons inside."

"Jovana," Kostya said, bowing low to the woman when

she stopped in front of us. "I assure you that we do not enter with any intention of violence."

"It is not your intentions I have argument with," she snapped, giving me a visual once-over. "Who is this?"

"Her name is Aoife. She is with me," he answered before I could do so.

"Your mate?"

I rubbed my arms against the chill of the darkened club and smiled at Kostya. He looked uncomfortable and was about to answer when the guy named Guillaume returned from his visit to the front door. "The ward is intact, Venediger. It is not weakened so far as I can tell."

Jovana's eyes narrowed on us. "How did you get through it? Is the Guardian outside? I have strictly forbidden her to tamper with my protections, and if she has disobeyed that order—"

"Aisling is at home," Kostya interrupted. "She has not aided us in entering the building. We are here, as I said, not to conduct violence but to get information. You are the Venediger; you are familiar with all the denizens of the Otherworld in Europe. We seek the services of a Charmer, preferably one located nearby."

She held up her hand to stop him, marching over to look at the door herself. "I do not understand how you got through the ward if no one was helping you. You will tell me how you achieved entry."

Worriedly, I curled my fingers into a fist and slid a glance at Kostya. He crossed his arms and looked bored, an act that made me want to cheer. I loved the fact that he wasn't in the least bit intimidated by this apparently all-powerful woman. "That is not pertinent to my request. Do you know of a Charmer who is reasonably close to Paris?"

"I know of two, one of whom has been in Lyon on assignment, while the other is in Seville, but their information will not be given to you until you satisfy me regarding this door," she answered, gesturing toward it.

Kostya raised one of his eyebrows at her. "We seek aid in ending the dragon war. You, yourself, have stated that you desire it to end so that you need not fear repercussions on the Otherworld. Our means of entry pale in consideration of that goal. What is the name and phone number of the Charmer in Lyon?"

"You will answer my question!" Jovana snarled.

"I am a wyvern," Kostya said, nostrils flaring in outrage. "I do not take orders—I give them."

"Not to me," she said, biting off the end of each word. She made an odd sort of gesture with one hand over another, and to my amazement, a blue-white fuzzy ball of light appeared in her hand. She flung it at Kostya.

I grabbed his arm to pull him out of the way, but he stayed put, reaching up to catch the ball of light just as casually as if she'd tossed him a softball. The light faded as the ball turned to dragon fire, which he then threw down to the floor. It spread in a pool around us.

"I am a black dragon," he said with a little smile. "Of all the dragonkin, we are the only ones who have an affinity with arcane magics."

She swore in a very scatological manner that had the prude in me pursing her lips. "Guillaume!" She made an imperious gesture. "Take them to my office. I will get the answer to my question there."

"Like hell you will," I said, and pulled hard on Kostya's fire, fully intending on using the ring to get us out of there.

Kostya kept his eyes on her but turned his head slightly

in my direction as he said softly, "Do not, Aoife. It is what she wants."

"She wants us to get the hell out of here?"

"No. She seeks to know the source of our power." He stopped when Guillaume approached hesitantly, obviously not wanting to get into it with Kostya but unwilling to disobey his boss. "We are content speaking to you here, Jovana. You must take my word for the fact that our ability to circumvent your ward has nothing to do with our intention to break the curse affecting the dragons and end the war that Asmodeus has declared upon all dragonkin."

She smiled, and for a moment, I wondered if she was related to Asmodeus's two demon bouncers. "I would not be a very effective Venediger if I believed everything that was told to me."

The door to the street opened, and sunlight streamed inside, making little motes of dust whirl and swoop in an intricate dance. Used to the darkness of the club now, I blinked at the bright sunshine, the light giving a stark look to the chairs and tables in its path. A strange noise followed the opening of the door, along with a blobby black shape that suddenly popped forward with an audible sucking sound.

"Fires of Abaddon!" the black shape swore, shaking himself before turning back to the door. "Man alive, Aisling! Is it going to be like this any time we go out? Because my fur is seriously rumpled, and I'm going to need a prolonged brushing to get it back to what it was."

"Jim!"

Jovana spun around at the entrance of Jim, her frown almost as potent as those normally worn by Kostya. "I thought you said that the Guardian was at home? And yet here it obviously is, complete with her demon, and you know well that I do not allow demons in G&T."

"Yo," Jim said, giving his shoulder a lick. "You don't have to talk about me like I'm some sort of genital wart. Aisling tells me I'm a good demon. I used to be some sort of a sprite or something, but I got booted out of the Court of Divine Blood—"

I nudged Kostya.

"The Court is what mortals think of as heaven."

"Gotcha."

"—and somehow ended up as a demon, although she wasn't very forthcoming about that bit because she said it was probably better if I didn't know all the shenanigans I used to get up to. Heya, Eefables. Heya, Slick. Aisling said you'd probably need some help. She's trying to keep Drake in the car, although I just bet that noise you hear now is him arguing with her and not doing as she said." There was another movement at the door, and Aisling popped through, followed by Drake.

I jumped in front of Kostya, my hands on his shoulders to keep him from lunging at Drake, but to my surprise, he didn't even tense up.

"Sorry, Pal, Istvan. I'm going to have to rest a bit before I pull you guys through. It really takes a lot out of you to push past a ward," Aisling called out the door; then she addressed Drake. "Sweetie, I told you that Kostya was going to be here and that it's just going to cause endless trouble if you come inside where you both can see each other."

"Hey," I said to Kostya, looking up into his face. He looked mildly interested at the newcomers. I released his shoulders and poked him in the arm. "How come you're not trying to kill your bro—"

I stopped and spun around to stare at Aisling. She was staring back at me. "I heard you," we both said at the same time.

"What the hell?" I added.

"Abaddon," Jim said, snuffling Guillaume's shoes before plopping down next to him.

"How—" Aisling turned to Drake. "How is this possible?"

"I strictly forbade you to force your way through the wards guarding the premises!" Jovana finally found her voice and marched over to where Aisling and Drake stood. "And what do you do? Exactly that!"

Aisling visibly straightened her shoulders at the same time that Drake took a protective step forward. "Hello, Jovana. I'd say it was nice to see you, because I'm a polite person, and I believe that it pays to be nice to people, but evidently you not only don't believe that, but you also forgot just who gave you the job of Venediger to begin with!"

She did a little head bob while she was talking that made me giggle.

"Oh, boy," Jim said, giving an excited wiggle. "Cat fight! Wish I had some popcorn."

"I have not forgotten," Jovana said, her voice cool. "That fact has no relevance here, whereas you disobeying my orders regarding dragons in G&T—"

"I'm a wyvern's mate," Aisling interrupted, clearly getting irritated. Drake murmured something and was about to step forward again, but Aisling held him back. "You don't have any right to give Drake or me orders. You can request that I do something, and I will—"

"You are a member of the Guardian's Guild!" It was Jovana's turn to interrupt, and she did so with vehemence.

"Thus you are bound to the rules of the L'au-dela, and that includes honoring my dictates."

I sighed softly to myself and asked under my breath, "What's a L'au-dela?"

"It is the formal name for the Otherworld."

"Why can't people just call things by one name?" I complained, but gave up my grousing to watch Aisling deal with the situation.

"You tell her, babe," Jim said, nodding his support. "Also, ask when the grill is going to open up, because that so-called lunch you had Suzanne give me isn't going to do the job, and I'm going to need my strength if you're going to want me to take down the mage."

"Take down the mage!" Jovana's voice went up an octave.

"I'd still like to know why Kostya and Drake aren't trying to kill each other, and why we can understand Aisling and vice versa," I said.

"I suspect it has something to do with G&T," Kostya answered slowly, giving Jovana a long look. "Perhaps the Venediger has done something to the premises that nullifies the curse."

"Can she do that?" I asked quietly.

"I believe we are looking at proof that she has done so."

"Yeah, what's up with that?" Aisling asked. "Did you magic up a safe zone or something? Drake, is there such a thing as a curse-free zone?"

"I have not heard as such," he answered, also giving Jovana a curious look. "However, it would appear that she can. The question is, how did she do it?"

"And why didn't she tell us about it? Do you know how hard it's been for the septs to talk to each other?" Aisling asked that last question of Jovana, who was once again talking quietly to her employee. Aisling sucked in some breath and added, "Oh! That's why she banned dragons from the G&T! She didn't want any of us showing up to find out that the curse wasn't effective here with whatever magic she's laid down! That's just mean!"

Drake slowly walked forward, his eyes on Kostya. I tensed, watching him carefully, just in case he was about to leap on his brother. He stopped about six inches away and stared at Kostya.

Kostya stared back at Drake.

Aisling and I held our breaths.

Jim licked his undercarriage.

Kostya said something I didn't understand, then reached out and grabbed Drake.

I was about to insinuate myself between them, fearing the worst, when I realized that the two men were hugging each other.

"Oh, that is so good to see," Aisling said, sniffling a little as she came up next to me. She squeezed my arm and nodded toward the brothers. "They haven't been able to do that for two years. Not that they're normally very demonstrative, mind you, but still, you don't know how much you miss being able to hug a sibling until that person tries to kill you every time he sees you."

"Touching," Jovana said, her face dark with anger. She nodded to her crony, who scooted around Drake and Kostya and disappeared into a back room. "The head of the Guardian's Guild will be sure to hear my complaint about your misbehavior later, Guardian. The question remains how *you* entered the club." She looked at me when she spoke the last sentence.

Aisling made a surprised face. "I didn't think of that. How *did* you get in, Aoife? You're not a Guardian or a Charmer. You're just...you."

"Thank you," I said. "I *am* just me, and really, I don't see why everyone has their respective knickers in a twist about how we got in. That's a minor point, surely."

"Gotta be the ring," Jim said, coming over to snuffle my hand. "Magic rings make everything better, huh, Eefies?"

"Jim!" I glanced at Jovana. She had been about to walk to the bar but stopped at Jim's words. "You're not supposed to blab that around."

"Ring?" Aisling asked, turning to her husband, who now stood having his own muted conversation with Kostya. "What ring? Drake? Did you know that Aoife has a magic ring? Oh!" She gasped on the last word and whomped me lightly on the arm. "You don't mean *the* ring!"

"One ring to bind them all," Jim quoted in a sepulchral tone.

Jovana's gaze sharpened on me.

"You have Asmodeus's ring?" Aisling asked, gawking at me. "The one every dragon, and all of Abaddon, has been searching for? That's it?" She pointed at my hand. "For Pete's sake, why didn't you tell us? Now you can end the curse! Drake, she has the ring!"

"I know," he answered, holding out a hand for her, which she automatically took, smooshing herself against his side. "It is that which Kostya offered for us to engineer his woman's release." The look he settled on me was decidedly sour. "She later reneged on that."

"There was no reneging. I didn't offer the ring; Kostya did, and it wasn't his to give." I clutched my hand to my chest. "The ring likes me. I tried to give it to him, but it didn't want him, so he had to give it back. Besides, it wouldn't do you guys any good since you can't use it while cursed."

"Convoluted logic much?" Jim asked, flopping on his side. "Belly rubs!"

"You are not my belly rub responsibility any longer," I told him.

"Jim, really! No one wants to rub your belly or see your outdoor plumbing. For heaven's sake, stop wiggling like that. You're making everything shake, and it's giving Aoife the heebie-jeebies."

"It is," I agreed, giving her a smile of thanks. "But mostly because he paraded around naked in man form so long. Where were we?"

"You were about to explain why you have come to G&T with the most powerful relic of the reigning prince of Abaddon without bothering to explain such to me," Jovana said smoothly, gliding over to where we stood. Her gaze dropped to my hand for a moment.

I braced myself for the inevitable, then decided that offense was better than defense, and said, "I suppose you expect me to give it to you, too?"

"No," she said quickly, her expression placid. "I am the Venediger. I have no need for its powers."

"Oh dear," I said softly, moving over to take Kostya's hand. Just the feel of his fingers on mine gave me comfort. "I don't like the sound of that."

Jovana considered me for a few seconds, then evidently came to a decision. "Come to my office," she told Kostya. "I will look up the information you seek."

"You're going to do what we ask? Without threatening

us anymore? Or trying to take my ring? Or attacking Kostya and me?"

The look of scorn she tossed my way made me feel petty. "Why would I desire to harm you? I have no desire to enter into the dragon war any more than I do the battle within Abaddon. I seek only to protect those in my charge, and since you possess the means to end the war that threatens us all, it is fitting that I offer aid to ensure your success. Come." She turned and marched to the back room.

"Well, she sure changed her tune fast enough," I told Kostya. "Do you think we should trust her?"

"Of course not," he said simply, pulling my hand up to his mouth to kiss my fingers before releasing them. "But I will accept the assistance she offers. Drake?"

"I will come with you." He leveled a look at his wife that had her making a face in return. "Aisling will remain here with your woman."

"I have a name, you know," I called after them as they followed Jovana, Jim at their heels. "Man, that irritates me. Is he always like that?"

"Yes," Aisling said with a fond smile. "He's annoying as all get-out sometimes, but he truly does love his brother, and I'm sure he'll come to love you as well."

"Yeah, not going to hold my breath on that one." I looked around the club and pulled two chairs off a table for us. "So, I guess we can use this time to get to know each other."

"We could," Aisling said, wandering around the club, her fingers trailing along the tables as she did so. "Or you can tell me about the ring and how you got it. Also, I'm not exactly sure what it does, so if you can tell me that, I'd be grateful."

"I'm afraid you're getting into the realm of *I have no freaking clue* on the last item. I can give you a quick run-down on how I got the ring, but anything more is kind of a gray area." I gave her a brief overview of how I had met Terrin and acquired the ring, although I left out the two years I spent in the madhouse, finishing with finding Kostya on the beach.

"That is so romantic," she said, having taken a seat while I was talking. She clasped her hands together, her eyes a bit moist. "I know I'm being emotional now because my hormones are going baby crazy, but that's just so sweet. You saved his life, Aoife. You truly were meant to be together."

"Yes, well, he doesn't seem to want to admit that."

"He's had a hard time recently," she said slowly.

"With his ex-girlfriend?" I nodded. "I gather that's the case."

"Cyrene? Oh no, that wasn't what I meant, although we all were surprised when he was so smitten with her. That sounds horribly rude of me, and I know I shouldn't tell tales to you about Kostya's previous love interests, but Cyrene..." She bit her lip for a moment before continuing. "Cyrene was kind of desperate to be a wyvern's mate. You see, her twin is one, and she wanted to be one, too, and so she saw Kostya and kind of got swept up in the whole mate-claiming situation." She waved a hand and gave a little shake of her head. "I'm not going to go into all that now; it's a long story and doesn't have anything to do with you and Kostya. What does is the fact that he was imprisoned so long. He was alone and at the mercy of some very bad outcast dragons for seven years. They tried hard to kill him by starving him, but he didn't give up.

So if he seems a bit stressed, and hypervigilant, and even emotionally distant, that's probably why."

"I can deal with most of that," I admitted. I certainly had enough experience dealing with my own emotional demons. "But it kind of grates that he refuses to admit that I'm his mate. I mean, I get that this other woman used him, but goodness, he can't paint all women with the same tar, now, can he?"

"I guess he can," she said, shrugging. "Men can be so blind sometimes. You didn't mention what sorts of things you've done with the ring. I take it you have been using it, yes?"

"Somewhat." I hesitated, unwilling to talk about it, even to Aisling, with whom I felt an unusual sense of kinship. "It got us in here."

"Hmm. I assume you're going to use it to help the Charmer to break the curse. I wonder..." She bit her lip again, a little frown wrinkling her brow.

"You wonder what?"

"I can't help but think if the ring is as powerful as everyone says it is—and you say that it likes you, although I've never heard of a sentient ring—then why can't you simply use it to break the curse yourself and bypass the middleman?"

"Aren't I a dragon now that I'm Kostya's mate? That would mean I can't use it to break the curse."

"Mates aren't dragons per se...we can't shift into dragon form, and we don't have a love of gold as they do, and all the other things that makes them dragons. We're just kind of extra bonus humans."

"Hmm." I looked down at my hand. "I wouldn't know how to begin to break a curse. What if I did something wrong and made it worse?"

"Oh, that's not going to happen," she said with a little dismissive laugh. "Trust me, I've done just about everything wrong that you can do, and it's all worked out for the best. I'm an old hand at this sort of thing. Tell you what, let's give it a shot while the men are out of the room, and if we are successful, then they can sing our praises for decades." She got to her feet and pushed a table aside, making a small clear spot in the middle of the room.

"And if we fail?" I said, slowly getting up as well.

"You're not going to fail. You have me to help you, and I'm a pretty sharp cookie when it comes to stuff like this, not that anyone would admit that, because it makes Drake nervous to have me using my Guardian skills. Let me draw a circle and call the quarters, and then we'll get you set up in it, so that you're protected."

"Protected?" I asked, a sense of hysteria quickly rising.

She gave me a toothy smile as she drew a circle onto the floor with what looked like a gold stylus. "Just in case something goes wonky."

"Eep!"

She laughed. "Such a worrywart! I'm here to protect you in case something does go pear shaped. Now I'll call the quarters. Do you have a favorite saying or family motto?"

I thought. "Live long and prosper?"

"Works for me. I always did have the hots for Mr. Spock—both original and remake." She turned to the north and chanted something in what sounded like Latin, then repeated it for the other three compass points before sketching a symbol in the air while saying, "Live long and prosper. All right, Aoife, the circle is sealed. Stand in the center, and tell the ring to do its thing."

A little zap of electricity ran down my body when I stepped into the area she indicated. The circle she had drawn wasn't visible, since she hadn't used chalk or something that would show up to the naked eye, but the air around it seemed to ripple, and I could certainly feel it when I got near it. Once inside, I felt bathed in warmth, as if the sun were beaming down on me. "I'm not sure I can get it to do that. It seems to like me being emotional before it works."

"Then you'll have to work up some emotions about something. What do you feel strongly about?"

"A lot of things. Animal abuse, women treated as second-class citizens, genocide—"

She made a face and began sketching symbols in the air around me. They glowed golden for a moment before dissolving into nothing. "That's so negative. Negative power isn't good to channel—I know that from experience. What about some positive things that you feel strongly about? You love Kostya, don't you? That should give you good grounds for stirring up some emotions."

I wrapped my arms around myself, not comfortable with talking about my feelings like that. Aisling might appear to be a reliable person, but she was basically a stranger.

She stopped, giving me a curious look. "I'm sorry. Did I touch a sore spot? Did I assume when I shouldn't have? You did say you were planning on marrying Kostya, didn't you?"

"I just . . ." I made a noncommittal gesture. "It's kind of hard to talk about—"

"Ah. I see. No, don't try to explain. I completely understand." She made a wry face. "Drake is forever telling me that not everyone is as willing to talk about their emotions as I am, not that I listen to him when it comes to making him open up to me, because honestly, if there is anyone more reticent than a wyvern, I don't know who it is. But still, you're entitled to keep things of such a personal nature to yourself."

"No," I said, standing tall and proud in my little circle of rippling air. "I'm being silly. I do intend to marry Kostya, and I think I am in love with him, although obviously, I haven't talked with him about that yet. I will use that emotion to generate whatever power the ring needs. Only—" I stopped to solidify in my head just what I wanted to say. "Only I'm not sure how to get the ring to work once I have built up an emotional head of steam."

"How did you get through the ward on the door?" she asked, drawing another symbol.

"I just backed us through it once I started kissing him."

"Did you visualize going through it? Imagine yourself taking him through the door? Picture the ward yielding to you?"

I shook my head. "I said to myself that I wanted to get through the ward and then backed through it."

"Hmm. It must have a verbal trigger, then. All right, put into words what you want, and then let's see what happens."

"I'll get charged up first," I told her, and proceeded to close my eyes, envisioning me kissing Kostya. I thought about how he made me feel, how much pain he had in him that I could ease, thought about how I felt when I was near him. I remembered the joy in his eyes when he embraced his brother after two years of the curse, of how the little silver flecks lit up when we made love. I dwelt on the sensation of his flesh against mine, of his scent, of the moment when our bodies worked together to drive us both over the brink.

"Wow. You're kind of glowing. Not bright light glowing, but it's like little motes of light are gathering around you. I assume that means you're nicely charged."

I opened my eyes and smiled at her. "What should I say?"

"Whatever it is you want the ring to do. I think it's probably more your intentions than the actual words, but I could be wrong about that."

"Well...I want the curse to end, naturally," I said slowly, trying to keep the warm, glowy feeling around me as I thought about what I wanted. The ring felt hot on my finger, and heavier than normal, as if it, too, was charging up.

"That's a good start."

But there was more, of course. "I don't just want the curse to end...I want everyone to be free of threat from the red dragons."

"Good, good." She nodded and continued to draw symbols every few inches in a circle around me.

Even that wasn't enough, I told myself, embracing the tingle of power that the ring was starting to send down my arm and throughout my body. What I really wanted was to get a hold of the root of the problem and stomp it into oblivion. "Only by disabling Asmodeus would the dragons ever really be free," I said softly.

Aisling looked at me, startled. "Whoa, now. I don't think—"

Yes, the voice in my head said, the thought of Kostya uppermost in my mind. Aisling was still speaking, trying to say something about demon lords and why it took a lot to destroy them, but I paid her little heed. I didn't want to destroy anyone—I simply wanted the war to end. I want to live with Kostya in peace, I told the ring. I want to wake up with him every morning and be able to spend my days without worry that someone will try to kill him. I want the war ended and the source of all the grief exposed, brought forth in judgment against all those he has injured, and tried for his crimes. "I want him here right now," I said aloud, my voice raw and trembling with emotion.

I hadn't realized that I had closed my eyes, but at a tremendous clap of thunder, I staggered to the side, suddenly horrified to find myself face-to-face with a man.

A strange man.

He looked just as startled for a second; then a sly look settled in his eyes, and he smiled.

Aisling shrieked and grabbed the back of my shirt, yanking me out of the circle. I collapsed, shaking, my body feeling as if all its energy had been suddenly drained.

Kostya burst into the room, skidding to a stop at the sight of the man in the circle, Drake on his heels.

"Are you all right?" Aisling asked, bending over me as I sat trying to catch my breath. "Are you hurt? Does anything feel wrong with you? Did he touch you?"

I shook my head, giving a wan smile when Kostya knelt beside me, pulling me to his chest. "No. I just feel... drained. A little weak. I'll be all right in a few seconds."

Kostya stared over my head at the man, then looked down at me. "Why?" he asked.

"Why?" I parroted.

He closed his eyes for a second, squeezing me so tight it was almost painful before letting me go and giving me

a little shake. "Why did you summon the most powerful
demon lord who has ever lived?"

"Huh?" I looked over at the man in the circle.

His smile grew.

"She summoned Bael," Aisling said, slumping against
Drake. "And after all the trouble it took to banish him to
the Akasha."

Seventeen

The man who stood in the circle—and who evidently went by the name of Bael—had wavy blond hair and a tiny little toothbrush mustache and wore a dark navy suit. He also had black eyes, not dark like Kostya's, but black, utterly void of color. They were also the coldest eyes I've ever seen, without the slightest hint of humanity in them. Just looking at his eyes made me feel as if little bits of my soul were being torn off and dissolved into nothing.

Kostya took me by the arms and glared down at me, his eyes bright with all sorts of emotions, but unfortunately, pleasure at seeing me wasn't uppermost. "What have you done?"

"It wasn't me! It was the ring."

"You summoned Bael!"

"The ring did," I started to say, but had to stop because one thing Dr. Barlind was very big on was not lying to oneself. "All right, I did, but I didn't mean to. I was trying to break the curse."

"You are not a Charmer," Drake said, his frown identical to Kostya's. I wanted to point that out to Aisling, because I had an idea she'd enjoy that fact as much as I did, but I figured now was not the time. "You cannot break curses by yourself."

"It would have been nice if someone had pointed that out before I tried," I said dryly.

"It's my fault," Aisling said, gesturing toward me. "I egged her on. I thought maybe if Aoife focused, the power of the ring would be enough. I didn't imagine that she would end up getting... *him*."

I avoided looking at Bael. "I'm really getting tired of always being the one who asks the questions, but I'm going to have to do it again. Who's Bael?"

"I am Bael," the blond man said, giving me a little bow. "I am the premiere prince of Abaddon."

"Was," Aisling said quickly. "You aren't the premiere prince anymore. In fact, you're not even a demon lord anymore. All your legions were absorbed by Asmodeus, or so I was told."

"You should not believe all that you hear, Guardian," he told her with a smile.

Aisling pressed closer to Drake in response.

I realized at that moment that Bael hadn't moved from the spot and that he was, in fact, being held within Aisling's invisible circle.

"WHAT IS THIS?"

The bellow came from behind us.

Jovana stomped forward at such a speed that Guillaume had to trot to keep up with her. "I come out to tell you that the Charmer you wished me to contact has informed me she is on her way here only to discover this!

Why is Bael in my club? *Why* is he in Paris? Who summoned him from the Akasha?"

She turned her eyes to Aisling, who held up a hand. "Not it."

"Then it must have been you!" Jovana said, swiveling to shoot laser beams from her eyes at me. Or at least that's what it felt like.

"I didn't mean to!" I protested, simultaneously worried and annoyed. "It's not like I deliberately set out to summon this dude."

"Bael," he corrected, frowning a little as he examined the floor around him.

"I mean, I don't even know who he is."

"I just told you who I am." He glanced over to Kostya, coolly examining him before moving on to Jovana. "A mage? This is who you chose to replace you as Venediger?" He shook his head. "And I worked so hard to take that position from you. Ah, well."

"I sense there is more going on than I'm going to be able to put my brain around," I said somewhat sadly.

"We have a bit of a history," Aisling said, her voice devoid of its normal warmth. She held on to Drake's arm as she spoke, her eyes narrowed on Bael. "He's the one who tricked me into becoming a prince of Abaddon."

I stared at her for a moment, then shook my head. "Nope. Sorry. I've reached maximum capacity of things I don't know, and I just can't handle one more thing."

"I dunno," Jim said, shaking in a manner that sent both slobber and dog hair flying over to splatter on Bael's legs. "You seem to me to have an infinite capacity for stuff you don't know."

"Silence, demon," Aisling and I both said at the same

time. We looked at each other, then giggled for a moment before Jovana reminded us that the situation was not one at all conducive to such things.

"Just what are you going to do about this?" she demanded to know, her arms tight across her chest. The look with which she pinned me back just about stripped the hair right off my head. "I insist that you remove this... this..."

"Prince of Abaddon," Bael supplied.

"...former demon lord from these premises, and from all of Europe. We have enough trouble from Abaddon thanks to you dragons, and I simply will not have any more of my people adversely affected by your battles."

"Holy garbanzo beans, lady!" My patience snapped, and I found myself standing toe-to-toe with Jovana, Kostya's fire whipping around me in a spiral up my body. "I didn't summon him on purpose, okay? And if you don't like him here so much, then you have my blessing to send him back to this Akasha place."

"Me?" She sniffed and stepped back one step when the dragon fire got a bit too close to her. I patted it out, not wanting to make the situation worse. "I cannot do that."

"Why not? I thought you were almighty and powerful?"

She gave me a look that I'd seen all too frequently in the last few days, one that said I should have known better. "I do not have *that* sort of power."

"No, she does not," Bael said, standing up. He had squatted down to examine the floor more closely, an act I thought was strange until I realized that he was looking at Aisling's circle. It really must be keeping him confined, a fact that made me relieved. Worry about just who and what Bael was had been growing to the point where I was now certain I had just done something seriously bad.

"Call whoever you must," Jovana said, giving me a glare before spinning around and marching to the back rooms. "But I want Bael out of my club in no more than five minutes. Make it happen, or pay the price of your folly, and I assure you, it will *not* be a price you will recover from."

I shivered at the threat that lay behind her words. The power snapped off of her, leaving the room filled with a charge.

"Wow. You pissed off the Venediger first time you met her. Smooth move, Ex-Lax."

I made a face at Jim. "I thought you had your brain wiped? Why is it you know about the Venediger?"

"I'm not stupid," he said, grinning. "I told you that I asked questions. Learned a lot in the last few days."

"Can you do something about him?" I asked Aisling.

"Jim? I can order him to silence."

"No, Bael."

She pursed her lips for a few seconds. "I'm a pretty good Guardian, but even I would probably have trouble banishing him to the Akasha on my own. There's Nora, I suppose." We both watched Bael, who was stretching his arms out in first one direction, then another, once again obviously testing the bounds of Aisling's circle. He seemed to have no trouble getting his arms past the boundaries, but I couldn't help but notice that his feet never left the circle. "Nora's my Guardian mentor, Aoife. She's very smart and has been of much help to me, although I'm not sure that even she and I together would be strong enough to banish Bael."

"You wouldn't," he said, still testing the limits of the circle.

"Confine him, yes. But send him back to the Akasha…" She looked at Drake, who shook his head.

"I would not want you to try without much assistance. It would be dangerous for you and the child."

"Well, I don't know this Nora person, but I do know that I'm right here, and I have a ring that evidently can do things that are pretty outstanding. Kind of." I took a deep breath and summoned up a smile for everyone but Bael. "How about we join forces? If I managed to summon him all by myself, then I'm sure if we pool our powers, we can send him back from whence he came." I left Kostya's side and marched over to Aisling, my hand with the ring outstretched toward her.

"I don't think so," she said, but stopped before continuing, giving the ring a doubtful glance.

"It's worth a try, isn't it? I mean, if everyone is saying it's going to be super difficult to send him back—"

"*Impossible* is, I believe, the word you seek," Bael said, his voice bland, but a little wave of anticipation seemed to ripple out from him.

"I suppose so," Aisling said.

"I do not like this," Drake said, facing her.

"Nor do I," Kostya agreed, giving me yet another frown. "It is too dangerous for Aoife. I will not have her risking damage to herself simply to oblige us."

"I'm the one who summoned this guy," I pointed out.

He turned to me, putting his back to the others. There was a look in his eyes that melted me into a puddle of love-struck goo. Oh, he was still frowning—I doubted if he'd lose that for a very long time. But his eyes were soft with emotion, deep emotion, one that made me feel like I was standing in a field on a hot summer's day. "I will not have you in danger," he said softly, so that only I could hear. "I would be upset should anything happen to you."

I swallowed back a sudden lump in my throat, wanting to tell him what was in my heart. I hesitated for a few seconds, unsure of what his reaction would be, but I couldn't stop myself.

I stepped forward, tilting my head to brush my lips against his, whispering, "I love you, Kostya the black dragon. I love you when you frown, and I love you when your eyes light up so it looks like stars against the velvety night sky, and I love you when you're stubborn and annoying and I just want to whomp you. And I'm beginning to believe I couldn't survive without you, too."

His eyes widened, and he slid a glance over my shoulder toward his brother, who was arguing in an undertone with Aisling. "You choose now to tell me this?"

"You started it. Besides, I thought you'd like to know," I said, smiling and rubbing my nose against his. "I just want you to know that you can scowl all you want; you can stomp around and be grumpy as hell—"

"Abaddon!"

"Stop listening, Jim. You can argue with me, and make me insane with lust, and cling to the wounds that I know still hurt deep inside you, but nothing is going to change the fact that I love you, wholly and utterly."

His jaw worked for a moment; then he grabbed me by the hips and pulled me up tight against his body, saying just before he stole all my breath in a kiss that damned near set the whole building alight, "You have the worst sense of timing of any woman I've ever met, and you're going to drive me mad, if I'm not already, but I'll fight to the death anyone who thinks he can touch my mate."

The heat from his kiss seemed to sear my blood, making my whole body tingle with desire and need and a whole lot of love, all dusted over lightly with the purest lust. Joy filled me, my heart singing a hallelujah at the knowledge that there really was a person in the world for whom I was meant, and who, despite his protests, was wholly mine, heart, soul, and body.

I told him how much that meant to me, how I would always cherish him, and protect him, and give him the love that he so badly needed. I promised to always be faithful and that I would move heaven and earth to make sure his life was a happy one. I swore that I would love him until the end of my days. I spoke not in words, but in the love that flowed from everything that I was, merging with his fire, which I directed back at him.

He was everything to me, and I knew at that moment that all the hell I'd been through had been worth it just to make sure I was there to bring Kostya back from the dark place he'd lived in for so long.

It was a wondrous moment, a profound realization of not just the meaning of love, but our place in the world. Unfortunately, it wasn't long-lived.

"Really, is this what I can expect from you? I had hoped for something a bit more entertaining," Bael drawled in a voice that fairly dripped boredom.

"I hear ya," Jim agreed. "Slick's just got his hands on her ass. It's much hotter when he's groping booby, and she has her hands heading for his zipper."

"That is not what I meant, demon. You, Guardian. Release me from this circle."

"Jim, will you stop staring at Kostya and Aoife? They're in love and allowed to do things like that. Although, good heavens, Kostya, really?"

"Hoobah! Now that's what I'm talking about. He's going to do the nasty right here in front of us!"

The words filtered through the emotions that swamped me, and the need I had to get Kostya to the nearest bed so I could do all the things that filled my mind, and I realized that somehow, I had managed to wrap my legs around his hips and was pulling on his hair in a demand for more...more fire, more of his kisses, more of everything he was...just *more*.

I pulled my lips from his, blushing wildly when I realized that everyone (except Bael) was staring at us.

"Oh. Um. Sorry. We got a bit carried away," I said, tapping Kostya on the shoulders so he would let me down. He looked like he was going to refuse but, in the end, sighed and allowed me to slide down his body until my feet were on the floor again.

I couldn't help but notice that the ring was charged up, glowing slightly and feeling extraordinarily warm and heavy on my finger. At least I wouldn't have to work up some emotions to get it to do what I wanted.

"Aoife is in love with me," Kostya told Drake and Aisling by way of an explanation. "It is only natural that she wishes to express her affection for me."

I reached around him and pinched him on his (adorable) behind. "You're not supposed to go blabbing that to everyone!"

"Why not?" He looked genuinely puzzled. "You just got done declaring your love for me. You can't have changed your mind so soon."

I looked silently at him for a minute, then turned to Aisling. She pointed at Drake. "Blame him."

"I am blameless in this," Drake said calmly. "Kostya's relationships with his women have nothing to do with me."

"Except when you insisted on stealing them from me," Kostya told him with a curl of his lip.

"I have never stolen a woman from you—"

"Paris, 1672. The barmaid with the red hair. She wanted to bed me, but you seduced her in the passage outside my door."

Drake became absorbed in picking a microscopic bit of fluff from his sleeve.

"Reeeeally," Aisling said, giving him a look that warned she would have more to say about that at a later date.

"Not to mention Ireland in 1711, when I was partaking of the dairy maids at a farm. I was all set to enjoy myself with the ripest of the maids, when you showed up, and not a single maid would give me a look after that. And then there were the triplets in Bavaria—"

"You know, I don't think this is having the effect you're hoping it will," I told Kostya, my arms crossed as I considered punching him. "Assuming you're trying to prove that you have suffered romantic disappointments over the years. It's just making me a bit ragey, to be honest."

"Did you believe me to be chaste before I met you?" Kostya asked me.

Drake choked on the word. Aisling had to pat him on the back in order to get him to stop.

"Of course not, no more than you believe I never had sex before I met you. But you don't see me trotting out a list of every single man I've slept with, do you?"

His eyes narrowed. "How many men were there?"

"That, sir, is none of your business. Or at the very least, it's a subject for discussion at another time."

"I wish to know their names," Kostya said. "You told me about the one who was so stupid as to spurn you, but now I wish to know the others who did not."

"Oh, come on," I said, distracted enough by Kostya's ridiculous demand to ignore Bael for a few minutes. "I appreciate the fact that you think being jealous is going to make me all swoony, but it's hardly realistic."

"Oh, Lord," Aisling said, giving her husband a weary look. "I'm afraid to tell you, Aoife, these guys don't think anything is at all wrong with going after exes. I had to put down my foot with Drake—he wanted to take out my ex-husband."

"The beach bum," Drake said, his eyes glittering wickedly. "I should have done as I desired; he would not then have been able to pester you with repeated demands for money."

"I told you, sweetie—murdering mortals is illegal, and I refuse to break it to the twins that their daddy is in jail because he got bent out of shape about a man who has meant nothing to me for more than ten years."

"You see?" Kostya told me. "There are valid reasons why I should have the information about your former lovers."

Drake nodded. "It is your right to locate and eliminate them."

"It is not... Oh, this is silly. I'm not going to continue the conversation. We strayed from the initial point, which was the fact that you blathered to everyone that I have nice feelings for you."

"Like I said, blame Drake," Aisling said, and when her husband protested again, added, "Or rather, blame his family. The men all think it's just fine and dandy to have women madly in love with them without once bothering to tell us that they reciprocate the emotion."

"Really?"

I turned to Kostya. He looked profoundly uncomfortable. "So, do you?"

"As you said, now is not the time for this discussion." He waved a hand toward Bael, who was apparently ignoring us and was drawing symbols of his own in the air in a circle around his torso. "We have Bael to deal with."

"Oh, do not worry about me. I shan't be here for long," Bael said, not bothering to look up from his symbol-drawing.

"What's he doing?" I asked Kostya in a whisper, watching the demon lord with growing worry.

"Attempting to break Aisling's circle with banes."

I sighed. I had a horrible premonition that I'd never get the hang of this whole-new-world business. "And a bane is...?"

"The opposite of a ward. Rather than protect, its intent is to do harm."

"Well, he can just stop that," I said loudly, walking toward him.

I intended on merely standing a few feet away and trying to stop him by means of the ring, but as I got close, Aisling, who had been arguing with Drake about his romantic liaisons in the past, suddenly stopped and yelled, "Aoife, don't get close—"

"Look," I said at the same time, about to unload a can of magic ring whoop-ass on Bael, "this isn't going to fly—"

Just as the words left my mouth, Bael's arm shot out, and he grabbed me, yanking me into the circle with him. I backpedaled wildly as Kostya yelled and lunged forward,

Aisling calling out a warning for him to stay out of the circle, but it didn't matter.

The ring grew tight on my finger as instinctively I pulled heavily on both it and Kostya's fire to protect myself. There was a moment of utter silence during which all life seemed to hold its breath; then a massive percussive blast sent me flying backward. I hit something hard and saw stars for a few minutes, my body not hurting, but my lungs scorched and my brain oddly numb and unable to function.

Dimly, from a great distance away, a voice said, *"Peracta vis est omnis!"*

"What's that mean?" I heard myself ask, even though I was blind and bemused.

The hard thing I hit shifted beneath me and groaned. "You don't speak Latin?"

I waited a minute until the wavy blackness that seemed to swim around me faded, and I could see. I rolled off Kostya and glared at him as best I could. "I'm a half-Senegalese, half-Irish woman who was born in America and raised in Sweden. Do you *think* I speak Latin?"

"I see no obstacle to you knowing it." Kostya groaned again as I got to my knees and started patting down his torso, putting out the fire that danced merrily on him. "The phrase translates to 'all power is marshaled,' and I believe it means Bael has just summoned whatever demons are in his control."

"Oh no. That was something I did, wasn't it? Hell." I waited for a moment, but there was no following "Abaddon" from Jim. Blinking, I realized that what I had taken for temporary blindness was mostly due to the air being full of dust and smoke. Around us, through the eddies of smoke, flames were visible, climbing the walls, moving across the floor, and consuming furniture that blocked its path. "Your dragon fire is everywhere. Does anything on you hurt like a broken bone or internal injuries?"

"That is not dragon fire, and no, I have no injuries. Do you?"

"None at all, thanks to you catching me." As he got to his feet, I winced at the Kostya-shaped dent in the plaster wall. The poor guy had cushioned me from the blast and taken the worst of it. I took the hand he offered and got to my own feet, mentally swearing at my stupidity, coughing and wheezing a little when he lifted me over a partially burned table.

"Kostya!" Drake's voice called out through the smoke and dust.

"We are here."

A large black shape moved in the smoke, resolving itself into Drake carrying Aisling, who he set down beside me. "You are both unharmed?"

"Yes. And you?"

"We're fine, although Jim's coat got a bit scorched," Aisling answered for Drake, slapping his hands when he started patting her down, obviously checking her for injuries. "Stop it, Drake! I've already told you that you shielded me from the worst of it."

"I wish I could say the same," Jim said, padding over to us. One side of his head was singed, but it was nothing to the look he turned on me. "Man, Eefies! If you were jealous of me being Aisling's demon, you could have warned me. You didn't have to release Bael. My coat is never going to be the same!"

"Hush, Jim," Aisling said, brushing herself off. Her face

was tight with worry, which just made me feel a hundred times worse.

"I'm so sorry. I had no idea that Bael would grab me and pull me into the circle. I didn't know he could do such a thing. What was that explosion?"

"My circle breaking." Aisling looked at Drake, who shook his head and consulted quietly with Kostya. "Which is a big surprise to me, since I hadn't the slightest idea that they could break. Not to brag, but normally, when I make a circle, they stay made until I undo them."

"Woot! Got me a badass Guardian as a demon lord. That's a lot better than a clueless wyvern's mate any way you slice it," Jim chimed in.

"You are beyond obnoxious," Aisling told him. "Apologize to Aoife right now. She took excellent care of you, and God only knows what she had to put up with from you."

Jim looked contrite. "Sorry, Eefies. Still wuv me?"

"Yes, not that you deserve it after kicking me when I'm down. Was it me going into your circle that made it break, Aisling?"

"No." Her nose scrunched up for a few seconds; then she shook her head. "No, there's no way having an addition to the circle would cause it to break. There was some other factor involved that caused the circle to explode."

"It was the ring," I said miserably, yanking a chair that wasn't yet on fire out of the path of the nearest blaze and setting it behind Aisling so she could sit. "I had no idea it would do that. It just happened of its own accord. But what it can do, it can undo. I'll just go find Bael and get the ring to zap him back to wherever he came from."

"I'm afraid it's not going to be that easy," Aisling said, waving a hand in front of her face. "The smoke is getting worse, which means the non-dragon fire is taking hold. Drake, we should probably get out of the building; I imagine the mortal fire department will be here soon."

"We can't leave, but you certainly will," Drake said, moving over to help Aisling. "Aoife will take you home."

"Why can't you come as well?" I asked Kostya, who was looking toward the back room. "Not that I approve of running away from a building I just blew up, because my parents always taught me to take responsibility for my actions, even if it's caused by a magic ring that I didn't tell to blow up a mystical circle, but still. The smoke *is* getting worse."

"Drake and I cannot leave because Bael has summoned demons," Kostya said, tossing aside a couple of tables and chairs that blocked the door to the back section. Jovana, her white suit stained black, coughed hoarsely as she crawled forward. At least I thought she was coughing until Kostya got her to her feet, and it turned out that she was swearing.

At me.

"Gods and goddesses all unite to smite the person responsible for this atrocity!" She panted a little, shook off Kostya's hold on her arm, and limped over to where Aisling and I stood. "You did this!" She shook her finger at me. "You have tried to destroy the club ever since you stepped foot inside it. I will have no more of it, do you hear me? I banish you from the premises! No more will you ever darken the doorway! No more will you— Are those *more* demons?"

She stopped haranguing me to shoot a glare into the smoke. A man-shaped form came through it, followed by six others, varying in sizes and shapes, and even colors, but all of them appeared to be human.

"Oh joy. Bael summoned some friends," Aisling said wearily, leaving a sooty mark when she rubbed her hand over her face.

"Can he do that?" Jovana asked, furiously punching the air toward the demons. "He is no longer in power!"

"No, but evidently there's still enough demon lord power in him to summon any demons who are not attached to another demon lord. Lovely. Now I have to banish them, too. Sweetie, I'm going to need help on this—"

"You will not banish anyone. It is too dangerous," Drake said, moving in front of her in a protective gesture.

"Well, then, how are we going to get rid of them?"

Kostya snatched up the nearest table, ripped off one of the legs, and passed the table on to his brother, who repeated the action.

"You have *got* to be kidding me," Aisling said.

"Man alive, dragon-on-demon action," Jim said, sitting next to Aisling. "This should be good. Not as much fun as seeing the red dragons jump Kostya while we were in Sweden, because that was just awesome, but I do love me a good fight where demons are beaten to a pulp."

"You *are* a demon," I reminded him.

"Yeah, but Ash here says I'm the good kind." He grinned at me. "Don't be jealous, babe. I said that I liked the fight with you and Slick more."

I rolled my eyes and dismissed him from my thoughts, returning to what was most important at that moment.

"Kostya, you can't possibly be serious about this." I tugged on the back of his shirt. Drake and Kostya had taken up a protective stance in front of us, the latter's table leg held firmly in his right hand. "Even I, with the tiny bit of knowledge that I have about the Otherworld, know you're not going to be able to beat up a demon with a piece of wood."

"Destroy them!" Jovana screeched, pointing dramatically at the seven demons, who had now formed a line. They glanced behind them and, at some unseen command, leaped forward.

A sudden spurt of fear made it feel as if my heart had been jerked into my throat. "Kostya!" I yelled, running after him.

"Guard Aisling!" he called back to me.

I skidded to a halt, a horrible vision rising in my mind of him lying dead on the floor while the building burned around him and the demons carried away Aisling and Jim. Panic gave me strength, sending me leaping onto the top of one of the remaining tables in a position where I could keep Aisling safe and yet monitor the situation with Kostya.

The demons, with harsh cries that made my skin crawl, divided themselves between Drake and Kostya, the latter of whom shifted into dragon form. Fire blasted the demons, but it evidently did them little harm, because it didn't stop their attack at all.

Drake's makeshift wooden sword whirled and danced in the smoky air, the thumps and cries of pain from the demons indicating that he was well versed in hand-to-hand combat. I stopped watching him, trying to pick out Kostya's dark form in the dim light, covered as he was with four demons. They snarled and spat invectives, and twice I heard Kostya grunt in pain.

I did an impotent dance on the table, wanting badly to go help Kostya but knowing that Aisling's state meant she needed extra protection. I did what I could by hurling balls of Kostya's dragon fire at the demons, but they paid absolutely no attention to it.

Behind me, Jovana alternated between shouting orders to Guillaume, who had staggered out from the back room, and hurling abuse at me and the demons. But she kept out of the range of both the battle and me, so I paid her little mind.

It wasn't until Bael himself strode forward that life seemed to sputter to a halt. He stood watching Kostya— now down to just two demons on him, the other two having disappeared into the floor—when he said something I couldn't hear, and suddenly a big-ass sword manifested itself in his hand.

"Thank you," he said, completely unexpectedly. His gaze was firmly fixed on me, making me feel like I was a bug pinned to a board. "You have fulfilled my expectations quite well. I will be forever grateful to you for freeing me."

He smiled and lifted the sword, obviously intent on killing the man I loved beyond all else.

I tried to yell a warning to Kostya, but my mouth was choked with fear and smoke and the horrible knowledge that whatever happened was due to my own ignorance. Once again the ring grew hot and heavy on my hand, and I fisted my fingers, pulling my hands in to my chest for a second before throwing them outward in a desperate attempt to fling away all of the badness.

The air in the club seemed to suck in to one tiny little point in the center of the building, then, with a noise that I will not soon forget, shot outward, destroying all in its path.

As I fell, I said a little prayer to whatever deity would listen to me for Kostya's death to be swift and painless.

Eighteen

It wasn't the shouts and cries that reached me first. It wasn't the sirens, or the rumble of the crowd, or even Kostya saying my name.

It was the sound of his heart beating beneath my ear, strong and true, in a rhythm that seemed to exactly match my own. I turned my face toward the sound, joy at the knowledge that whatever else, we were together. Kostya's delicious scent sank into my bones, making me feel both oddly safe and incredibly aroused.

"You're not dead," a rough, cracked voice said. It occurred to me that it was me who spoke, and I put my hand up to my mouth to see if I still possessed such a thing.

"I told you it was difficult to kill a dragon. Are you hurt, dearling?"

I opened my eyes at that, smiling a little to myself at the sight of Kostya's face a few inches from my own. The silver flecks in his eyes were as brilliant as polished starlight, glittering at me in a way that warmed me to the tips of my toes, which was odd considering that I was wet and cold. I reached up and moved a lock of hair that had fallen down over his forehead. "Dearling?"

"Answer my question," he ordered, his brows pulling together.

"Do you know, I wouldn't recognize you if you weren't scowling," I said, laughing, and tipped my head so that I could kiss him. "I'm not hurt, no, and I like the dearling. Can I call you dearling, too?"

He looked slightly horrified. "No! It is not suitable for you to refer to your wyvern by such terms. I should not have done so in a public place, but my emotions got the better of me."

"Good. We'll have to let your emotions run away with you again." I pushed back on his chest until he moved away enough for me to sit up. I looked around, the sounds suddenly rushing in to me. Three fire engines sat a block away, water playing on the burned remains of G&T. The street between us was filled with police cars, a fire official's car, tons of bystanders, and three ambulances, only one of which was doing any business. "What happened? Is Aisling okay? And why am I soaking wet?"

"Aisling is fine. Drake has taken her home. You are wet because I was unconscious when the mortal fire department arrived and began spraying everything in sight with water. And as for what happened—apparently, you blew up the entire building."

I pulled my gaze from the milling crowd and emergency workers and turned to gawk at him in openmouthed astonishment. That's when I noticed the gash on the far side of his face and the remains of blood that had obviously been hastily wiped up. The gash was still bleeding, but sluggishly now, and was about the size of my palm, running from his temple down to the middle of his cheek.

"Kostya! You're hurt! You must let the ambulance guys take care of you."

He gave a wry twist to his lips before answering. "It will heal of its own accord."

"Did you get hit with something when I— Holy frijoles, I blew up the building? Did you get hit by a flying piece of furniture? Oh, man, I feel terrible now. I was just trying to blow everything away from us, not having it backlash and hit you."

"This isn't due to the explosion." He got to his feet and helped me to mine. I wobbled for a few seconds and was quite happy to clutch him in order to steady myself. "I dragged you from the remains of the building first, then helped Drake and his bodyguards recover Jovana and her assistant. That's when Drake and I realized the truth."

"What truth?" I ripped off a bit more of my shirt and dabbled at Kostya's wound.

"That we were outside the bounds of the club." He touched the side of his head and grimaced. "Drake found the table leg I'd been using while I was ensuring you weren't harmed."

My eyes just about bugged out. "He hit you? Oh! That rat bastard! I'm so going to have a few things to say to him!" I flexed my fingers and twirled the ring. "We'll just *see* who takes unfair advantage of a situation."

To my surprise—and utter delight—Kostya gave a short bark of laughter and pulled me close in a bear hug, saying into my hair, "Dearling, you can't use your ring against my brother. Not only is he my kin, but also Aisling would gut us both if we did anything to harm him."

I giggled into his neck, then gently pulled his head down so I could let my lips do a few things to his. "All right, but don't think I'm not going to have Rene or Jim tell Aisling what he did. Were Jovana and Guillaume hurt? I don't suppose there's any chance that Bael was, either?"

"Jovana was slightly injured. Her assistant has been taken away to the mortal hospital, so I do not know his status. As for Bael..."

A little shadow passed over my mind at the last word, accompanied by a bad feeling in the pit of my stomach.

"He is free," Kostya finished.

It took a second for me to process that. I blame the couple of explosions in a short period of time for the lack of brainpower. "Free? As in loose in the world?"

"Yes." Kostya's eyes darkened, the silver bits dimming as he glanced over toward the blackened remains of G&T. "Do you recall what he said just before your explosion?"

"Not really." I frowned into the distance, trying to sort through the feelings that roiled around unhappily inside of me. There was worry in there, and anger, and something worse, something that made me sick to my stomach...guilt.

I sucked in my breath, memory flooding my mind. "He thanked me for freeing him! He said I met his expectations." I grabbed Kostya's shirt with both hands and shook it. "What expectations? How did he know me? Sweet sardine sandwiches, Kostya! What did he mean?"

Jim emerged from the crowd, padded over to us, and snuffled my legs. "Heya. Charmer just got here and is talking with the Watch dude who is taking notes about what really happened, while making the mortal police think it was just a gas explosion. You okay, Eefums? You look a bit frazzled around the edges."

"I feel frazzled," I said, releasing my death grip on Kostya's shirt. "I'm fine. And thank all the gods and goddesses that the Charmer is finally here. I can work with him to get the curse broken right away."

"Her. It's a chick. I told her you were over here." Jim tipped his head to the side and eyed Kostya. "Drake really brained you, huh, Slick? Good thing Pal and Istvan were outside and pulled him off. I thought you were a goner for sure. Hey, you think that café is doing business? I could do with a sandwich or two. Oh, there's the Charmer. I'm going to check out the café and see if the owner is too busy to notice a handsome, yet scorched, Newfie mooching around the kitchen."

I dabbed a bit more at Kostya's face, making tsking sounds until he took my hand, kissed my fingers, and said softly, "I appreciate the concern, Aoife, but my wound is minor and will heal shortly. Do you feel up to speaking with the Charmer, or would you like to rest first?"

"Hello," a voice behind me said, somewhat breathlessly. "Are you Kostya? Jovana said you had an emergency job for me. I see you've been having some excitement here."

I froze at the words, for three seconds my entire body feeling as if I'd been magically converted to a marble statue. Slowly, I turned to face the Charmer.

She stared at me in outright astonishment. "Aoife?"

I nodded, speechless for a moment.

"You know the Charmer?" Kostya asked, his voice expressing disbelief. "Why did you not tell me that you were acquainted with one? We could have avoided asking Jovana for help."

I stared at the woman in front of me, her face almost as

familiar as my own. "Bee, what...how can you...you're a Charmer?"

Her gaze moved from me to Kostya and back. "You're with a dragon."

I nodded again, sliding my arm around Kostya's waist. "I am."

"Aoife is my mate," Kostya said matter-of-factly, pulling me tighter against his side.

I stopped staring at my sister to gaze at him in equal surprise. "Oh, you pick now to finally admit it?"

A little flash of humor flitted through his eyes. "Yes. I thought you'd like to know."

I pinched his side to let him know I appreciated the irony in him throwing my own words back at me.

"You're a wyvern's mate?" Bee's face twisted in amazement. "I just can't believe... I left you in Sweden."

"How do you know this woman?" Kostya asked.

"She's my sister." I took a deep breath, giving Bee a long, long look. "The very same sister who helped have me committed to a loony bin because she said the things I saw at the Faire couldn't possibly be real, when all the while she knew very well they were. *That* sister."

"Ah." Kostya was silent for the count of eight, then gave me a little squeeze. "That situation is not of prime importance at this moment. We will deal with it later. Come, Charmer. We have much to discuss."

During the trip to Drake and Aisling's house, I turned inward, unable to chat with Bee. My anger was so hot, I literally set fire to Rene's car three times before I finally managed to get a handle on it. It was the hurt that filled me, though, a deep, scarring pain, at the knowledge that my own sister would betray me as she did.

I'd always loved my sister and looked up to her as someone who seemed to so easily make her way through life. But now...now she seemed like a complete stranger. Someone who looked familiar but was replaced by a person I no longer knew.

Bee made a few efforts to engage me in conversation, but I couldn't discuss the situation with her. Instead I sat silent, drawing strength from Kostya pressed to my side, struggling with my own sense of worth.

I looked out the window of the taxi, not really seeing anything of the streets we drove down. I was aware that Bee expressed amazement when Kostya told the tale of our recent adventures, but not even her statement that the ring couldn't be in better hands drove me to converse with her.

Ten hours later the sun finally set, leaving the section of Paris containing the remains of the G&T lit with soft yellow streetlights, the air still smelling of smoke, but the burned shell of the building no longer hot enough to burn us when we shuffled in through what had once been a door. Only two walls remained, and they looked about ready to fall in. Kostya, Drake, and the bodyguards cleared a spot on what had once been a small dance floor next to the bar and set up a couple of folding chairs they had brought in their car.

"Thank God the magic still works," Aisling said as she took a seat. She gave me a grim smile. "It's been a hell of a day, made all that much worse because we couldn't talk once we got back home. Kostya, how is your face?"

"Not of any concern," he told her, and placed a chair for me, holding out a hand. I took it, not looking at my sister, who sat on a chair that Drake set up. Pal and Istvan arranged a few more chairs, forming a circle.

"We are all here?" Drake said, looking around. "Good. We shall begin, then. Rene, would you tell us what you found out earlier?"

Rene, who had just sat on the other side of Kostya, stood up again and cleared his throat. "It took some doing, but I eventually traced Bael to the house in Provence where we know Asmodeus to have an entrance to his palace in Abaddon. Whether or not he has returned to Abaddon, I could not tell. I simply know that he has access to it via the house. What his actions will be are just as impossible to guess." He sat down again, looking tired.

Voices grew and ebbed as a couple of people strolled past the burned-out club.

Drake, evidently nominating himself as chairperson of this meeting, waited until their footsteps faded away before saying, "Thank you, Rene. That was quick work, considering the circumstances. We will naturally dispatch as many dragons as possible to watch Bael's moves. Jim?"

"I wasn't licking my balls for the fun of it!" Jim said quickly, straightening up from where he had, in fact, been licking his noogies. "It's called grooming and is perfectly normal for a dog to do! There's nothing kinky or weird in it at all."

Drake sighed. "What do you have to report to us?"

"Oh, that." Jim shook and sat down, donning an officious expression. "Aisling sent me to Abaddon to see which way the wind was blowing there, but there wasn't the slightest whiff of Bael or even a concern that he was out of the Akasha. I don't think anyone knows, although I can't imagine that's going to be the case for long. Demons like to talk."

"So he's not in Abaddon." Aisling spoke slowly, a little line appearing between her eyebrows as she puzzled out the situation. "But he's in Asmodeus's house, which has access to it. Well, I think Drake's right, and it's foolish to guess what he's going to do. Surveillance is our best bet."

"Kostya, you are in agreement?" Drake asked his brother.

"Yes. I will provide a detail of black dragons to take turns watching Bael."

"I don't understand why you want to keep tabs on him," I said softly to Aisling. "You said he was booted out of Abaddon to the limbo place, so isn't he pretty much neutered, magically speaking?"

Aisling shuddered. "I doubt if anything but outright destruction could neuter Bael. Even crippled by being removed from Abaddon, he's still a dangerous person."

"Dangerous to dragons, or other people?"

Her eyes met mine in a long look filled with bleak despair. "Everyone."

"Great. And I let him out."

Drake ignored our whispered consultation. "Excellent. We will get word to Bastian and Gabriel so that they may also provide dragons to watch Bael."

I elbowed Kostya. He leaned over and whispered in my ear, "The wyverns of the blue and silver dragon septs, respectively."

"There's more than just the three septs?" I asked, a little surprised by that fact.

"There is a sixth sept as well, but they have only five members, two of whom are children, so they cannot provide extra dragons to monitor Bael."

"Pardon me for interrupting," I said, raising my hand. Everyone turned weary faces toward me. "Why is Bael so dangerous? From what you've all said, he's a former demon lord. Yeah, he summoned a few demons, but you said they were destroyed and sent back to their holding bin. Or wherever demons live when they aren't doing demon things. I don't understand why you guys are so concerned about Bael being out and about."

"He's a master trickster," Aisling said at the same time that Drake answered, "In his prime, he was infinitely more powerful than the current reigning prince."

"But he's no longer in charge," I argued.

"It doesn't work that way, Aoife," Bee said, her face tight with worry. "Even though he doesn't have his full powers, he's still pretty awful."

Aisling nodded. "The head of the Guardian's Guild is going to have a lot of things to say when I tell him that Bael is back. We're supposed to protect mortals from demons and demon lords, and if Bael, the most powerful of all of them, is now running around in our world…" She shivered and rubbed her arms.

I felt sick to my stomach. "And I let him loose."

"You did not do so intentionally," Kostya said in a comforting tone.

"No, but that doesn't really matter now, does it." I sank into a miserable silence while Drake continued on with the meeting.

"Now we turn to Bee Ndala, the Charmer who has kindly consented to help break the curse." Drake made a little bow in Bee's direction. "I understand that you have a connection to Aoife?"

"We are sisters," Bee said, her voice and manner subdued.

I slid a quick glance at her but couldn't look for long without almost choking on the sense of betrayal.

"How felicitous. It will make working with Aoife that much easier. What do you need from us in order to break the curse?"

"Normally, nothing external to what I can do by myself, since it's usually just a matter of untracing the curse, but with this one . . . I'm sorry, but curses by demon lords are much more involved than lesser curses. The curse laid on all of you is going to require something more."

"You can't break the curse?" I asked, a bit exasperated. "Are you sure you're a Charmer?"

"I've been a Charmer a lot longer than you've been a dragon's mate," my sister answered in a snippy tone.

"Do not speak to my mate in such a manner," Kostya warned her. "She does not deserve it."

"Mate?" Drake's eyebrows rose.

"Yes." Kostya looked more than a little pugnacious. "Do you have anything to say about that?"

"Not I." Drake looked like he wanted to laugh but managed to control his lips.

"Well I certainly have something to say!" Aisling gave a little cheer and beamed at Kostya and me. "I'm so glad you finally saw the light, and I just know you both will be as happy as Drake and I are. A new mate! I can't wait to tell May and Ysolde. They will be thrilled to welcome you to the union. Did I mention the mates have our own union? We used to meet once a month to discuss things, but of course that got put on hold with the curse. I can't wait to get back to the meetings—we always have such fun at them. What?"

The last word was addressed to Drake, who was giving her an odd look.

"You are babbling," he told her.

"I'm allowed to babble. This is a big occasion! But I will attempt to stem my enthusiasm until after the curse has lifted. Go ahead, Bee."

Bee lifted her hand in a helpless gesture. "I can't."

"Why not?" Kostya asked.

She made a regretful face. "It's the nature of the beast. With a normal curse, I could unmake it without any outside help. But with the origination lying with a demon lord who is in the mortal world, I'm going to need a token, something personal belonging to the one who laid down the curse. And then there's Aoife's ring." She slid a glance toward me. I lifted my chin. "I would like to tell you all that I'm capable of handling the curse by myself, but I'm afraid that such a thing is beyond any Charmer. The ring is going to be a necessity. It will need to be relinquished to me, and I'm sure Aoife won't want to give it up. It will be up to you all to take it from her—"

"You bitch!" I spat out, leaping to my feet.

A shocked silence followed.

I was too furious to care. "How dare you imply that I won't do everything in my power to save the dragons from this curse? What sort of person are you that you think I wouldn't give everything I owned to let the dragons live in peace again? Wait, what am I saying—I *know* what sort of person you are. You're someone who throws your sister, your own flesh and blood, into a lunatic's asylum even though you knew full well I was telling the truth. You're that sort of person, so I guess it shouldn't surprise me that you think I'm made of the same traitorous, self-centered, egotistical material!"

Aisling's eyes were round as she watched me.

Kostya stood up when I did, but he said nothing, just stood close enough behind me that I could feel his heat, feel his fire simmering below the surface.

"Whoa," Jim said sotto voce. "I didn't see that coming. Eefable's sister is the one who had her committed? Bad form, Charmer Sister. Seriously bad form."

"It wasn't bad form at all," Bee suddenly snapped, jumping up and stomping over to face me. "I was trying to protect you, you ninny!"

"Protect me?" I sneered. "By telling me I was crazy and having me locked up for years? What was it really, Bee? Were you jealous of me? You're the one who was always gallivanting off helping third-world people, while I just stayed at home and took care of the house. What was it I had that you wanted? Huh? Go ahead and tell me. I'd dearly love to know what drove you into betraying me."

She took a deep breath, then turned to Kostya. "Do you know who gave her the ring?"

"No," he admitted. "Obviously, he must be a member of the Otherworld, but beyond that, I do not know of him."

"His name is Terrin, and he's a steward in the Court of Divine Blood. I don't know how he got Asmodeus's ring, but the second Aoife told me who her boyfriend was, and what had happened at the Faire that night, I knew that she was in danger, terrible danger."

"Oh, sure you did." I crossed my arms and felt the ring grow hot on my hand. I wouldn't be human if I didn't admit that for a second, just a tiny little second, I thought about using it against her. But fortunately, my sense of morality and Kostya's warm presence behind me kept me from doing anything rash.

The look she gave me was almost as cold as the one I had laid upon her. "You won't believe me, of course, and there's little I can do about that except tell you that I had no way to protect you from what was sure to follow. I knew about the dragons being cursed; we all knew about it. And here was the ring that not only all the dragons were seeking, but also all of Abaddon, in my little sister's hands. I had business to attend to and my little sister was in grave peril from a number of fronts. I did the only thing I could do—I made sure you and the ring were hidden away from both the dragons and Asmodeus."

"You sent me to a nuthouse!" I yelled, waving my hands in the air. "You let me believe I was crazy!"

"It was the only thing I could do!" she yelled back. "All the Otherworld was in an uproar. I had no way of knowing what the dragons would do if they found you possessed the key to their salvation, but I did know what would happen to you should Asmodeus's demons run you to earth." She took a deep breath. "And believe me, I would not wish that on my worst enemy, and especially not on my little sister. Oh, Aoife, don't you see? It was the only thing I could do given that situation."

I stepped back into Kostya's embrace, his arms strong around my waist, his chest solid behind me. Tears that I hadn't known were flowing made my throat ache. I rubbed away the wetness on my cheeks and swallowed the rest of the tears. "I don't know what to think other than there must have been another way. One *not* involving shock treatments."

Her gaze dropped to her hands, which were clutched together, her knuckles showing white. "I'm sorry about that. I had no idea they would do something like that to you. The woman running the facility assured me that you would be treated very gently."

Kostya's arms tightened in silent support and comfort. I put my hands on his and leaned back against him. "It's a moot point, I guess. What's done is done, and the important thing right now is to break the curse. Despite what you think, it will not be necessary to have the ring taken from me. You can have it."

I pulled it off my finger and was going to hand it to her, but Kostya stopped me.

"No," he said, putting it back on my finger. "The ring chose you, Mate. It is you who must aid your sister in destroying the curse. It will not work for her."

I turned in his arms. "You don't know that."

"I do." His eyes were back to glowing with that mercurial light from the depths of black velvet.

I couldn't help but smile. "You just want me to have to deal with my emotional issues, don't you? I know how you think, Kostya, and I'll agree on one condition—that you do the same."

"Work with the Charmer?"

"No." I bit his chin. "Deal with your issues. Namely, me."

The familiar martyred look came over his face. "You're going to make me say it, aren't you?"

"Yes."

"Right here, in front of witnesses?"

"Uh-huh. It's better that way."

He squeezed my behind. "Better for who?"

"Say it, Kostya."

"I've already mentioned the sun and moon."

"And that was lovely, something I'll always cherish, but I need more."

He sighed dramatically, then tilted my head up and kissed me, saying, "You have my heart, Aoife, and all the love that I possess. You are life to me. Without you, I would cease to exist."

"What's that?" Aisling said, smiling as she held a hand to her ear. "I didn't hear you, Kostya."

"Do not be cruel, Mate," Drake said, a pained look on his face. "It's bad enough when you make me say it, but at least you don't require me to declare myself in public."

Jim hooted in laughter while Aisling pointed at her husband. "You're just lucky I'm secure enough in the fact that you're crazy wild in love with me so I don't make you say it right now. Kostya, however, is still new to all of this. Go ahead, Kostya. Say it so we all can hear it."

"Once," Kostya said against my lips. "I will say it once."

"Every day," I countered.

He looked horrified. "In public?"

I laughed, and bit his lower lip before moving out of his arms and gesturing toward the others. "No, just the once in front of witnesses, and the rest of the time in private. Okay?"

He sighed again, then said quickly, "Very well, but I will remember this when we are alone, and you are vulnerable to reciprocation. I love you. Now can we get on with plans on how to get whatever item is needed for the Charmer so that my brother will stop trying to kill me?"

Aisling and Rene applauded. Drake, with a roll of his eyes, nodded at his men, who left to go fetch their car.

Bee gave me a long look, then said simply, "I'm sorry that you suffered, Aoife, but I'm truly delighted to know that you have such a bright future." Her gaze shifted to Kostya, and she said in a bossy voice that was very familiar, "You had better treat my little sister right, dragon, or you'll have my brother and me to answer to."

Kostya was about to make a snarky answer in return, I was fairly certain, but I stopped him by putting my hand on his chest and leaning into him, rubbing my nose on his as I said, "No. It's not important right now. The fact that you've finally realized that you can't get along without me is, however, and if we're done here, then I suggest we hurry back to Drake and Aisling's house so we can get into our bedroom before they come home, and you can tell me again how much you love me."

He pulled me close, kissing me with a passion that lit my own into an inferno, Kostya's dragon fire spiraling up our bodies. "Drake was right. You're going to make my life a living hell."

"That's right," I said, not paying any attention to Aisling's laughter or Jim's mumbled "Abaddon." "And you're going to love every single minute of it. Just as I will love you making me crazy. Kostya?"

"Yes?"

"I love you, too. Let's go see just how fireproof Suzanne's bedroom is."

Constantine has always been
supernaturally unlucky in love.
But when he encounters a beautiful,
blue-eyed woman imprisoned in a
dark dimension, he soon finds *he*'s the
one in need of being saved…

Please see the next page for
a preview of

Dragon Storm.

Coming in November 2015

One

"Baaaaa."

Constantine of Norka, once the famed warrior leader of the sept of the silver dragons, jerked upright from where he had been dozing in the weak morning sun. The air in the small sitting room was still and quiet, the gas fireplace gently blowing warmth into the room, leaving him with a sense of being frozen in an endless moment of time. He cocked his head and held his breath, wondering if his mind had been playing tricks on him.

"Baaaaaghhh." The distant noise started out in a tinny, mechanical approximation of a sheep's bleat but ended in what sounded like the cough of an asthmatic toad. One with a heavy smoking habit.

"Constantine!" The bellow that followed the horrible noise all but shook the stone walls of the castle. The gas jet sputtered as if in sympathy with the noise.

With a martyred sigh, Constantine got to his feet, taking

a corporeal form despite the desire to fade into the spirit world where no one could see him.

"Is it too much to ask you to keep your deviant sexual aids from my son?"

Constantine pursed his lips, crossed his arms, and leaned against the wall as the dark-haired, dark-eyed man strode toward him, a fast-deflating blow-up sheep clad in fishnet stockings clutched in one hand.

"What makes you think that belongs to me?" Constantine asked in a conversational tone. He'd found through centuries of experience—not including the time while he had been inconveniently dead—that doing so had the tendency to enrage Baltic even more. And there was nothing Constantine liked better than to push Baltic's buttons. It was payback, he felt, for all that he had suffered at the hands of his once friend, later mortal enemy, and finally, reluctant acquaintance. "That guard of yours—what is his name? Pablo? Pachebel? You know who I mean, the one who enjoys both sexes—he has many such things. You do me wrong to accuse me when it likely belongs to him."

"His name is Pavel, as you well know," Baltic said, breathing heavily through his nose.

Constantine gave himself two points for the loud nose-breathing. He wondered if he could get Baltic to grind his teeth—that was a worth a full five points, and getting that would push his daily Aggravating Baltic score to over twenty. It would be a new high, and one which he had long sought. "Pavel? Are you sure?" Constantine rubbed his jaw as if he was considering the fact. "Doesn't sound very likely to me. You've probably gotten it wrong. Such things happen when you get old, you know."

Baltic took a deep breath. "I don't know why I bother

conversing with you. You never have anything of intelligence to say, and simply use up air."

"You talk to me for the same reason you begged me to join your sept—you know I am the superior wyvern."

"You are deceased," Baltic said, enunciating with deliberation. "You are a former dragon. You no longer exist. You are, in effect, a nonentity, and the only reason I went against my better judgment to include you in the sept of the light dragons is because Ysolde—*my* Ysolde—pleaded with me to do so in order to keep you from being without a sept."

Constantine sniffed. He disliked the way the conversation was going, and said the one thing he was sure would derail it. "Perhaps Ysolde got that sheep with the charming garters and stockings to distract your lusty attentions. Perhaps she is tired of you but is too kind to tell you. Perhaps she desires another. Say, for instance, me..."

"Out!" Baltic bellowed, pointing dramatically at the door. The sheep gave a feeble "Baaagh" before the last of the air slid out of it with a rude noise.

"Out?" Constantine brushed his fingernails along one arm and lazily examined the results. "Out of what? You speak in riddles, Baltic. Is your brain addled?"

"Out of my castle! Out of my sept, and my hair, and most of all, out of my life!" Baltic yelled, glaring at the sheep when it uttered one last rude noise before falling limp in his hand. He flung it to Constantine's feet.

Baltic strode off before Constantine could goad him further.

"Fourteen points," Constantine said sadly to himself, idly looking through the window to the wilderness beyond. Dauva, the home of Baltic and Ysolde and all the rest of the light dragons (whose numbers totaled six, including Constantine), was situated outside a remote town in Russia. Constantine had been born and raised in a region that was now Poland, but he much preferred the South of France and its balmier climate.

"Only fourteen, and I used my strongest verbal weapons. What has gone wrong with my life that I find myself here, at this time of year, cold even when it's sunny? I am unwanted, undesired, and alone," he said aloud. No one answered him, which was exactly what he expected. All too frequently he'd found himself on the outside of the family that was made up of Baltic and Ysolde and their two children. Even Pavel, Baltic's right-hand man, was a part of the family, whereas he, Baltic's oldest friend, and once mated to the lovely Ysolde, existed on the fringes of their attention. He'd never felt so ghost-like and insubstantial as he had the last few months. Lately, there were days when he didn't even bother to slip into his corporeal state.

A woman with long blond hair bustled into the room, speaking as she did so. "...told him that we do too have to worry about it, but will he listen to me? No, he won't." Ysolde de Bouvier stopped in front of Constantine, a toddler perched on her hip. "Honestly, there are times when I could just whomp him on the head with the nearest blunt object."

"If you're speaking of Baltic, I would be happy to be of service. Bashing him over the head is always high on my list of things to do," Constantine said, rising and making a formal bow before chucking the child under his chin. Constantine had a love of babies that led him to making secret forays into the child Alduin's chambers, bringing toys that he thought would amuse.

Alduin said, "Uncle Connie!" and held out his arms for Constantine.

"Lovey, Uncle Constantine doesn't want to hold you, not after you've been helping Uncle Pavel make baklava. You are one sticky little boy and are going to have a bath just as soon as I'm done here." Ysolde set the boy down and gave him a mock look of regret before turning a smile onto Constantine. "Good morning. Do you have a moment, or are you busy planning something with your blow-up doll? If so, please let me talk first. It's really most important. I want to talk to you about this curse."

Constantine frowned. "The one affecting the dragons, or is there a new curse?"

"No, that's the one." Alduin clasped the deflated sheep to him with a cry of delight. Both Ysolde and Constantine ignored the sheep's plaintive *baa*.

"Did they find Asmodeus's ring, then?"

"I gather so, or they wouldn't have a Charmer lined up to break the curse. Evidently, they are looking for something that belongs to Asmodeus to use to help break it . . . a talisman of some sort."

Constantine scratched his chest. "What has this to do with us?"

"I told Aisling that you'd get the talisman."

He gawked at her, outright gawked, something he never did. "Ysolde—"

"Now, hear me out," Ysolde interrupted.

"Even deceased, former wyverns have some standards, after all," he said with a sniff. "Just because I don't actually lead a sept anymore doesn't mean I don't have important demands on my time."

Ysolde pursed her lips and raised an eyebrow at the deflated sheep.

Constantine sniffed again and looked away.

"I know you have lots of important things to do," Ysolde said soothingly. "But don't you see just how ideal you are for the job? For one, you think well on your feet."

He had opened his mouth to protest, but at the words of praise, he hesitated. "This is true. But—"

"And you can blink in and out of the physical world, which no other dragon can do."

"Yes, but—"

"Not to mention the fact that you are clever enough to get in and out with the artifact before anyone even knew you had been there."

"Again, you speak the truth, but I must point out—"

"And you would be saving all dragonkin," Ysolde ended triumphantly. "You would be a hero!"

"I'm already a hero," he protested. "I am the wyvern of the silver dragons!"

"Constantine," Ysolde said in a distinctly chiding tone of voice. Constantine did not care for it at all. "I can't believe you'd be such a coward."

"Coward?" he asked on a gasp of disbelief. "Me?"

Ysolde brushed a bit of lint from her sleeve. "Well, what else am I to think when you, a brave and heroic dragon who has sworn himself to my eternal service, won't even do this one simple little task for me?"

"If you think such ridiculous statements are going to bait me into jumping to your command, you are mistaken," Constantine said dryly, but despite that, he began to seriously consider her request. He didn't want to do it for a number of reasons, but he had to admit that when he reached the state where the high point of his day was irritating Baltic, he should reassess his life plan. Perhaps a little adventure would be just what he needed to shake himself of the sense of gloom that pervaded him of late. "You say this object belongs to Asmodeus? Asmodeus is sure to be in Abaddon."

"I assume so."

"I don't like going to Abaddon," he said slowly, still considering the idea. "All I would need to do is find this object, a talisman? Is there one in particular, or will any item do?"

Ysolde picked up her child and pulled a strand of her blond hair from his sticky grip. "Aisling didn't say it was one in particular, and she would have if that was the case, so I think it's safe to say you can get anything that suits the bill."

"Which means any object of a personal nature to the being in question." Constantine thought about this. He added, more speaking aloud to himself than to her, "I suppose I could get in Asmodeus's palace and find an object quickly enough. I wouldn't have to spend any time in Abaddon, not that—" He remembered he wasn't alone, and once again bit down on his words. With a brief nod at Ysolde, he added, "Very well. I will undertake this quest for you, my beloved former mate. But will ask for a boon upon completion."

"What sort of a boon?" she asked suspiciously. "You know Baltic would go ballistic if you tried to do anything… intimate … with me, not that I'd let you to begin with, but I'd rather avoid getting him all bent out of shape."

He shrugged. "I do not yet know what reward I'll ask for, but if I take this mission for you, then you are indebted to me. Do you agree?"

She rolled her eyes briefly. "Dragons. Always bargaining. Yes, very well, I'll owe you one if you do this, although really, I'd think bringing about the end of the curse would be reward enough."

Slowly, so Ysolde would not notice, Constantine nudged the deflated sheep behind him. "I will pack my things. Where must I go to accomplish this burdensome task?"

"You are the cutest sticky child in the world," Ysolde said to her son when he started to sing in a high, sing-song voice. "Hmm? Oh, the Charmer is evidently in Paris, but you could get into Asmodeus's palace by any of its entrances. I don't know where they are, but I'm sure you can figure it out."

Ysolde dropped a kiss on her son's head and started toward the door. "Thank you so much for doing this, Constantine. I would tell you how much I appreciate it, but it's so much more than just my wishes at stake here. You'll free all the dragons, and then we can get back to having the world be a normal place with all the septs able to talk to each other again, and no one at war. It'll be heaven compared to how things are now. All right, my darling child, it's to the bathtub for you …"

Constantine's frown grew darker as he absently watched the love of his life leave the room, his thoughts, for once, not on his own grievances but instead reaching back in time to his youth. "I wouldn't do it if Bael were not safely confined in the Akashic Plain," he said softly to himself. "But as he is, and has no way to get out, then I will act the hero. I will save the dragonkin. I will take my place in the annals of modern dragon history. I will do this for the glory of the silver dragons."

With a little nod at his noble intentions, he took the sheep to his bedroom, already planning the items he would need on the trip. It didn't occur to him until later that he never once thought of undertaking the job for Ysolde's sake alone.

Enjoyed reading *Dragon Fall*?

Discover Katie MacAlister's scorching
Silver Dragons series . . .

Book one of the Silver Dragons series

The heat is on . . .

Despite her unique ability to protect herself by
hiding in the shadows, May's on the run for breaking
Otherworld law. And she's also in hiding from her
demon boss, Magoth, who is absolutely determined
to seduce her.

But then May meets Gabriel. The most gorgeously,
broodingly, handsome piece of trouble you can
imagine. Sparks fly – quite literally – when she
discovers he's actually a shapeshifting dragon.
And the passion that burns between them makes it
look like he could be the one to take her out
of the shadows for good.

That is, until Magoth orders May to steal one of
Gabriel's treasures. And she really does have to decide
if she's up to playing with fire . . .

Available from Hodder in ebook and paperback

ISBN: 978 0 340 99302 6

Book two of the Silver Dragons series

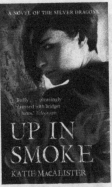

The sparks are flying . . .

Being held hostage by a demon lord is getting
considerably chilly, especially when May Northcott's
heart still burns for Gabriel Tauhou, the flaming-hot
leader of the silver dragons.

Destined to be together and yet pulled apart . . . will
there ever be a way to overcome what separates
them without disaster?

Thankfully Gabriel has a plan to rescue his beloved
mate. But it's risky – and would also force May
to become a pawn in a very dangerous game
involving hell, fire and all of humanity, in
order to secure her freedom.

She insists she'd do anything to be with Gabriel.
But if the deal falls through and things get too
hot, will she be able to withstand the blaze? Or will
her life go up in smoke?

Available from Hodder in ebook and paperback

ISBN: 978 0 340 99301 9

Book three of the Silver Dragons series

May Northcott is at the end of her tether. Her demon boss has moved in and is making life hell. Her scorching hot dragon lover seems to think everything can be solved with a fiery kiss. And worse still, she's being shadowed by her ditsy twin sister – a naiad who simply can't seem to stay out of trouble.

The arrival of a nearly-dead man on May's doorstep could be the final spark that sets light to their tinder-box world. And with dragon war imminent, it's looking increasingly like it will be up to May (and her watery shadow) to stop it before the fire consumes them all, and their lives end up in smoke . . .

Available from Hodder in ebook and paperback

ISBN: 978 0 340 99300 2